Devil's Game

PATRICIA HALL

First published in Great Britain in 2009 by
Allison & Busby Limited
13 Charlotte Mews
London W1T 4EJ
www.allisonandbusby.com

A CIP catalogue record for this book is available from
the British Library.

10 9 8 7 6 5 4 3 2 1

13-ISBN 978-0-7490-7959-8

Typeset in 11/16 pt Sabon by
Terry Shannon

has ... on ...urced

AVAILABLE FROM
ALLISON AND BUSBY

In the Ackroyd & Thackeray series
Skeleton at the Feast
Deep Freeze
Death in Dark Waters
Dead Reckoning
False Witness
Death in a Far Country
By Death Divided
Devil's Game

Other novels
The Masks of Darkness

ALSO BY PATRICIA HALL

In the Ackroyd & Thackeray series
Death by Election
Dying Fall
In the Bleak Midwinter
Perils of the Night
The Italian Girl
Dead on Arrival

Other novels
The Coldness of Killers
The Poison Pool

CHAPTER ONE

She drove into the forest with her heart thudding as usual and smiled to herself. It was always like this, the raised heartbeat, the clammy hands on the wheel, the slight breathlessness as she tried to hold the small car steady on the uneven track through the close-packed ranks of trees. It was a moonless night and not even a star could be glimpsed overhead between the swaying branches, but she kept her headlights dipped. They all knew better than to attract attention to themselves, at least until they were well away from the main road – although here, high in a plantation on the slopes of a Pennine hill long after dark, they were unlikely, she thought, to be noticed. Little moved up here at night, not even the scattered sheep on the open moors above them.

She could just see the rear lights of a car ahead of her making for the usual meeting place, and in her mirror she caught a glimpse of someone else following behind, the lights dipping up and down in tune with the rutted track. She hoped there would be a good turnout tonight. It was the variety of these encounters which excited her, the not knowing who would be there, whose hands would touch her, the knowledge that she would not know tonight, or ever, who she had been with. She smiled at the thought of the pleasures to come.

They were beginning to obsess her, these nights when her husband thought she was safely at work on the late shift, to the point where she wished they would come round more often. She was beginning to anticipate for days in advance the long drive, not usually alone but tonight there had been no choice, the bumpy track through the woods which in itself aroused her, and then the climax in the circle of headlights, the thrashing bodies, the shouts and cheers of the onlookers. The fact that Terry, and the rest of her family, her workmates and friends and neighbours, would be appalled at what she had fallen into almost by accident, only made the excitement greater. They would never know, she thought, and anyway, what the hell did it matter to them? Why should she live out her life with no thrills, no excitement, stuck in the chronic boredom of a dead-end job, a couple of kids, and a husband whose idea of a great night out was the quiz at the local pub?

It was a workmate who had introduced her to these meetings, at the end of a fag break in the yard which had ended up with a ritual moan about the lack of excitement in their lives, and especially in bed, since the kids had been born.

'D'you want summat a bit different?' Charlene had asked, leaning forward confidentially. 'A bit out o't'ordinary?'

'What do you mean?' she'd asked.

'A bit o'dogging?'

'Dogging?' Karen had no idea what Charlene was talking about.

'You must ha' read about it.'

'You mean doing it in public, like? Wi'people watching? I don't think Terry'd go for that.'

'You go on your own, silly. That's t'whole point. It's quite safe. There's lots of people there. You can go wi'any bloke you fancy but you're not on your own. Far from it. It's safety in numbers, like. You can't get hurt or owt like that. You can come wi'me, if you want. It's a right turn-on, if that's what you're looking for.'

'What'll I tell Terry?'

'Tell him you're on a girls' night out. Wi'me. There's nowt wrong wi'that. You will be, won't you? But it'll be a bit more bloody exciting than most girls' nights out, I can tell you.'

So she had gone with Charlene that first time, on her girls' night out, in Charlene's car, driving out of Bradfield and up into the high hills, and down this same long winding track through the conifers, to this same clearing she was just pulling into, but on her own this time, taking her place in the circle of cars and feeling nothing but exhilaration at the prospect ahead. Perhaps the bloke who had turned her on until she screamed last time would be there again tonight, she thought. But it didn't really matter. So far, it had worked for her every time. She had not been disappointed. The pool of light created by the encircling headlights had lived up to expectations and she only wished that the meets, every couple of weeks, could happen more often. She pulled on the handbrake and switched her headlights to full, illuminating the centre of the circle like a stage. This, she thought, as she slipped out of her coat and got out of the car in hot pants and a top which barely covered her nipples, was what life should be like.

* * *

The newsroom at the *Bradfield Gazette* was abnormally hectic that morning, as reporters struggled with garbled first reports of a major pile-up on the motorway during the rush hour in which there had been fatalities and serious injuries. Insulated slightly from the hubbub by her concentration on the deadline for the feature she was writing on a local school which was being considered as a prospective academy, Laura Ackroyd bashed her computer keyboard urgently, blotting out the distractions around her. By ten o'clock she had finished and pressed the key that sent her work to the sub-editors who would fit it into the feature pages, and to the editor, Ted Grant, who looked very unlikely to take much notice of her efforts. He was almost galloping around the room, reading over one reporter's shoulder after another as they put together the details of the motorway smash for the front page. His comments and advice were never less than trenchant and this morning, with a very tight deadline, they bordered on the manic.

She leant back in her swivel chair with a sigh, letting the tension drain out of her shoulders as she surveyed the controlled chaos of the newsroom, something she loved and resented in almost equal measure. How much longer would she be here, she wondered, driven out not by her own ambition as she had once expected, nor even by Ted Grant's relentless aggression, which she had occasionally feared, but by a wholly new obsession which was beginning to dominate her every waking hour. Soon, she thought, for the hundredth time, she must resolve this. She could not go on much longer as she was.

Her brief respite was suddenly interrupted by the unexpected sound of her name hurled across the newsroom in the editor's usual stentorian tones. He had retreated to his glass-walled office now, she noticed, and was beckoning her urgently in his direction from the doorway.

'Who is this beggar, Sir David Murgatroyd?' he asked without preamble as she came into the cluttered space from which he directed his reign of terror over his staff. Laura could see that he had the feature she had just completed on his computer screen in front of him.

'He's some sort of venture capitalist,' Laura said cautiously. 'I thought you might have known him. He claims to have come from these parts originally.'

'Never heard of the beggar,' Grant said. 'Why's he getting involved in one of our schools then? Everyone I talk to reckons Sutton Park should be closed down, and good riddance to it.'

Everyone you talk to in the Clarendon bar, Laura thought cynically, where she knew from past experience that the assembled wisdom of Bradfield's ageing and wealthy conservatives, with and without a capital C, was distilled into a particularly potent racist and sexist bile.

'The inspectors say the school has improved out of all recognition over the last few years,' she said mildly. 'A new head, better discipline, exam results going up. As I say in my piece, the teachers and parents are not best pleased at the idea of handing the place over to some peripatetic millionaire. The scheme would throw loads of money at the place, which can't be bad, but control would go to this man Murgatroyd. And he's a fundamentalist Christian by all accounts, so I don't know where that leaves all the Muslim kids who go to Sutton Park now.'

'Aye, well, you've said all that here,' Grant said dismissively. 'I reckon what this piece needs, before we use it, is a profile of this Murgatroyd bloke. Let's find out who he is and what his motives are, shall we? We'll hold it for the minute. How can I write a leader one way or t'other unless I know what sort of alternative he thinks he's offering? And you might ask him what he thinks he's going to get out of it, an'all. It seems a funny sort of thing to do with your money, however much of it you've got, propping up a run-down comprehensive.'

'I'll do some digging around then, shall I? See if I can get an interview with him?' Laura asked, not displeased with the idea. 'If you like, we could do a full page about it next week if I have any luck. I've got something Jane did on the plans for the Mela which could just as well go in today.'

'Aye, do that. People keep telling me I need to keep the flaming ethnic minorities happy. We'll use this school stuff later when we've got summat a bit more meaty to go on. You should have thought of that yourself. I don't know why I'm having to teach you to suck eggs after all this time.'

Unmoved by Grant's parting jibe, which she knew was at least partly justified, Laura went back to her desk and began an intensive trawl of the Internet for details of Sir David Murgatroyd's career. He was right: she should have done this before, she thought wryly. She must focus better, at least while she was within range of Ted Grant's unforgiving surveillance, and not let her own private obsessions interfere with the job. If she was going to leave the *Gazette,* she wanted to leave under her own steam and at a time of her own choosing, not booted out ignominiously for making mistakes that only a cub reporter could be forgiven. She owed herself more for the years she had spent here, locked into her home town by quite other considerations than the nature of the job.

* * *

DCI Michael Thackeray glanced up slightly wearily as DS Kevin Mower entered his office. The bullet wound in his back, which had nearly taken his life the previous year, had been playing up in the night and he had slept only fitfully, lying rigid at the side of the bed hoping that he would not wake Laura.

'Quiet night?' he asked hopefully, taking in the sheaf of papers Mower carried.

'Traffic's up the wall, guv,' Mower said. 'A lorry careered into a queue of cars at the M62 junction and there's complete mayhem out there. As far as CID's concerned it was quiet enough. A burglary in Southfield, place ransacked when the owners came home from the opera in Leeds. Forensics are out there now so we may get something from them. But the lads are getting wise to DNA. The canny ones are wearing coveralls, and gloves and masks, would you believe? There was one toerag nicked red-handed in Harrogate by an off-duty DI who said it could have been one of our own forensics team on a murder inquiry the way he was all dressed up for the job.'

'It's lucky they're not all quite as bright as that,' Thackeray said. 'We might have to shut up shop.'

'And a good job most killings are spur of the moment. The last thing on your average murderer's mind is whether he's leaving DNA behind.' Thackeray nodded, his own mind obviously not really on what the sergeant was saying.

'So, no other overnight excitement then?' he asked eventually.

'Uniform are talking to some bloke whose wife didn't come home after work last night, but it sounds like another domestic. She's got bored with the husband and kids and has done a runner, I expect. They'll keep me informed if it looks like anything more dodgy.'

'A day to catch up on the paperwork, then,' Thackeray said, glancing at the pile of files in his in tray without enthusiasm. More likely, he thought, another day with time to wrestle with the problem Laura Ackroyd had set him and which he knew would have to be resolved soon if their relationship was to have any future. Her desire to have a family was growing, that was all too obvious, while his own reservations only deepened. And he did not know how to tell her that.

'Thanks, Kevin,' he said. Mower glanced at him warily. He knew better than to probe too deeply into Thackeray's private life but he had known his boss and Laura long enough to recognise the signs that things were not going well. It really was time those two sorted their future out, he thought unsympathetically as he closed the door carefully behind him. They'd had time enough.

On the other side of town, on the edge of the new housing complex that was still being built to replace the dilapidated blocks of flats on the Heights, known not just to its inhabitants but to the whole town as Wuthering, young police constable Nasreem Mirza was sitting uncomfortably on the edge of Terry Bastable's sofa. She was by now well aware that whatever it was that worried Mr Bastable, whose broad face looked pale and drawn, he really did not want to fill her in on the details. And she knew exactly why she was unwelcome, even though Mr Bastable had called the police himself and she had been dispatched to see him within half an hour. She had spotted the small, fading red, white and blue BNP poster in the front window, no doubt left over from the last council election campaign, and drawn her own conclusions even before the man had opened the front door and she had seen his face harden into hostility rather than welcome or relief. He was a muscular figure, in a tight T-shirt, revealing several indecipherable tattoos and with a close-shaven head which in itself exuded aggression.

'Are you the best they could send?' he muttered as he led her into the house, his expression surly. Nasreem knew better than to respond and settled herself in an armchair without being asked.

'So tell me what's happened, Mr Bastable,' Nasreem said, her Yorkshire accent as broad as Terry's own. 'We can't do owt about it unless you tell me the facts.' She got out her notebook and pencil and busied herself trying to impart a sense of calm efficiency, in spite of the fluttering anxiety in her stomach. Whatever he thought about the colour of her skin, he had no choice but to deal with her, but she knew that this antagonism, which she met every day from some local people, only added an edge to the need for her to do a good job. If anyone was going to mess up her career by making a complaint, she thought, it would inevitably be one of these racist bastards.

'She told me she were on t'late shift,' Terry mumbled. 'I look after t'kids when she's working late. She takes the car and is usually back about midnight. I had a few bevvies and fell asleep on t'sofa. I didn't wake up till gone seven this morning, and didn't realise she'd not come back till I went upstairs with a cup of tea for her about half past. She weren't in bed and the car's not outside.'

'No messages?' Nasreem asked. 'Phone, text…?'

'Nowt,' Terry Bastable said. 'And when I rang Shirley's, which is where she works, they said she weren't on t'rota for last night any road. She weren't supposed to be at work at all till tomorrow.'

Nasreem sighed. Anyone asking the questions she knew she had to ask would be unwelcome, she thought, but her interrogation would be more unwelcome than most to this man who sat bolt upright on the sofa, rigid with a fury which she guessed was pretty equally aimed at his errant wife and her own unwelcome presence in his house.

'Has she ever done anything like this before?' she ventured.

Bastable shook his head irritably.

''Course not,' he said. 'She's steady, is Karen. Not like some.'

'And have you been getting on well together? No domestic problems which might lead her to go off on her own for a bit?'

'We're happily married, aren't we?' Bastable said. 'As far as I know, we are, any road. No, no domestic problems, none at all.'

'No hint that she had begun to see anyone else?'

Bastable glowered at Nasreem, his face beginning to look flushed, and shook his head vehemently.

'Nowt like that,' he snapped.

'But she said she was on the late shift, when she wasn't...'

'Summat must have happened to her. Summat bad,' Bastable said, and Nasreem could see the fear in his eyes. 'She went off in t'car. I always make her go by car because she comes back late. Maybe she thought she was on shift... Made a mistake like, with the rota, and summat happened on the way there or on the way back. You hear of women getting abducted, don't you? Women disappear. It's not just kiddies who get taken.'

'It's unusual, Mr Bastable,' Nasreem said gently. 'Most adults who disappear go of their own free will, you know. Generally we wait for a few days, just post them as missing, and they turn up again. In this case we can also look for the car, if you give me the details. It would also help if you could tell me what she was wearing when she left the house.'

Bastable looked at her blankly.

'I didn't notice,' he muttered. 'Her coat, I suppose. It were chilly last night, weren't it? Her coat's dark…blue. No, green. That's right, green wool, but dark, almost black. Fits a bit tight, like. I don't know what she had on under it.'

'Have you looked to see if she's taken a suitcase or holdall? Whether all her clothes are still here?' He shook his head dumbly.

'Could you check that for me, d'you think?' Nasreem asked. Rigid with suppressed emotion, Bastable got to his feet and went thundering upstairs, where Nasreem could hear him opening cupboards and drawers and slamming them shut again. She glanced round the living room of the small house with its large flat-screen TV and PlayStation in one corner, computer games strewn where the children must have left them before they went to school, and she wondered if they had any idea where their mother might have gone. Judging by the school photographs of a blond boy and a red-headed girl on the mantelpiece over the gas fire, they must be ten or eleven, probably still at primary school. Wherever Karen Bastable was, they would no doubt be devastated if she never came back. She sighed and waited until Terry Bastable came back into the room and slammed the door behind him.

'I can't see owt missing,' he said. 'She's got a lot of stuff up there, stuff I've never even seen before, bit saucy, some of it.

But if she'd gone off by her own choice she'd have taken some of her new stuff. Stands to reason. She'd been out shopping just last weekend for holiday gear because we're going to Majorca as soon as t'kids finish school for Easter. Some of the stuff's still in t'Primark bags, not even taken out yet. And all the suitcases are still in t'cupboard on the landing. I don't believe she's run off. It's not what Karen would do. She loves the kids even if...' He didn't finish the sentence although his sudden doubt about his missing wife's commitment to him was written in his face.

'Even if you have your problems?'

'We don't have problems,' Bastable said loudly. 'What would you know about it with your arranged marriages and all that bollocks, any road? My marriage is grand.'

But Nasreem did not believe him. She changed tack suddenly.

'Do you have a bank account? Can she draw money out that you can check on?'

'There's never owt in our account to draw,' Bastable said bitterly. 'We've paid for us holiday, so there's even less than nowt.'

'But you'll check?'

'Aye, I'll check, but it's wasting time, isn't it? I need to know where she is, what's happened to her, the kids need to know. I need you lot to start bloody looking. She'd never go off like this without a word.'

'But it does look as if she might have had plans last night which she didn't want to tell you about, if she said she was going to work and didn't,' Nasreem said. Bastable scowled and clenched his fists, a baffled bull, but said nothing.

'I'll complete a missing person report for her,' Nasreem

went on quickly. 'And I'll log in the details of the car. That's really all we can do for now.'

'Well, it's not enough, is it?' Bastable said angrily. 'You're not taking it bloody seriously.'

'I'm sorry, Mr Bastable,' Nasreem said. 'If you're unhappy about the procedure you can always come down to the station and talk to my sergeant. But you'll get the same answer, I'm afraid.'

'You've not got enough time for folk like us now, all the hours you're putting in tracking effing terrorists and illegals and God knows who in this country,' Bastable shouted, jumping to his feet so suddenly that Nasreem flinched. She stood up herself and deliberately turned her back on the angry man although her heart was thudding as she walked to the door. She turned briefly, her hand on the handle.

'I'm sorry, Mr Bastable. I'll do what I can. Let me know if she comes home, will you? That's the most likely outcome, you know. Honestly it is.'

'Paki cow,' Bastable spat as she closed the front door behind her.

Karen tried to move but she had been secured too tightly for that. She was still wearing the thin clothing she had stripped down to in the forest clearing as she moved back to her car as the meet in the forest began to disperse. She was surprised when a man she had not noticed before, with a scarf pulled up over the lower half of his face, approached her just as she was reaching for her coat.

'Do you feel like another quick turn?' he had asked, his voice muffled by the scarf, and when she had hesitated, he had suddenly seized her from behind pushing her head down, and before she could scream or attract anyone's attention, he had pulled a heavy bag over her head. She had seen pictures of hooded prisoners on television and had never imagined just how suffocatingly disorienting the procedure could be. She had struggled for breath and drawn in only dust and fibres and found herself choking helplessly within seconds. Even as she tried to fight him off, she felt her arms being strapped to her side, and soon knew that she was being bundled into the boot of a car. She tried to scream, but the thick material around her face muffled her cries and she was dimly aware the noise of departing vehicles was fading away. There was nobody left to hear her.

She had no idea how long the journey had lasted but eventually the car stopped and there was complete silence. How long she lay there she had no way of telling. She thought she fell asleep at one point, but could not be sure. She groaned occasionally as her limbs cramped, and she felt freezing cold. And then at last she glimpsed a dim light even through the thick fabric across her face and realised that the boot was being opened and she could see it was already daylight. She had been in the boot all night, she thought, trying to get a good look at the man who was gazing down at her, but he tugged her blindfold down lower so that she could only glimpse him from the waist down.

'You bastard,' she stuttered, through the thick fabric. 'What the hell are you doing?' But he did not respond and she was shivering so convulsively now in the sharp morning air that however much she wriggled and tried to struggle she could not resist the strong arms which took hold of her and dragged her out of the boot and along the ground so violently that she cried out in pain. Eventually she managed to lash out with her feet and catch her attacker so sharply that he too cried out.

'Bitch,' he said, flinging her to the ground in frustration. 'Bloody whore.' She tried shouting and screaming again but the sound seemed to get lost without even penetrating the suffocating mask, and eventually she simply accepted that there was no one to hear her anyway, just as no one had heard her in the forest. She could hear her attacker breathing heavily now, as if in the grip of some overpowering emotion. And she simply began to moan, a high, keening sound, equally muffled, but she was by then beyond rational thought, the hard ground beneath her cold and wet, with sharp stones which tore at her half-naked body.

'Please, please, let me go,' she said, sobbing in despair. 'Please, please don't hurt me.'

But as if he needed to hear her beg, her pleas seemed to act as some sort of trigger and her attacker pulled off the suffocating hood and stood over her, his face still barely visible behind his scarf and a hat pulled low over his eyes.

'Now, you little cow,' he said. 'You still seem to be gagging for some more fun and games. And I can't bloody wait.'

It was then that the pain began, and there was nothing left for Karen to hear except her own gasping, panicking breath and then her desperate screams as the uncaring sun rose faintly and looked down from a pale, misty sky and she begged him in the end to kill her quickly.

CHAPTER TWO

Laura Ackroyd picked at a piece of toast at the breakfast table and watched Michael Thackeray pour himself coffee. He looked tired, she thought, and she knew that he was still occasionally sleeping badly, the residual pain of his gunshot wound keeping him awake. But she was sure that there was more to it than that. What she wanted to discuss – and perhaps soon must – would not help at this time of day, she decided, spooning marmalade onto her plate. Given his present mood, she would leave it until later.

'You're not in a hurry this morning?' he asked, sipping hot coffee and pulling on his jacket.

'I'm going straight up to the Heights to talk to Joyce,' Laura said. 'Part work, part social.'

Laura's grandmother Joyce Ackroyd still lived resolutely on her own on the housing estate she had helped to create in her political heyday in the Sixties and Seventies, unwilling to accept her increasing physical frailty and showing no sign of diminishing mental energy as she pursued one cause or another close to her very old socialist heart.

'What's she up to now?' Thackeray asked with a smile. He approved of Joyce in spite of Laura's anxieties about her obstinately independent lifestyle, in the teeth of encroaching arthritis and the reduction of her neighbourhood to a building site.

'I want to know what she knows about David Murgatroyd, or Sir David, apparently. He was knighted in the last honours list for services to education. He's the one who wants to turn Sutton Park into an academy, but he's an elusive fellow. I know he was born in Yorkshire and has one of his homes here. That's on top of others in London and Monaco and the Caribbean, no less. But when you try to track him down or find out how he made his millions, or maybe billions for all I know, it's like hitting a brick wall. I know Joyce has got herself involved with the Sutton Park governors who don't want to be taken over, so I thought she might have gleaned a bit more info than I've been able to so far. Ted is very keen on a profile but I could write it on the back of a postage stamp so far.'

'I thought you could find out anything about anyone on the Internet these days,' Thackeray said.

'Not this lad,' Laura said. 'Date of birth, the names of his companies – all private equity jobs so almost no details – and a few cuttings on the six academies he's sponsored so far. That explains the recent knighthood, of course. That's about as much as I gleaned yesterday. Another couple of academies and he'll get a peerage, no doubt.'

'Such cynicism in one so young,' Thackeray mocked, pulling on his coat and kissing the top of Laura's copper curls by way of farewell.

'Michael, will you be home reasonably early tonight?' she asked quietly. 'We need to talk.'

He looked at her for a moment, the light draining from his eyes.

'I'll try,' he said, but as he closed the door behind him she wondered if he really meant it.

Later that morning, in her grandmother's tiny living room, nursing a cup of instant coffee as she flicked through the pile of paperwork Joyce had presented her with, Laura marvelled at how efficiently she managed to keep in touch with the various protest movements and campaigns she thought worthy of her political experience and commitment. And surprisingly, Laura thought, in spite of the advance of the smart new politicians of all persuasions who now seemed to dominate the town, there were still people who seemed to value Joyce's old-fashioned wisdom, though her knees would no longer let her wave a banner at their protest marches as she once had.

'The person you want to talk to is Steve O'Mara,' Joyce said. 'I'll give you his phone number. He's one of the parent governors and he's really angry about the whole affair. I think he was on the panel when the new head was appointed and he reckons she's doing a brilliant job. He's afraid that the new regime will simply ignore the local kids who go to Sutton Park now, and go all out to recruit middle-class youngsters from further away to make the place look good. That's what's happened in other places by all accounts. And the parents will lose what little say they have now in how the place is run. This beggar Murgatroyd will control the governors, the school rules, appointments, the lot. Where's the accountability in that? And from what we've been able to find out from the other schools he's taken over, he's one of these born-again Christians.'

'I know, I know,' Laura said. 'I've heard most of this already. What I want now is to get hold of Murgatroyd and put some of these objections to him. But he's an elusive man, is Sir David. He claims to have local connections but I've not tracked down anyone who knows him, or even remembers him from way back. Have you heard of him?'

'There used to be a David Murgatroyd out Eckersley way years ago. Too long ago to be this one, but maybe a relation. All I can recall is that he was a county councillor for a while, Tory of course, and was one of those who tried to stop the West Riding going for comprehensive schools in the Sixties because it meant closing Eckersley Grammar. Made no difference, of course. There were only a handful of Tories on t'county council back then when Harold Wilson got in. Not like the other ridings where they still ruled the roost, of course: all those landowners and farmers. Mind you, they all went comprehensive in the end, when they realised how much money they were wasting on all those small grammar schools and bog-standard secondary moderns. Maggie Thatcher closed more grammar schools than anyone else, you know.' Joyce chuckled in satisfaction.

'But Murgatroyd...' Laura edged her grandmother back to the matter in hand. Her knowledge of the politics of her beloved county was encyclopaedic but inclined these days to be rambling.

'Aye, David Murgatroyd,' Joyce acquiesced amiably enough. 'I don't reckon he was involved in politics for very long. As I recall he resigned quite quickly. I think there was some family tragedy, but I really can't remember what it was. You might find something in the archives at the *Gazette*, I should think. Bradfield Council and the county never had a right lot to do with each other. We were textiles, they were mining and the rural bits in between. We didn't have a right lot in common, even in the Labour Party. We weren't in the pockets of the miners' union, like some.' Laura could see the pain of old battles lost in her grandmother's eyes, but she had more urgent things on her mind and she pressed on.

'So if that David Murgatroyd is my man Murgatroyd's father, he could well have been born in the county. According to *Who's Who*, which has a very brief entry, he was born in 1960, so he would have been a small child when his father was involved in politics.'

'Look in your own archives,' Joyce said. 'It's sure to be there. Eckersley wasn't part of Bradfield in them days but it was close enough for the *Gazette* to keep an eye on.'

'I'll do that,' Laura said. 'And I'll catch up with Steve O'Mara. What about the new head at Sutton Park? Is she really doing a good job?'

'Debbie Stapleton? Yes, I reckon she is. Steve's no fool and he rates her very highly. And the exam results are getting better, for what that's worth. You should talk to her, too. Steve said she's absolutely gutted with what's happening. Feels she's been sold down the river by the council, which seems to have fallen for this scheme hook, line and sinker.'

'I bet she does,' Laura said, finishing her coffee. 'Right, I'd better get into the office or Ted Grant will think I've jumped ship.'

Joyce glanced at her granddaughter, with her red hair and green eyes, a combination of colouring and character which reminded her so sharply of her own impulsive youth that it brought tears to her eyes, and eventually asked her the question that kept her awake at night.

'And are you? Thinking of jumping ship?' Laura shook her head sharply.

'Of course not,' she said. 'What gives you that impression?'

'Oh, I know you, miss,' Joyce said enigmatically. 'Do you think I can't tell when you're unhappy?'

'I'm fine,' Laura said firmly.

'And that man of yours? What's he doing? Is he going to make an honest woman of you?'

Laura laughed at the question although she knew that she wanted it answered a hundred times more urgently than Joyce did.

'We're fine,' she prevaricated. 'Always busy, but fine.' Joyce did not believe her.

Back at the office, Laura took Joyce Ackroyd's advice and delved back into the paper's own dusty archives and soon found some of what she was looking for. David Murgatroyd had indeed been a county councillor in the mid-Sixties and had resigned before his four-year term of office was up. But it was the reason for that resignation which intrigued Laura. Murgatroyd, who had died suddenly in 1974, had been a wealthy textile manufacturer who, like many before him, had abandoned the smoky environment of Bradfield, where he had amassed his millions, and bought a country pile, Sibden House, just outside the small market town of Eckersley, ten miles or so up the valley of the Maze and well out of sight of the belching mill chimneys of the industrial belt. Once there, he had apparently established himself as lord of the manor and local politician. But as Laura flicked through the cuttings, it soon became apparent that his comfortable lifestyle was built on sand.

His wife, younger than he was, had given him two children

in his middle age: a son, and a daughter six years later. Exactly what happened was not fully spelt out in the archive. Local papers had none of the intrusive carelessness with people's private lives that the tabloids had begun to wallow in after the birth of Murdoch's *Sun* years later, and the details of the family tragedy in the *Gazette* were minimal and muted. But it was clear from the inquest report that Murgatroyd's wife had suffered some sort of breakdown – post-natal depression Laura guessed – and had drowned herself and the baby in a reservoir not far from their home. The jury had returned a kindly open verdict. Mrs Murgatroyd had left no note.

Laura felt suddenly cold. The stark details recorded by the coroner were close enough to Michael Thackeray's bitter experience to make her shudder. This was one investigation she would not be sharing with him in much detail, she thought. But she was intrigued to uncover whether the younger David Murgatroyd, whose life story she was investigating and who seemed still to have a house in the county, was in fact the son of the late county councillor and had been left motherless at seven and an orphan in his teens. It was quite possible, she thought, that he still owned his father's house and the simplest way to find out might be to go up to Eckersley and ask.

Ten miles above Bradfield, where the fells rose sharply towards the lowering, windswept watershed which separated the steep industrial valleys of West Yorkshire from the more rolling plains of industrial Lancashire, two men bounced on a tractor along the rutted track through a conifer plantation. They were pulling a long, low trailer, which swung wildly if the driver accelerated too fast, as he often seemed tempted to do. The two men wore earmuffs, which insulated them not just from the roar of the heavy diesel engine but also from the natural rustle and sough of the forest floor, littered deep with pine needles; not much of a habitat for birds but home to a few small creatures who scuttled beneath the trees, and to an occasional deer which had strayed to this upland retreat from its more fruitful pastures lower down the valley.

The tractor eventually reached its destination, a clearing where the sun could just penetrate and some thin green vegetation survived, and where stacked piles of felled logs were waiting to be loaded onto the trailer and taken to the sawmill. The driver killed the engine, took off his ear protection and hard hat and glanced at his companion.

'Who the hell is that?' he asked, waving at a compact blue car parked almost out of sight beneath the trees and partially obscured by bushes. His companion shrugged and jumped down from the cab and sauntered over to the car, which turned out to be an elderly Astra. He was followed by the driver, who was lighting up a cigarette and sucking in the smoke gratefully.

'No one here,' his mate said, peering through the misted windscreen. 'Someone left their coat.' A dark-coloured item lay crumpled on the front passenger seat as if it had been discarded in a hurry. He tried the passenger door and looked surprised when it swung open.

'Careless beggar,' he said, peering into the interior. 'Gone for a walk, d'you reckon?'

'Bloody funny place to come rambling,' the driver said, glancing round the clearing and the almost impenetrable ranks of trees which enclosed it. 'Any road, it's nowt to do wi'us. If they've not come back when we finish up this afternoon we'll report it in.' He paused for a moment and looked at the ground more closely. 'There've been a few cars up here since last week,' he said thoughtfully. 'Look at them tyre tracks. Summat funny's been going off.'

'Darren said he thought cars were coming up here at night,' his partner said. 'Noticed it a few times, he said. I've not seen owt missen, but then rain washes out tracks pretty fast.'

'You'd not think they'd come all this way for a bit of nooky. Even in my day we made do with the edge of Broadley Moor and most of t'kids seem to be happy with a bloody car park these days. They don't care who sees them at it.'

'At it like bloody rabbits, teenagers today,' said his companion, a small grey-haired man, with a sour look. 'We'd best get a shift on. We'll be up here all day, else. And there's no overtime to be had, you can bet on that, no bloody fear.'

The two men returned to the trailer and set about their day's work, casting only an occasional glance at the apparently abandoned blue car. Only when they left the clearing with their last trailer load of logs did they mention it again.

'I'll drop you off, and tell Gordon about it when I get back to t'yard,' the driver said. 'It's a bit odd, that.' But when he had unloaded and completed his paperwork, Gordon has already gone home, and he promised himself he would report it the following morning. If he remembered.

Laura was glad to be out of the office. She had made another call to the only number she had for David Murgatroyd's business enterprises and had met a brick wall for the fourth time. Mr Murgatroyd did not give interviews, she was told by a press officer. Mr Murgatroyd's interests were private. There were no public companies and so no public information. There would be no change in that position however many times she approached them.

Irritated, she had reported her failure back to Ted Grant and got his reluctant acquiescence to a trip out of town to attempt to discover where the mysterious would-be benefactor of Sutton Park School had quite possibly started his life.

Now, with the weight of Ted's hostility off her shoulders, she determined to forget her private worries and enjoy the trip up the valley of the Maze towards Eckersley where, just beyond the gargantuan and monstrously ugly building society offices which dominated the small town, a monument to the Yorkshire tradition of thrift and canny investment, she turned off the main road and headed up into the steep hills above the river.

The small village of Sibden lay a mile or so from, and five hundred feet above Eckersley, in a narrow wooded valley where a beck tumbled vigorously down from the moors to the river below. A cluster of stone cottages huddled around a pub and beyond that a high stone wall commenced on the left-hand side of the narrow lane. Laura continued slowly up the hill alongside the wall, until it was broken by a solid stone archway and high wrought-iron gates, firmly closed and, she could see even from the car, with an electronic keypad to one side and under surveillance from CCTV. There was no indication what or who lay beyond the gates, and nothing to be seen through them except a well-kept gravel drive which disappeared into rhododendron shrubberies and trees. She guessed that this must be Sibden House, the former home of

David Murgatroyd senior, and still quite possibly, given the level of security, of the man she assumed to be his son.

She pulled off the road and into the entrance and got out of the car. Whoever lived here, she thought, neither wanted nor expected casual callers. In fact, as she looked at the high stone wall more closely, they seemed quite determined to deter them. The wall was topped with several strands of vicious-looking razor wire.

Without much optimism, she pressed the bell push at the top of the keypad and was quite surprised when a male voice asked her who she was and what she wanted. She introduced herself and was rewarded with a prolonged silence. Then the voice came back sharply.

'Sir David Murgatroyd is not in residence,' it said. 'And he does not give interviews to the Press. Please take this as a final answer.'

Laura made to protest but the intercom had been switched off at the other end and she was left fuming, with a chill wind whipping round her making her glad she had put her jacket in the car. She reversed out of the entrance in front of the forbidding gates and drove slowly back to the village and found a parking space outside the Leg of Mutton, a dilapidated-looking public house with a few mildewed picnic tables at the front and only a glimmer of light inside to indicate that it might possibly be open to the passing traveller in search of a drink and a bite of lunch. No gastropub here, she thought wryly, and guessed it would not be long before an establishment like this either closed or was transformed into something a bit more stylish. The door creaked as she opened it and she found herself in a shabby barroom, with beer-stained tables, and no other human presence in sight. She stood at the bar for a moment, uncertain how to attract attention but eventually a middle-aged man, with a beer belly hanging over his jeans, slouched from the murky regions at the back and scowled at her.

'We've nowt to eat,' he said. 'Delivery's not turned up this morning.'

'I'll have a drink then,' Laura said quickly. 'Can you do me a Bloody Mary?'

The publican looked startled, as if this was something he had seldom concocted, but turned to the vodka optic accurately enough and shuffled through the soft drinks until he found a can of tomato juice so dusty that it looked as if it had sat on his shelves untouched for years rather than months. Laura decided against asking for ice, in case it turned out to be an unwarranted provocation.

She paid for the drink and leant on the bar to take a sip.

'I've just been up to Sibden House,' she confided. 'I wanted to see David Murgatroyd but they say he's not there very often.' The publican stared at her stony-faced, his small blue eyes betraying not a scintilla of interest.

'Oh aye?' he said.

'Do you know him? Mr Murgatroyd? Or Sir David, as he is now.'

'Nobody knows *him*. He's never there, is he?'

'Doesn't do much for the village, then?' Laura asked.

'Why would he? Most o't'old village has gone, any road. It's all weekend cottages now. Come for that new golf course Joe Emmet has opened on what should be good grazing land. Bring their food with 'em from Marks and bloody Spencers, they do, and bugger off back to Leeds first thing Monday morning. Never set foot in here.' Laura thought that the landlord's complaint might be better justified if he made more effort himself to smarten the place up and attract customers, but she said nothing, sipping her drink slowly.

'So does Sir David come for weekends, then? Is this just his country pad?' For some reason her last question unlocked the publican's tongue.

'I don't know what it is,' he said, looking even more surly, but evidently provoked by some anger which Laura did not comprehend. 'It were left empty for long enough after his father died, my mother said. This one were only a little lad then and he got sent away to school when his mam topped herself. You know about that, do you?'

Laura nodded non-committally.

'It were only about ten years back young Murgatroyd turned up again and did the old place up. It had gone to rack and ruin by then, but brass were no object. He brought in big contractors from outside. No work for t'locals, was there? And like a bloody fortress when he'd finished. Alarms, cameras, the full bloody monty. And even now we never see him. I don't know what he's got hidden away in there, that needs all that security. But they say he's a millionaire now so maybe t'place is stuffed full o'gold bullion. You can bet your life he pays no tax on it, if it is. They don't, do they? It's poor sods like us who get screwed while folk like him get all the breaks.'

'You won't remember his father, I don't suppose?'

'My Mam spoke highly of him.'

'Is she…?' Laura probed.

'Passed on, didn't she? Last year.'

'I'm sorry,' Laura said.

'Don't be,' the publican said with finality. 'She had a stroke.

Couldn't bloody speak for three years and we got no help wi'her to speak of. It were a blessing when she went.' That was another path Laura did not wish to tread, so she simply nodded sympathetically.

'Is there anyone left in the village who might remember the older Murgatroyd, this one's father?' she asked quickly.

'You could try old Fred Betts. He were a gardener and I think he worked up there way back. But he's in an old folks' home now, so I don't know how much he'll remember. He may have gone ga-ga, for all I know.'

'Which home?' Laura asked.

'Old Royd, down in Eckersley, on t'road up to Broadley over t'moor. You can't miss it. They say on a bad day you can smell it from half a mile off.'

Laura took a deep breath and pushed her drink away. She had not wanted it in the first place and now she knew she could not take another sip without gagging. She turned towards the door without a word and left the bar, hoping she never had to set foot in the place again. If the landlord was typical of Sibden, she thought, it was no wonder that the weekend visitors had as little as possible to do with the pub. The place exuded decay and rancour and she wondered how far the Murgatroyds, son and possibly father, were responsible for that.

She drove thoughtfully back into Eckersley, joined the old main road and turned off over the bridge that crossed the bypass to climb the steep hill up the opposite side of the valley, towards Broadley and the open moorland which lay between Eckersley and its more elevated neighbour. Before the suburban bungalows gave out and the cattle grids signalled the approach of the sheep-friendly open road, she pulled into the car park of Old Royd Nursing Home. The place had been the subject of a scandal not so long ago, she recalled, when the owners had been accused of sedating some of their residents in the interests of a quiet life for the staff. It was under new and, she hoped, better management now. The door was answered by a young woman in a blue overall who seemed surprised when she asked to see Fred Betts.

'He's likely asleep,' she said. 'He does a lot of sleeping, does Fred.' It was an unwise comment, Laura thought, in view of the place's history, but the girl was young enough perhaps not to know what had gone on a few years previously. She was led down a long corridor which, in spite of the publican's comments, smelt fresh enough – in fact somewhat over-disinfected – but that was undoubtedly better than the alternative, and when her guide knocked on one of the doors she was answered by a voice which sounded unexpectedly vigorous.

'You've got a visitor, Fred,' the girl said, and left Laura in the doorway to face a small, wrinkled man muffled up in blankets in his wheelchair, who gave little sign of life beyond his eyes, which were bright blue and piercingly alert.

'I thought it might be my daughter,' Fred Betts said sharply. 'But I expect she's too busy.'

Laura smiled, knowing that she could not make up for a daughter, though at least she might break the monotony of life in a home for a while. She explained who she was and why she was here and saw the old man's eyes become distant as he considered events which he could probably remember more clearly than he could recall what had happened yesterday.

'He were all right, were old Murgatroyd,' he said at length. 'A fair boss and a fair man, but obsessed with his work. Never enough time for people was his trouble and it did for him in the end. Not that I'm saying he deserved what happened to him, mind. No one deserved that.'

'I'm writing about his son,' Laura said. 'But it's very hard to make any contact. The house is locked up and he doesn't give interviews, apparently.'

'He were always a close one, the lad, even as a babby. Never said much. And after his mother died he were sent away to school. And then his dad passed on an'all, died of a broken heart, they reckoned – and I don't think young David ever came back to Sibden after that. I never saw him, any road. The staff were laid off soon after the old man went, and the house was just abandoned. The gardens turned to a jungle. It were a crying shame after all the work that went into them previous. A terrible waste.'

'What happened to his mother exactly?' Laura asked.

'She were a lovely lady. A bit nervy, like, even in t'beginning. She near jumped out of her skin one day when I came up on her unexpected, like, in the gardens. And she were left alone a lot in that big place. Old Murgatroyd had his ambitions and he were away a lot. But she never got over t'second baby. A little girl, it were. Jennifer. The lad were about six or seven by then, and the housekeeper said he doted on t'baby. But his mother never recovered. She went a bit funny. And one night she took the little lass, and just walked into t'reservoir on Broadley Moor with her. They found them the next morning, the baby's hands tangled up in her hair, they said. Lovely red hair she had, a bit like yours. Both drowned. Ten months old, the baby girl were. What did she ever do to hurt anyone?' Even after all those years, the old man's eyes filled with tears. 'A crying shame, it were,' he said.

'I read the inquest report,' Laura said. 'But the boy? He must have been devastated.'

'He got sent off to boarding school as soon as he were old enough – if you think eight's old enough. His father never had much time for him, and after that he were more interested in burying himself in his political work than looking after his lad. By the time the boy were fourteen or so, the old man were dead any road. Left the lad a small fortune, but there'd been little love lost. When he came home for t'holidays he used to mooch around the house and garden on his own most o't' time. Came chattering to us working in t'garden, as if we had time to listen. Never brought friends back and he had no friends local, like. Not so far as I could see, any road. A lonely lad in a lonely, sad house. Like his mother were a lonely wife. I don't think old Murgatroyd meant any harm. He never saw it coming with his wife, that's for sure, but other folk did.'

Laura drove back to Bradfield slowly and headed straight home. She was not sure that Michael Thackeray would keep his promise to come back early, but she planned a meal which would survive until he eventually arrived. Then, she thought apprehensively, they really must talk. Soon it would become obvious that the worry that had oppressed her for the last few weeks had become a certainty, and she had absolutely no confidence that he would greet the news that he might be about to become a father again with anything other than horror. And with the tragic story of David Murgatroyd's loss of his wife and baby daughter fresh in her mind, Laura was only too aware of why that might be so.

CHAPTER THREE

DS Kevin Mower had no doubt about the mood his boss was in when he went into his office the next morning. Difficult would have been the most charitable adjective he could ever conjure up for Thackeray after all the years he had worked for him, which did not mean that Mower did not have respect and even affection for the older man, but these were feelings he had learnt to keep to himself. And this morning the atmosphere resembled one of those days when a threatening sky seems to press down on the world and lightning can be seen flickering on the horizon.

'Guv,' he said tentatively, closing the door behind him. 'You've seen the reports on this missing woman?'

'Why wasn't I told about this yesterday?' Thackeray said. 'It seems to have been obvious enough to the young copper who interviewed the husband that something serious was up.'

'Well, she told her sergeant that, but he didn't agree, played it down, so it didn't go in her written report. There was absolutely no evidence that Karen Bastable hadn't left home of her own free will. They filed a misper report and circulated the car number. When I spoke to him he was still a bit dismissive of PC Mirza's worries. She told him Bastable was a racist bastard and he's obviously got up her nose. That may be why he discounted her concerns.'

'Do you know PC Mirza?' Thackeray asked.

'I've met her actually,' Mower said. 'She was with "Omar" Sharif at a race relations course at HQ a couple of months ago.'

'And...?'

'She seemed a sharp cookie,' Mower conceded. 'Sharif seemed to rate her too. Reckoned she'd do well.'

'Right. So talk to her before you go and see Bastable. Get her take on the situation. If this woman's car's been found ten miles from home and a couple of miles into Bently Forest, which is not exactly a spot you'd go for a picnic at this time of year, it casts a whole new light on her disappearance. And if I've got to persuade Jack Longley to start a major search in that sort of terrain, I'm going to need all the facts at my disposal. What time did the forestry workers report this?'

'The message came in at about 8.30 this morning from their foreman. But they actually saw the car yesterday morning parked in the clearing where they were working. Apparently they just thought someone was walking in the woods but when no one had come back by the end of the day they decided to report it to the foreman, but he'd gone home, so they did the same. They only mentioned it this morning when they went in to work.'

'So we've already lost twenty-four hours?' Thackeray said incredulously. 'Don't they carry mobile phones, these silly beggars?' Mower shrugged.

'If they do, they obviously didn't think it was worth calling in. Incredible. Though to be fair, you're lucky to get a decent signal in some of those remote areas.'

'Did it rain up there last night? It was pouring down when I got home.'

'I think it was pretty general. So forensics will have a hard time finding anything useful at the scene,' Mower said.

'Right. First things first. Get uniform to make sure the car is still up there, and cordon it off,' Thackeray said. 'We don't want anyone putting muddy fingerprints all over it before we've had a thorough look. Then talk to PC Mirza before you go to see the husband. Take her with you if you like. She might be useful in spotting if he's changed his story at all. There's only two possibilities, if she drove to a remote spot like that. She's either still up there, alive, or quite possibly dead. Or she left in someone else's vehicle. Again, she could have gone off willingly with someone. Or perhaps not.'

'Guv,' Mower said.

Thackeray sat immobile for a long time after Mower had closed his office door behind him but his mind was not on the possible disappearance of Karen Bastable. He had not gone home early the previous evening, as he had promised Laura, and when he finally arrived he had found her already in bed reading.

'Have you eaten?' she had asked ungraciously, when he had pleaded pressure of work. But he had shaken his head, then slumped in a chair watching TV and not gone to bed himself until he had been sure she was asleep. He guessed that she wanted to talk about a commitment he had rashly made a few months before, a last desperate throw, he thought now, to keep Laura with him and one which he had come to regret.

Now life had returned to something more like normal, he realised how hard that commitment would be to keep, how much, in fact, it terrified him. However much Laura wanted a child, he did not think that he could possibly become a father again.

Sergeant Kevin Mower warmed to PC Nasreem Mirza. She described her interview with Terry Bastable with a glint of humour in her dark eyes.

'You don't let the racist bastards get you down, then?' Mower asked.

'You can't, can you? They'd only think they were winning. It's been worse since the London bombs, of course, but I'm not going to be blamed for what those idiots did.'

'Do you want to come with me to talk to him again? You obviously weren't happy with what he told you.'

'It was more that there was something I thought he wasn't telling me,' Nasreem said. 'I'll certainly come if you want me to. If my sergeant's happy.'

The sergeant was happy enough, but it was obvious that Terry Bastable was not when the two officers arrived on his doorstep.

'Have you found her?' he demanded as he reluctantly let them into the house, reserving his glare for the Asian PC and addressing himself entirely to Mower.

'We've found her car, Mr Bastable, apparently abandoned, but there's no sign of your wife, I'm afraid.'

Bastable threw himself onto the sofa and ran a hand across his forehead, as if to wipe something away.

'I've not had a bloody wink of sleep,' he said. 'Couldn't stop thinking about her, where the hell she might be.'

'You've heard nothing, I take it?' Mower asked. 'You'd have called us...?'

'Nowt,' Bastable said. 'She's gone without a bloody word. She wouldn't do that, would she? Not our Karen. Summat bad must have happened or she would have got in touch. The kids are up the wall...'

'Have you any idea why she might have driven up to Bently, that big Forestry Commission plantation beyond Haworth?' Mower asked.

'I've no bloody idea,' Bastable said. 'I didn't know there was a plantation beyond Haworth. I've never bleeding heard of it.'

'Well, in view of the fact that her car was found abandoned in such a remote spot, we'll have to start a search up there,' Mower said carefully. 'There's still no firm evidence that anything untoward has happened to your wife, Mr Bastable, but it's looking more likely than yesterday.'

'I told this P—, this *officer*, that summat untoward had happened, didn't I?' Bastable spat back. 'Karen would never have just gone off wi'out a word. Never.'

'There is just one thing you could do at this stage to help us,' Nasreem said calmly. 'Would you let me have a look round the house, just to get an idea of what she was like, the sort of clothes she wore, that sort of thing?' It was obvious from Bastable's face that he wanted to say no, but he glanced at Mower's implacable expression and thought better of it.

'I suppose so,' he said, addressing Mower again. 'Though I've told *her* already.' He scowled in Nasreem's direction. 'She's taken nowt with her that I know of.' PC Mirza glanced at Mower, who nodded, and she left the room to go upstairs. From below they could hear her moving quickly around the bedroom above them, opening drawers and cupboards. Bastable sat forward, as if tensed to spring out of his chair. His hostility to Nasreem Mirza was palpable and Mower determined to warn her sergeant not to send her here on her own again.

'Calm down, Mr Bastable,' he said. 'This is all just routine.'

'Not for me, it's bloody not,' Bastable grunted.

'So tell me some more about Karen. What about her friends?' Mower asked. 'Have you contacted anyone to ask if they know where she might have gone?'

Bastable glared at Mower for a long moment before he replied.

'What friends?' he asked. 'You mean a boyfriend? You mean she might have a boyfriend?' His colour rose and for a moment Mower thought that he might take a swing at him with one of his fiercely clenched fists.

'I didn't mean that,' Mower said quietly. 'Though if you've any evidence...?' He left the question hanging in a heavy silence. Bastable did not reply and gradually he sank back into his chair, deflated.

'I meant her friends, girlfriends, workmates perhaps, or women she goes out with occasionally. Anyone she worked with who she might have talked to?' Mower persisted. 'She must have some women friends, surely.'

'Girls' nights out, you mean? She doesn't do owt like that,' Bastable said. 'I don't like gangs of women out to get pissed. That's no way for a married woman to behave. Mind you...' He stopped again. 'Just recently, she's been out a few times with Charlene.'

'Who's Charlene?'

'I've not met her. She talks about someone called Charlene

at her work,' Bastable said. 'You'd have to ask at Shirley's.'

'Right, I'll check her out,' Mower promised. PC Mirza came back into the room and shook her head imperceptibly and the sergeant got to his feet.

'We'll launch a search around where the car was found, probably later today, Mr Bastable,' he said. 'But it's an isolated spot and it'll take some time. We'll keep you in touch with what's happening, and if there's anything else that you think we should know, don't hesitate to contact us, will you?'

Bastable had slumped in his chair now, his eyes closed.

'She wouldn't have gone of her own free will,' he muttered. 'Not Karen. Summat bad's happened to her. I know it has.'

Back in the car, Mower glanced at Nasreem.

'What did you think?' he asked.

'It all looked perfectly ordinary upstairs,' she said. 'Though she's got a lot of sexy underwear, I will say that. A few things I'd never seen before. Must have come from one of those special shops. My parents would go potty if I came home with anything like that.'

'Perhaps she and Terry have an exciting sex life,' Mower said mildly. Nasreem shuddered slightly.

'Rather her than me,' she said.

'Are you married?' Mower asked tentatively.

'No, I'm the despair of my parents' life,' Nasreem said, with a shrug. 'It's not as if they're particularly religious. There was no nonsense about covering my head, or anything. And they were happy to support me at school and college and with my career. It's just that at my age, most Muslim women are married with kids. It's obvious they'd like grandchildren. They always do, don't they, parents?' She shrugged and glanced at Mower. 'It's just the problem of finding the right man. The longer I'm independent, I guess, the harder it's going to be.'

'I know the feeling,' Mower said, the image of the beautiful Indian girl he had once loved and then lost flashing briefly into his mind. He seldom thought about her these days. Their affair had been brief and had ended tragically. But that was as close as he had ever got to marriage, he thought, and he could not imagine that it would ever happen again.

'Right,' he said. 'Let's go and chase up Mrs Bastable's friend, Charlene, and see if she knows anything about where she might have gone or who she might have been meeting.

Sutton Park School occupied a motley collection of dilapidated buildings on a steep hillside overlooking the centre of Bradfield. Its core, originally a boys' secondary school, was a grim stone pile which in the expansionist Sixties had proved inadequate for its new mixed intake as a comprehensive school, and had been surrounded and almost overwhelmed by extensions and temporary classrooms. As Laura Ackroyd drove into the car park and reversed into a solitary slot marked for visitors, she pulled a wry face. She knew the temptation there must be here to accept a multi-million pound rebuilding programme and began to wonder why the governors and staff could possibly object to what they had to give up in return for becoming an academy. Could passing control to Sir David Murgatroyd be so dreadful that they would rather continue to live and work in this municipal slum? On the surface, it seemed like a small price to pay.

She locked her car and followed the notices which led her to a cramped reception area and then to the office of the head teacher, Debbie Stapleton, a smartly dressed plump woman

with a warm smile in spite of the lines of strain around her
eyes.

'Come in,' the head teacher said warmly, holding out her
hand. 'Your grandmother said you would give us a fair
hearing in the *Gazette*. We could certainly do with some
support.'

'Tell me about it,' Laura said, accepting the chair Debbie
waved her into and switching on her tape recorder. 'Why have
you been singled out to be an academy?'

Debbie waved a hand at the view from her window, where
puddles of rainwater stood on flat roofs and scaffolding
surrounded a dilapidated outcrop from the original stone
building, although there were no workmen in sight.

'The place is falling down,' she said. 'And we'll get no
money for rebuilding for years and years unless the council
goes for academy status.'

'That sounds a bit like blackmail,' Laura said.

'You said that, not me. I couldn't possibly comment.'
Debbie Stapleton's face relaxed into a smile. 'I'm not allowed
to.'

'So what's so bad about it?'

'There are two objections, really,' the headmistress said.
'One of principle, the other specific to this school. In
principle, I personally don't think that control of schools
should be taken away from the local community. The
governors here are not political apparatchiks. They represent
all the people who have a stake in the school, and the whole
of the community we serve: local business, the minority ethnic
groups, we even have the local vicar on board, plus parents,
staff, students. That would all go. The governors would be
appointed by the sponsor. But to be honest, if that were the

only objection I don't think I could carry the existing governors with me. They'd look at the plans for shiny new buildings, computers, laboratories and the rest and they'd go for it.'

'So what's the second objection?' Laura asked.

'David Murgatroyd,' Debbie said. 'The second objection is personal. This is a multi-ethnic school. We take most of the Muslim children from around Aysgarth Lane. Plus most of the white children from the Heights, and quite a lot of black youngsters. They have all sorts of problems, but we're beginning to make a success of it. They do well here. Exam results are improving. Discipline is improving. The inspectors are happy – or much happier than they were before I came, anyway. We don't need Murgatroyd. He's some sort of born-again Christian. He's been accused in Parliament of forcing his views on the academies he's already running. They're imposing rigid regimes and throwing out anyone who won't conform – children or staff. Where will our difficult kids go if they can't come here? St Mark's is very successful at filling its places with middle-class kids. Who's going to look after the rest if we don't?'

'I'm trying to write a profile of David Murgatroyd, but he's a very elusive man. I've not been able to get near him for an interview.'

Debbie Stapleton laughed.

'No one can get near him, according to my teachers' union people. The closest anyone gets is to one of his bag carriers, a man called Winston Sanderson. He's been to talk to our governors but they were less than impressed. Not because he's black, which he is; Jamaican heritage, I think. People simply don't like his uncompromising views, which presumably echo his boss's. Intelligent design, no proper sex education, homophobic prejudice...you name it. Of course, we have some parents who'd go along with some of that, especially some of the Muslims, but we've succeeded here so far by emphasising tolerance of difference. You can't realistically ban bullying because of the colour of someone's skin and then let it rip if they have a different sexuality. Bullying is bullying, in my book, and we don't put up with it here.'

Laura was surprised at how passionate Debbie Stapleton suddenly became. She flushed and glanced away for a moment and Laura saw that her eyes were filled with tears.

'I was bullied at school myself,' she said quietly. 'This man Murgatroyd stands for everything I hate.'

Laura paused for a moment to let the headmistress compose herself.

'Would you survive the change yourself, as head, I mean?' Laura asked.

Debbie shrugged. 'I'd have to apply for my own job. I shouldn't think my face would fit.'

'Do you have any contact details for this man Sanderson? Maybe I can get to Murgatroyd through him.'

'You could try,' Debbie said. 'He left me a mobile number. Apparently he travels a lot. Murgatroyd himself is based in London.'

'He is a Yorkshireman, by birth anyway, apparently, and he has a house up here,' Laura said. 'He seems to have hung on to the family home in Sibden, but he wasn't there when I went up to see if I could catch him.'

'Right,' Debbie said. 'Mr Sanderson did say they stay there sometimes. In any case, David Murgatroyd is coming here in a week's time. Sanderson said his boss would want to talk to the governors himself after they gave him quite a rough time at the last meeting. It's scheduled for the 16th. You ought to be able to catch both of them then.'

'Fine,' Laura said. 'I'll certainly try to pin them down then if I can't make contact before that, though my editor is pressing me for something sooner rather than later.' She wrote down Sanderson's mobile number carefully.

'These people can't career around the country taking over schools without explaining to people exactly what they have in mind for them, can they?' she asked.

'Oh, I wouldn't bank on it,' Debbie Stapleton said. 'That seems to be exactly what David Murgatroyd is doing. And I don't anticipate being here very long myself if he gets away with it at Sutton Park. As I said, I'm quite sure I'll be the first to go.' She gazed out of the window for a second, with a weary expression. 'All that work here and that's the thanks I get,' she said quietly.

'You must have succeeded Margaret Jackson as head,' Laura said. 'I met her when a boy was killed here some years ago. Did you know about that?'

'Oh yes, that was one of the reasons my partner said I'd be a fool to take this on. But it was ancient history, really, and it wasn't anything to do with the kids here, was it? I think they were much more affected when Margaret died so soon after she left. That upset a lot of them.'

'Yes, I knew she had cancer,' Laura said. 'It was a bad time for the school. They were lucky not to be closed down then, I think.'

'They've been on the brink so long that I think the staff have got used to it. But we have made real progress in the last couple of years. That's what's so galling about this takeover bid. But people will be seduced by the promise of new buildings. You can see what a dump the place is. It may be blackmail, but it'll probably work.'

'Well, good luck,' Laura said. 'I'll give you a call about the 16th if I haven't succeeded in tracking Murgatroyd down before then.'

Karen Bastable's friend Charlene Brough was not at work when DS Kevin Mower and PC Nasreem Mirza went looking for her. She was off sick, according to her supervisor, who reluctantly provided an address for her on the other side of the Heights from where the Bastables themselves lived – a tightly packed warren of newly built houses with tiny gardens that had been intended for first-time buyers but which were almost all occupied now by families with young children, trapped there by the housing market.

Mower knocked at the white PVC front door and glanced upstairs at the tightly curtained bedroom windows.

'If she's really sick, she could be asleep,' he said. He knocked again and eventually the door was opened a crack by a woman in a black lacy negligee. She hesitated for a moment when Mower introduced himself before grudgingly easing the door open to let them in. She led them into an untidy living room and waved them into chairs before lighting a cigarette and drawing the smoke deep into her lungs. She was a small woman, pale and thin to the point of emaciation, with untidy blond hair still uncombed and smudges of black make-up around her eyes that only accentuated the deep hollows of tiredness.

'I'm sorry to bother you if you're not well, Mrs Brough,' Mower said. 'But we're becoming increasingly worried about your friend Karen Bastable.'

At the mention of Karen's name Charlene shuddered and flung herself down on a chair by the fireplace, drawing hard on her cigarette. But she said nothing.

'Have you any idea why she might have taken her car up onto the hills and abandoned it in the middle of a forest?' Mower asked, an edge of anger in his voice. He had seen many guilty men and women and he had no doubt that this woman sprawled in front of them, oblivious to the fact that her negligee had flopped open to reveal her bra and thong, was as guilty as hell.

Charlene gazed at the glowing tip of her cigarette before stubbing it out and lighting another and belatedly pulling her wrap more closely around her as she began to shiver.

'I should have gone with her,' she said. 'I should never have let her go on her own.'

'Where did she go? And why?' Mower asked.

'You heard o'dogging?' Charlene asked and Mower nodded impassively, although Nasreem looked startled.

'That's what it were. Karen and me got into it a few months back. People were meeting up there, in them woods, every couple of weeks. We always went together but last time I got close to a bloke and he wanted a bit more, wanted to see me again, so I didn't go that night. I met him here instead.' She glanced at the ceiling above their heads where sounds of movement could be heard.

'He were here again last night. My husband drives a long-distance truck. He's away a lot.' Her explanation was matter-of-fact, as if that excused everything.

'So Karen went on her own?' Mower asked.

'She must of, mustn't she? She wouldn't want to miss, I know that. She loved it.' She noticed Nasreem's appalled gaze and flushed slightly. 'It were just a bit of fun,' she said. 'Just a bit of a laugh. Nowt serious.'

'I'll need a full statement, from you and your boyfriend,' Mower said. He had no right to criticise with his record, he thought, but this industrial-scale adultery made him shudder. 'I'd like you both to come down to the police station and give us all the details you can.'

'There aren't any details,' Charlene said. 'You never know who's going to be there, who you'll go with. No names, no details. As I said, just a bit of fun.'

'Well, it may not have turned out so funny for Karen,' Mower said. 'I need to know whatever you know about the men who turned up there, what they looked like, what cars they were driving, anything else you can recall. And the same from your boyfriend, if that's where you met him.'

'Do you have to get him involved?' Charlene asked, her reluctance obvious. 'That'll be the end of a beautiful friendship, that will.'

'Karen could be dead,' Mower said flatly. 'I need you both to cooperate. Will you go and get dressed now, please, and tell him to do the same? If you don't come with us voluntarily I won't hesitate to arrest you both.'

CHAPTER FOUR

Superintendent Jack Longley gazed at his DCI in disbelief.

'This isn't a joke, is it?' he asked.

Thackeray shook his head.

'We've got chapter and verse from Karen Bastable's workmate and the bloke she picked up on one of these dogging expeditions. Married man, of course, terrified we'll shop him to his wife. Unusually, he arranged to see Charlene again after they first met up there in the woods. Generally the whole thing's completely anonymous.'

'I'm getting too old for this job, Michael,' Longley said, his broad face crumpled with incomprehension. He ran a hand over his shining bald head. 'I thought I'd heard it all, but this beggars belief. It's like something out of ancient Rome. And in this climate! Where do they go when the weather's bad, for God's sake? They can't have orgies up there in the middle of winter, surely.'

'In the village hall if wet?' Thackeray suggested mirthlessly. 'I'm sure we'll find out when we get hold of more of them and find out who does the organising. Charlene Brough said she and Karen had only been up there half a dozen times previously and it had been fine weather every time. She thinks it's been going on for a considerable time.'

'So how do they arrange to meet, then?' Longley asked sceptically. 'Someone must be organising it.'

'Box number in the *Gazette*. Simply a time and day,' Thackeray said. 'Signed Pan. Someone who's had some sort of education, obviously. We've still got Charlene downstairs. I'll get Mower to press her on how she got involved in the first place, if he hasn't already. Someone must have told her about it.'

'And there must be a record of who put the ad in? That's a lead,' Longley said, but Thackeray shook his head.

'We already checked that out,' he said. 'Someone simply handed it in over the counter on one of those forms they print in the small ads section. Paid for in cash. There's nothing illegal about printing a time and day, so no one ever queried it. I've got someone talking to all the people who work the desk to see if they recall what the advertiser looks like, but I don't hold out high hopes.'

Longley whistled gently between his teeth.

'There must be something we can throw at them all, once we get hold of them.'

'I'm sure there is if we do get hold of them. They can hardly claim it's in private, however far from the road they were. But the more urgent thing is to find Karen Bastable. Or her body.' Thackeray's face was grim. On the evidence of what Karen's friend had told them he had little hope of finding Karen alive. The dogging rendezvous was a perfect place for a sexual predator and he had no doubt that at least one had been present the night she had foolishly decided to drive to the Bently Forest alone.

'I don't think we've any choice, have we?' Longley said grudgingly. 'Get a major search organised. I'll talk to county about the overtime budget. If it turns out to be a major investigation, we'll be all right. If we end up having searched half the Pennines while the lass is holed up somewhere with a boyfriend, we'll have egg all over our faces. But I don't see that we've got any choice, so you'd best get on with it.'

'I'll get the troops organised. Will you talk to uniform?'

'Oh aye, they're going to love this,' Longley said. 'There'll not be enough overtime money in the kitty to make up for being stuck up there.' He glanced out of the window to where they could see dark clouds tumbling down towards the town from the high Pennines. 'Especially in the bloody rain.'

Thackeray went back to his own office and set the wheels in motion for a search of the whole forested area around where Karen Bastable's car had been found. Then he went to the interview room where Sergeant Kevin Mower and PC Nasreem Mirza were still talking to Charlene Brough. The three of them looked at him inquiringly, the officers impassive, their witness pale and red-eyed, clutching her packet of cigarettes as if her life depended on it.

'I'll sit in now, Nasreem,' Thackeray said and the PC nodded and reluctantly gave the senior officer her chair. Thackeray introduced himself.

'Do you think Karen is still alive?' he asked. Charlene shook her head.

'I don't know, do I? Can I have a fag? These bastards won't let me smoke.'

'You can go outside for a cigarette break shortly,' Thackeray said, knowing as a smoker himself he was likely to have been more sympathetic than his colleagues. 'Just tell me what you think might have happened to your friend.'

Charlene's face crumpled.

'I don't know, do I?' she said again. 'It were just a bit o'fun. She were really up for it. She were right bored wi'her husband. Have you seen him? If you see him, you'll know what I mean.'

'Could she have made a more serious commitment, like you did? Gone home with someone? Did she give you any indication she wanted to go out that night to see someone in particular? Or was it just...' Thackeray hesitated, lost for words, unable to hide his distaste. 'Was it just random?' he asked after a pause.

Charlene shook her head.

'She never said owt about anyone special,' she whispered. 'It were just a bit o'fun, no strings, no names, just a quick shag or two, or three sometimes, a quick drink – people brought their bottles of booze – and off home.'

Thackeray caught Nasreem Mirza's eye and saw the same incomprehension there he knew must be in his own. The young PC was still hovering by the door.

'You can go now, Nasreem,' Thackeray said, and she slipped out looking grateful. The DCI turned back to Charlene Brough, feeling weary.

'You say that the cars in the circle had their headlights on,' he said. 'So whatever was happening was well illuminated.'

'Yeah, well, that were the point, really,' Charlene said. 'The audience, like.'

'So, given that it was quite light you can give us descriptions of the people who were there.'

'I suppose,' Charlene said grudgingly. 'Some, any road.'

'And you can tell us who invited you up there in the first place.'

Charlene looked even more mutinous at that.

'I mean it,' Thackeray snapped. 'You must realise that what was going on up there is illegal. What we decide to charge you with will depend very much on how cooperative you are today. I want a list of everyone you can remember, and whatever you can recall of the cars, with the dates they were there, if possible. We'll ask your boyfriend to do the same. From the sound of it, neither of you want to be appearing in court tomorrow. It's the sort of case which would be meat and drink to the newspapers. The *Globe* would be up here like a shot. Your friend Karen could have been abducted or even killed, remember. We need this information and we need it now.'

Charlene stared at him horrified, cigarette halfway to her mouth in a trembling hand. She licked dry lips.

'I'll see what I can remember,' she whispered.

Bob Baker, the *Gazette*'s crime reporter, was a dab hand at seizing Ted Grant's attention. And this morning, this had been simply achieved by coming back from police HQ with his own interpretation, which was far from the official one, of the disappearance of Karen Bastable.

'It's bound to be the husband,' he told Grant confidently. 'They've started a massive search up on the Forestry Commission plantation on the Nelson road. Word is that she had a boyfriend, hubbie followed her up there when she went to meet him and bingo – she never came back. I wouldn't be surprised if they find two bodies. The boyfriend probably copped it as well.'

'So that's the official line, is it?' Grant asked.

'Not yet, it isn't,' Baker confessed. 'That's from my own

sources. All they're saying officially is that they've started a search, and the husband will give a press conference later today. Hankies out for that, of course, but we all know how good killers are at playing the grieving relative. We've seen enough of them. You can't believe a word they say.'

Grant glanced at his computer screen thoughtfully.

'You'll only get a couple of paras in today. Tell the subs to make a bit of space on the front, give it a trail if you think it's a serious runner. We'll follow up big time tomorrow, by which time you'll have the press conference to get your teeth into, and hopefully a body.'

'Right,' Baker said. 'I'll go and do a bit of doorstepping, see what the neighbours know about the Bastables. And there's a couple of kids, apparently. And I'll have a quiet word with Laura. She might have picked something up on that pillow grapevine she runs.'

'You'll be lucky getting anything out of Laura,' Grant said, his expression sour. 'She's as tight as a Saudi virgin with information from that source.' Baker grinned.

'We'll see,' Baker said. 'I get the feeling that liaison's not as cuddly as it used to be. She may be susceptible to a bit of charm.'

But when he approached Laura, with a friendly hand on her shoulder, she looked at him with incomprehension.

'Michael never mentioned a missing woman to me,' she said sharply, removing the offending hand with a sharp shrug. 'And if he had, I wouldn't be telling you about it. You should know that by now.'

'It's the sort of story you should be interested in – missing mother of two, husband likely to be the prime suspect. After all that stuff you did about domestic violence recently, this looks like it might be another instalment. Just thought you might like to know.'

'Thanks,' Laura said. 'I'll bear it in mind. Have they found a body, then?'

'Not yet, but they've launched a major search up at Bently. Husband's giving a press conference later. So it's looking bad.'

'I might come to the press conference if I've got time,' Laura said grudgingly. 'I want to do a follow-up on the Julie Holden murder case before it comes to trial. I'm furious that they've charged her at all, really. It was an obvious case of self-defence.'

'You've been called as a witness?'

Laura nodded, her face grim, not wanting to relive the moment she saw a domestic dispute end in tragedy.

'Really not where I want to be,' she said. 'But I'm sure you'll enjoy the cross-examination.'

'I'm sure we all will,' Baker said with an unfriendly smile. 'A bit embarrassing for your copper, wasn't it, all that?'

'He'll cope,' Laura snapped, not even wanting to think about her private life in close proximity to Bob Baker.

'Well, I may see you later, lover,' Baker said. 'It looks like this is another domestic gone badly wrong. Right up your street. *Ciao* for now.'

Laura sighed. She never intentionally tried to get close to the cases Michael Thackeray handled, but again and again their paths crossed, making their respective professional lives almost always more difficult than they needed to be. And the Julie Holden case had been a particular disaster as she had ended up witnessing what could have been a preventable death. She logged off her computer screen and picked up her jacket. She had, she thought, different, if not bigger, fish to fry, and she knew Ted Grant's gimlet eyes were on her as she left the office. Life, since she met Michael, had never been easy, but she had a depressing certainty that it was about to get seriously worse.

This time when Laura Ackroyd arrived at Sibden House, the electronically controlled gates swung open in response to her call, and she drove up the gravelled drive and parked outside the portico of a squat Victorian mansion overlooking manicured gardens which stretched as far as the eye could see. It must have taken more labour than Fred Betts could provide, she thought, to have kept this estate in good order before the advent of the garden machinery that now kept the lawns as smoothly striped as a first-class cricket ground. As Laura got out of her car she was conscious of a CCTV camera on the corner of the portico, no doubt recording her every move. As the landlord of the Shoulder of Mutton had said the first time she came to the village, the security was high tech and extensive; only the most determined burglar would gain access here.

The front door was opened before she had time to reach the top of the steps leading up to it and she found herself face to face with a tall, slim black man in a smart suit whose smile of welcome did not quite reach his dark eyes.

'Winston Sanderson,' he said, holding out his hand in Laura's direction but only allowing the briefest of touches when she responded. 'And you must be the persistent Miss Ackroyd. I'm David Murgatroyd's personal assistant and he's asked me to give you some help with your article. Do come in.'

He led her into a broad tiled hallway, furnished with

antique furniture of lustrous beauty, which no doubt justified the security systems. The solid oak doors on each side were closed and the hall ended in a broad, branching, oak staircase which rose in shallow steps to the upper storeys. Sanderson opened a doorway to the left of the front door and led Laura into an equally elegantly furnished sitting room, overlooking the front drive.

'A beautiful house,' Laura said, as she took the seat Sanderson waved her into.

'It wasn't much to look at when he decided to refurbish,' Sanderson said, pausing with his hand over a bell beside the marble fireplace. 'Would you like tea?'

'Not really,' Laura said, slightly reassured that there was someone in the house to make it. 'You said you hadn't much time.'

Sanderson hitched his trousers carefully and sat down opposite her. 'I have to leave for London at three,' he said. 'So perhaps you're right. Let's concentrate on how I can help you. But I must warn you. Sir David is a very private person. He really dislikes personal publicity.'

'He's proposing to take over one of Bradfield's schools,' Laura objected. 'People will expect to know who he is and what his plans are.'

'Of course,' Sanderson said, his expression bland. 'But there are limits to what he is prepared to talk about, that's all I'm saying.'

'Right,' Laura said. 'So can we talk about his local connections first? That's naturally what a local paper is interested in. And then perhaps we can talk a bit more widely.'

Sanderson waved a hand around the room.

'As you can see, he has a home locally, his family home,

which he inherited from his father. His business interests are international, of course, but he gets here a couple of times a year at least.'

'So I can write about the house, can I?'

'No reason why not. I'll give you a quick tour before you go. It's a fantastic old place, built about 1860, I believe, by some textile magnate, and bought by Sir David's father in the 1950s. No one was interested in these old places back then.' Sanderson glanced around the room with a proprietorial air. 'He got it for a song, apparently.'

'But it must be worth a fortune now,' Laura said, wondering just how wealthy Murgatroyd was. No expense had been spared on the meticulous period detail around her.

'Absolutely,' Sanderson said, with satisfaction.

'Mr Murgatroyd was left an orphan at quite an early age, I understand,' Laura said.

'He had a tragic early life, but he really is not prepared to discuss that publicly. I think you could safely say it left him deeply traumatised, and it has taken him a long time to come to terms with what happened. That's his father over there.' He waved a hand at a portrait of a stocky man in a dark three-piece suit, with piercing blue eyes and a proprietorial expression.

'And his mother?' Laura asked, glancing around and seeing no other family pictures.

'I've not seen a photograph of his mother,' Sanderson said.

'Is he married?' Laura pressed on.

'No,' Sanderson said, and it was obvious he was not going to expand on that answer.

'And his business interests are what, exactly?' Laura asked.

'He's in private equity,' Sanderson said, confirming what Laura had already discovered. 'He buys companies, improves their productivity, then sells on. You could say he was a moderniser of British industry when he started, now it's a worldwide enterprise. He has set up various private companies over the years, but is tending to take a back seat now, in favour of his educational and religious interests.'

'Financially, he's done very well, then?'

'You could say that,' Sanderson said. 'But he is more interested now in doing some public good than amassing further money. That, I think, is what he would like you to concentrate on.'

'So why schools?'

'Mr Murgatroyd is a firm Christian believer, as I expect you know. And he feels that children and young people can only benefit from exposure to Christian belief at an early age. It is something that he feels he can give back to society.'

'Give me a child before he is seven? Is it the Jesuits who say that?' Laura suggested. 'But these will be teenagers. They may be harder nuts to crack.'

'We haven't found that to be the case,' Sanderson said, betraying just a hint of irritability. 'It's possible to turn lives around.' He sounded, Laura thought, as if that was something he knew about.

'Was religion something he had in his own life, maybe? Or something he lacked?' Laura asked, not wanting to get sidetracked if Sanderson's time was short.

'I think that is the sort of question Sir David would not wish to answer,' Sanderson said firmly.

'The family's off limits?'

'Exactly so.'

'So, in the public domain, then. He runs his academies as faith schools?'

'Of course,' Sanderson said. 'Very much so. That's the whole point. If you have heard the good news, you're duty-bound to pass it on.'

'Do you think the parents at the schools he takes over are aware of the way their character will change?' Laura asked, doubtfully.

'They are aware of how dramatically the schools will improve,' Sanderson said. 'This is about improvement, Miss Ackroyd, physical, academic and spiritual improvement. It's a wonderful thing we are involved in, believe me. One would hope that in future all schools will take the same path. Sir David sees himself as a torch-bearer, leading the way where others can follow. There is not enough philanthropy in the world, and certainly not enough Christian philanthropy. Bradfield is indeed blessed in gaining a Murgatroyd academy. I think that should be the thrust of your article.'

Laura drove back to Bradfield deep in thought. There had been nothing unpleasant or overbearing about Winston Sanderson, but the interview had still left her uneasy and dissatisfied. He had refused point-blank to arrange an interview with David Murgatroyd himself, claiming that he was out of the country. There had been no obvious reason to disbelieve him but Laura was still left wondering why the house had been opened up, heated and evidently staffed – although she had seen no physical sign of the supposed tea maker while she was there – if Sanderson himself was about to go back to London and his boss was abroad. It felt to her much more likely that the master, like some Jane Austen gentleman returning to the country for the shooting season, was about to come home, if he had not already done so. But

Sanderson had effectively kept the gate tightly closed, which was no doubt his job.

Glancing at her watch as she pulled into the *Gazette*'s car park, she decided to follow Bob Baker to the press conference that was about to begin at police HQ. She had been deeply upset by the recent case of domestic violence she had been involved in and would have to give evidence about it in court. She could not help hoping that this latest disappearance of a married woman was not another variation on the same dreadful theme.

The uniformed constable opened the door to the conference room for her and she slipped unobtrusively into a seat on the back row, with a partial view past a handful of reporters and photographers and the paraphernalia of local TV and radio news that clogged the area in front of the conference table. There were three people at the table: DCI Michael Thackeray, who caught her eye only briefly, and with absolute neutrality, as she quietly took her seat; a woman in a smart black suit, whom she recognised as a press officer from county police HQ; and a nondescript, heavily built man in a blue sports shirt, his broad face pale and stressed, his hands fiddling compulsively on the table in front of him, but oozing aggression nonetheless. This must be the husband, she thought, and she could not help feeling sorry for him as the TV crew switched on some powerful lights that almost immediately made Terry Bastable sweat. Behind him, on a board, was a blown-up and slightly blurred photograph of a pale-faced woman with a head of auburn curls, not a beauty exactly, but striking enough, Laura thought with some fellow feeling for someone of her own colouring, to stand out in a crowd.

There was a brief, dispassionate introduction from

Thackeray, setting out the facts of Karen Bastable's disappearance, and the search that had been launched for her. At this stage he chose not to reveal all the police knew about her reasons for heading to Bently Forest, and his private conviction that she was dead, preferring to let the husband make his appeal for her to make contact, on the off chance that she still might do just that. He turned to Terry Bastable and nodded, and Bastable began to read slowly and hesitantly from a piece of paper in front of him.

'I just want to say to Karen that if she's gone away of her own free will, me and the kids, we want her back. We're broken-hearted she's gone, and we want her to come home. And even if she can't do that straight away, she should call us. We need to hear from her, we need to know she's all right, we need to talk.' He hesitated, obviously on the verge of breaking down, and desperately not wanting to reveal that sort of weakness. The press officer put a hand on his arm sympathetically for a second but he pushed it away. But he was content to let her take over.

'What I think Mr Bastable wants to say is that he doesn't know why his wife would go off like this. And he wants to appeal to her to make contact. Perhaps we could give Mr Bastable a moment, and DCI Thackeray could take your questions. Thank you.'

Bob Baker wasted no time, and Laura could see the faintest expression of distaste on Thackeray's face as he nodded to the crime reporter when he leapt to his feet.

'Mr Thackeray, can you tell us how the search for Karen is going? Are you looking for a body?'

'The search is going as well as can be expected, but there are three hundred acres of thick woodland, with very few clearings, where Mrs Bastable's car was found, so it's not a quick process. And no, we're not looking for a body, as such. We have no idea where Karen is and still hope very much that she is fit and well somewhere. That is, after all, the purpose of this press conference, based on the hope that if she hears her husband's appeal she will make contact.'

A young reporter from the local TV station whom Laura knew by sight was next, the camera swinging towards her as she spoke. 'Does Mr Bastable know of any reason why Karen would have left home of her own free will?'

Bastable shook his head vigorously.

'No reason,' he said. But Bob Baker was not letting it go at that.

'No problems at home?' he broke in. And again Bastable shook his head. 'Come on, Terry. Everyone has some problems at home. Did Karen have a boyfriend, by any chance? Is that what this is all about?'

Thackeray stepped in at that, not bothering to hide his anger. Laura could see the tension in every inch of his body as he struggled to remain the dispassionate chairman.

'These are questions we can't answer at the moment,' he said. 'As my colleague here has already said, Mr Bastable doesn't know of any reason why Karen would have left home deliberately and, as you can see, he is very distressed, and so are his two children. What we are hoping is that you'll be able to help us in terms of space and time and give extensive coverage to the family's appeal. We depend on you all in this sort of case. We have photographs of Karen, and the children, for you...' But Bob Baker was not happy with this approach.

'Terry, what did Karen say before she left home on Tuesday evening?' he broke in again.

'She said she was going to work,' Bastable said.

'Which is where, exactly? Mr Thackeray didn't say.'

'Shirley's, the big bakery up Ecclesfield. She's been there six years, does nights now and again. She takes the car when she does nights.' Bastable's voice was a touch stronger now, and he was beginning to regain some of what was obviously his natural belligerence. That, Laura thought, might be his undoing if he himself had anything to do with his wife's disappearance.

'Should she have gone to work that night?' Baker persisted.

'No, they weren't expecting her,' Bastable said, revealing his anger now. 'She wasn't on t'rota.'

'So she lied,' Baker said triumphantly. 'So where might she go? Or, more importantly, who might she go to see?'

'I don't know, do I? I've no bloody idea. Someone's got her. She's come to some harm. She'd never have left her family of her own free will.'

Laura could hear the ripple of excitement amongst the reporters, as the TV camera tightened its angle on the husband and a couple of cameras flashed. The room was very hot now, and she could see a trickle of sweat running down the side of Bastable's face. And it was obvious from Thackeray's expression that Bastable was straying fast off the police script.

'So she could have gone to meet someone?' Baker asked, but DCI Thackeray, rather than Terry Bastable, answered this time.

'That is one of the lines of inquiry we are investigating,' he said. 'But by no means the only one. There must be some reason why Karen Bastable's car was driven ten miles from her home into a remote area, but so far we have absolutely no idea what that reason was, or even if she drove it there herself. We're hoping that the media's input will clarify some of these points, and I appeal to anyone who knows anything about Karen Bastable's movements after she left home at six on Tuesday evening and the time her car was first spotted in Bently Forest – though unfortunately not immediately reported to us – the following morning. You've got full details of the make and colour of her car in your press release. And if Karen herself hears this appeal, I would just like to reinforce the point. Please get in touch with us or with Terry. We really need to know if you are safe and well. Nothing is as important as that. Your husband and children need to hear from you. I think that's all we can give you for the moment, ladies and gentlemen. Thank you very much for coming.'

Thackeray got to his feet, quickly followed by his colleague who helped the glowering Terry Bastable to his feet and ushered him out of the room. Laura sat for a moment as the TV crew began packing up their equipment until Bob Baker turned away from a brief flirtation with the attractive TV reporter and bore down in her direction.

'What did you make of that little performance?' he asked.

Laura shrugged. 'Mr Bastable looked genuine enough, even if he is a bit of a thug,' she said. 'But you can never tell, can you?'

'Damn right you can't,' Baker said. 'Remember Ian Huntley? All smiles and deep concern for bloody weeks until they found the bodies of those little girls. We don't even know if this beggar is telling the truth when he says Karen went off on her own. He could have killed her and driven her body out there to dump it.'

'So why leave the car there?' Laura objected. 'It was the car that aroused suspicion. It could have been weeks before anyone started searching up there for a body, if they ever did. Without the car, a corpse could lie up there for years. It doesn't make sense.'

'Well, I don't know. Maybe she did meet a boyfriend up there and Bastable followed her in another car. Who knows? What I do reckon is that your lover boy's appeal for her to get in touch was all a waste of breath. He knows far more than he's letting on at this stage. She's dead, is Karen Bastable. I'd put money on it. So, chop-chop. Another nice little murder mystery to entertain the readers. I reckon this is going to be quite a juicy one.' And with that Baker bustled away, tape recorder in hand, leaving Laura wondering why Michael Thackeray had been so obviously cagey that even the generally insensitive Bob Baker had noticed.

CHAPTER FIVE

'So what did you make of that, guv?' Sergeant Kevin Mower asked the DCI as they made their way back to their offices after Terry Bastable's appeal to the press. They had sent Bastable home in a taxi after his performance, still protesting that there was no way Karen would have abandoned him and his family voluntarily.

'Not a lot,' Thackeray said bluntly. 'But until we find a body, it's going to be difficult to prove that he's harmed her. Nothing's come back from the search teams, I don't suppose?'

'The place where her car was found was thoroughly churned up by up to a dozen vehicles, including the forestry workers' heavy tractor and trailer, plus it's been raining heavily, so they're unlikely to get any usable tyre tracks. Are you sure it was wise to keep the lid on the dogging angle? We might get something from the other people who must have been up there if they realise that someone has gone missing after their fun and games.'

'Fat chance,' Thackeray said. 'If they went to all the trouble of meeting in a remote spot like that you can bet your life none of their partners know what they've been up to. Even leaving murder out of the equation, there won't be many of them volunteering for an interview with the police.'

'But we'll have to trace them,' Mower said. 'If the husband's the prime suspect, as usual, that group must provide the rest of the cast. Do you want me to start inquiries door to door up there? Or farm to farm in this case, I guess. It's not exactly inhabited, in any real sense of the word, is it?' For all his years in Yorkshire, Mower still had the mindset of a Londoner unable to grasp with any certainty the concept of wide open spaces, like those that surrounded the town of Bradfield, hemmed in by rolling hills and moors.

'Give it twenty-four hours,' Thackeray said. 'By that time, we may have found her body, or she may have called in to say she's run off with the milkman, or whoever.'

'I suppose the car details may jog someone's memory,' Mower said. 'Someone may have seen her driving up there. Or they may nudge the conscience of someone who was up in the forest with her. People are pretty shameless about sex these days, but I think death at a dogging party's a bit over the top for your average swinger.'

Thackeray glanced at the sergeant with a hint of amusement in his eyes.

'I didn't think anything shocked you, Kevin,' he said.

'You'd be surprised, guv,' Mower said. 'Though I suppose this could still turn out to be a missing person; a bit of extramarital that's run into extra time. Let's hope so.'

'Let's,' Thackeray said.

But within hours of the decision to wait for a public reaction to Bastable's appeal, Thackeray and Mower found themselves driving once more to Bently Forest, summoned by the search team which was slowly combing through the plantation from its western edge, near the summit of Bently Pike, one of the high fells that separated Yorkshire from Lancashire, to the valley floor, where Bently Beck tumbled down from the hills to join the River Maze.

'You've found her?' Mower had said, not able to hide a momentary excitement when he fielded the call from the uniformed inspector in charge of the search.

'No,' his colleague said. 'But we've found summat a bit odd near the clearing. I think you ought to take a look. It looks as if the party had an audience, someone who didn't want to be seen.'

Thackeray had decided to make the trip himself, as much to get out of the office as because he thought his presence would be useful. He had spent most of the morning, since Terry Bastable had been sent home, staring out of his office window across Bradfield's town hall square, where the trees were just beginning to bud, smoking cigarette after cigarette and wondering how he could prevent Laura from tearing herself apart at the state of their relationship. He knew only too well what she wanted, and was equally certain that he could not give it to her.

'Damnation,' he muttered under his breath suddenly, as Mower swung the car sharply up the hill towards Bently.

'Sorry, guv,' Mower said, thinking his driving was to blame for his boss's discomfort. 'Bit sharp, that turn. Didn't see it coming.'

'What?' Thackeray said, sharply. 'Sorry, I was thinking about something else.'

Mower shrugged. He was getting used to Thackeray's abstracted self-absorption, guessed the cause, and worried about where it would lead. In some ways, he thought, Laura and Thackeray himself, much as he liked them both, deserved better than each other. He had always doubted their compatibility and his reservations only increased with the passage of time. It was what it would do to both of them when they finally split up, as he was sure they would, which haunted him.

They drove into the forest, down the track marked with police tape, and pulled up on the very edge of the clearing where Karen Bastable's car had been found. A uniformed sergeant approached, walking carefully around the edge of the area that had been churned up by vehicles.

'Over here, sir,' he said to Thackeray, and led the way to an area of brambles and rough scrub on the far side of the clearing.

'There are tyre tracks here, a bit apart from the rest. Not very clear because they're mainly on the grass, see?' He indicated where a vehicle had crushed the vegetation. 'And then here, look, someone's been standing right here. Maybe more than one person. We thought maybe they were watching what was going on, a grandstand view, as it were.'

'Any chance of a tyre print?' Thackeray asked.

'I doubt it, but I've asked forensics to take a look. You never know. A vehicle might have left some other trace in this sort of terrain. It's not where I'd risk the family car, let alone anything more upmarket. You'd be bound to scratch the paintwork.'

'So that's it, is it?' Thackeray asked, irritated at having been tempted to come so far for so little.

'Not quite, sir,' the sergeant said. 'Whoever parked up here got out of the car and left some footprints, which are quite a lot clearer than anything else we've found. Over here.'

He led the two detectives to a spot overlooking the rest of the clearing but where a couple of bushes provided a screen. A patch of damp ground was carefully cordoned off and a white-suited forensics officer was crouching on the ground.

'Anything useful?' Thackeray asked. The young woman looked up.

'I think so,' she said. 'Someone stood here for quite some time. The prints are quite deep and didn't get too damaged by the rain because of the overhanging vegetation. And they were made by a man, not a woman, judging by the shoe size. About a ten, I'd say. I should be able to get a good cast. And this is quite clearly someone wearing shoes, not the ubiquitous trainers that a thousand people are wearing within a square mile. Shoes last longer, wear in particular ways, are much more individual, in other words. If you can match the cast to a shoe, you've a good chance of identifying who stood here.'

'And the shoes will have got muddy,' Mower ventured.

'That too. I'll take samples of the ground and the vegetation.'

Thackeray nodded and glanced at Mower.

'So what do you make of it?' he asked. 'You get a large group of people up here intent on public sex. And someone keeping out of sight and watching them. Was he standing here wondering whether to join in? Or was he a voyeur who was satisfied simply by watching other people? Or was he a predator who wanted to keep his car out of sight before picking up his victim and driving away with her?'

'We need to push Charlene and the boyfriend some more,' Mower said. 'They're our only link to what was going on. They may have noticed a car being parked away from the main circle on previous occasions. Or seen someone joining in, apparently arriving on foot, which would be a bit unusual, to say the least. Until we find someone who was here this week, we'll have to rely on what they can recall happened on a regular basis and what, if anything, seemed unusual.'

'The other possibility, of course, is that it was the husband spying on Karen, trying to find out exactly what she was up to before intervening,' Thackeray said.

'Except, as far as we know, he had no transport, guv,' Mower objected. 'She'd taken the family car.'

'Transport's not difficult to get hold of if you really try,' Thackeray said. 'I think at the very least we'll have a look at Terry Bastable's footwear. He may think he's washed the mud off, but you can bet your life that if he was up here, there'll be traces forensics can find. Clothing too. If he's been in amongst this thick vegetation, there'll be traces of that on his clothing as well.'

'He won't be very pleased if we go round raiding his wardrobe,' Mower said with a small grin. 'He took offence when we looked at Karen's stuff. I'll get the heavy mob to do it, I think.'

'Straight away,' Thackeray said. 'Before it occurs to him to get rid of anything incriminating.'

Laura kept her head down as Ted Grant made one of his regular sorties round the newsroom, peering over reporters' shoulders and generally making them uneasy even if he offered no overt comment on what they were writing. When he got to Bob Baker's desk, where the crime reporter was pounding his keyboard as if his life depended on it, Grant made a close study of what he was writing.

'So, do you still think the husband did it?' he asked at length. Baker glanced round and shrugged.

'I took a turn round Greenwood Close, after the press conference. That's where they live. There weren't many neighbours about, all out at work, of course. But I did have a chat with one woman who reckoned that the Bastable marriage was on the rocks when I told her Karen had gone AWOL. She lives opposite and said she'd heard shouting at all hours. Her husband went and banged on the door once when the noise got too bad. Got a mouthful from Terry for his pains. All sorts of threats, she said. She reckoned Terry's a violent bastard and she wouldn't be surprised what he'd done. Either he's done Karen in or she's scarpered for her own good, she reckoned. Of course, she didn't want to be named, but I reckon I can get some of it in as neighbours' speculation, that sort of thing.'

'She's no idea whether she had a boyfriend on the side?' Grant asked.

'No sign of anyone that she'd seen,' Baker said. 'But I might go back later, when they're all home from work, and see what else I can dig up.'

'Good lad,' Grant said and turned towards Laura, who had been listening unashamedly to this exchange.

'And you, miss?' Grant said, obviously irritated. 'Have you tracked down our mysterious Sir David Murgatroyd yet?'

'Not yet,' Laura admitted. 'I've made contact with his PA, but he doesn't hold out much hope of an interview. Says he hates personal publicity.'

'Well, let's come at the beggar another way,' Grant said. 'Go to one of the other schools he's taken over, why don't you. Isn't there one in Leeds? The budget will run to that. See what

they think of him over there, how it's working out in practice.
You may find it's the best thing since sliced bread for all I
know. These objectors in Bradfield may all be closet commies,
rent-a-mob, green weirdos, who knows what? Get the facts,
girl, and then we'll see where we are, shall we? Don't hang
about. I don't pay you to sit around playing solitaire on your
bloody computer all day.'

'Right,' Laura said, smiling faintly at the jibe, and flicked
back to her notes to find the names of the other schools David
Murgatroyd had sponsored. The head teacher of the nearest
academy was very willing to see her the next morning to give
her a tour of his empire, but she reckoned that it would be
useful to get more than one view of a new academy, so she
rang her grandmother to see if the campaign in Bradfield had
any unofficial contact with the Murgatroyd Academy in
Leeds.

'Talk to the union secretary,' Joyce said. 'She'll fill you in.'
And she gave her a name and a number. 'You haven't
forgotten I'm off to Portugal in the morning to see your mum
and dad, have you?'

'Are you sure you're OK getting to the airport?' Laura
asked, feeling guilty because she had completely forgotten.

'All fixed,' Joyce said. 'Taxi at six-thirty.'

'So have a wonderful holiday,' Laura said. 'And all my love
to them both.'

'Aye, I'll pass on all the news. Take care, pet.'

Laura called her grandmother's contact and made an
appointment to meet her next morning in a coffee bar close to
the school.

'If they catch me talking to the press, I'll be for the chop,'
the union rep said. 'Strictly against the rules, that is.'

'Tomorrow at eleven, then,' Laura said cheerfully, knowing from experience that the more people were forbidden from airing their grievances to the press, the more willing many of them were to do it.

'I'll slip out in my free period. And hope no one sees me. It's like Alcatraz round here.' Laura hung up and decided to call it a day. There was something she had to resolve and she needed to get home in good time today to do it.

Less than an hour later, Laura gazed at the blue line on the testing kit without much surprise but with a sense of foreboding which almost overwhelmed her. She had been sure for several weeks that she was pregnant, but had been putting off the moment of truth, which she knew would present Michael Thackeray with a decision that he desperately did not want to take. She guessed it would make or break their relationship and she blamed herself bitterly, knowing that it was her own carelessness that had led to this. Thackeray was the last man in the world who would be pushed, or bounced, into something he did not want to do, she thought, and although he had made quite a different promise not long ago, she was sure that he still did not want to become a father again.

Laura groaned, and pushed the testing kit back into its packet, took it into the kitchen and buried it at the bottom of the rubbish bin. But she knew that the dilemma she faced would not be so easily disposed of. She glanced at her watch. It was six-thirty and Thackeray had not called to say that he would be late, as he often did, so she began desultorily preparing a meal. The efforts she used to make to persuade her partner to take an interest in cooking had run into the sand when it became obvious that she was always home long before he was. He had also, she realised sadly, resisted most of her efforts to persuade him to shift from his preferred diet of meat and two veg. She took chops out of the fridge; she would have hers with a salad and she would cook chips for him. She should, she thought, feel elated at the thought of the new life inside her, a life she passionately wanted to bring into being, but instead she felt deeply depressed and on the edge of panic.

On an impulse, she called her friend Vicky Mendelson.

'Are you at home tonight?' she asked. Vicky sounded surprised.

'David's out at some dinner,' she said. 'I was going to wash my hair once the kids are asleep.' Laura and Vicky had been at university in Bradfield together, but once her first baby arrived, Vicky had opted to be a stay-at-home mother with no apparent regrets about the legal career she had abandoned. Laura half envied and half despised her choice, but unequivocally adored her three young children.

'I'll come round later,' she said. 'I need to talk.' She hoped Vicky might be able to put what was happening to her into perspective before she broke the news to Michael.

She heard Thackeray's key in the lock as she was peeling potatoes and he came up behind her and kissed the back of her neck.

'I saw you at the press conference,' he said. 'You're not writing about it, are you?'

'No, that's Bob Baker's territory,' Laura said. 'You'll no doubt get some lurid speculation on the front page in the morning.'

'It'll be even more lurid when he finds out where we think she went that night,' Thackeray said. Laura turned towards him, intrigued.

'And where was that, Chief Inspector?' she asked. 'Strictly off the record, of course.' She listened, astonished, as Thackeray explained briefly why they thought Karen Bastable had driven to Bently Forest.

'That's a bit over the top. I knew things like that went on, but I thought it was just kids in car parks.'

'This seems to be much more organised than that,' Thackeray said. 'But I doubt very much that anyone will be rushing forward to tell us about it. God knows what they got up to up there. If she's dead, the whole thing is going to be very messy.'

'And you think she's dead?'

'Why would she abandon her car miles from anywhere unless she's come to some harm? We have to go through the motions with her husband appealing to her to get in touch, but privately I think it's a waste of time.'

'I didn't warm to Terry Bastable,' Laura said.

'I don't think anyone warms to Terry Bastable,' Thackeray said, thinking of Nasreem Mirza's furious reaction to the man. 'He's a racist thug, by all accounts. But that doesn't mean he necessarily murdered his wife, whatever your feminist instincts tell you.'

'You know I'm a bit off violent husbands, after the last one I met,' Laura muttered, turning away quickly as she realised she had said too much. She busied herself serving their meal.

'I'm going over to see Vicky later,' she said eventually. 'Is that OK with you?'

'Of course,' Thackeray said, chomping happily on his supper. 'Give her my love.'

* * *

'So what's the problem?' Vicky Mendelson asked bluntly, after settling Laura down with a cup of coffee in her sitting room later that evening. 'You look dreadful.'

'There's nothing like an honest friend to improve morale,' Laura said wryly.

'Is it Michael? Is he messing you about again? Sometimes I feel really guilty about introducing you to that bloody man.'

'I'm still crazy about him,' Laura confessed, with a faint smile that lit up her wan face.

'So, what then?' Vicky persisted.

'I'm pregnant,' Laura said. Vicky relaxed and hugged Laura to her.

'That's marvellous,' she said. 'Aren't you pleased? I thought it was what you wanted. You have such a silly grin on your face every time you see Naomi, I thought you were terminally broody.'

She stopped suddenly, seeing the tears in Laura's eyes.

'Michael doesn't want it,' Vicky said, the excitement draining out of her as she suddenly realised her friend's predicament.

'I haven't told him yet,' Laura said, her voice dull. 'He said a while ago we'd go for it, but then...' She shrugged dispiritedly. 'Silence. He's never mentioned it again.'

'So how...?' Vicky ventured.

'An accident. I didn't do it on purpose. I missed a couple of pills. But he won't believe that, will he? He'll think it was deliberate and I don't know how he'll react. Oh God, Vicky, I don't know what to do.'

Vicky leant back on the sofa and put an arm around Laura, as she let the tears come.

'I didn't want it to be like this,' Vicky said gently. 'And I'm sure you didn't. I wanted us to celebrate when you decided to have a child. I wanted you to be as happy as I was when we had ours. I was over the moon with every one of them.'

'I remember,' Laura said. 'I was jealous, even though I wasn't ready then.'

'But you are now, aren't you?'

'Yes,' Laura admitted. 'I want this baby, desperately. I'm ready, but I want to keep Michael as well, and I just don't know how he's going to react.'

Vicky sighed.

'He really ought not to put you in this situation,' she said. 'Are you afraid he'll pressure you into getting rid of it?'

'No, no, not that,' Laura said vehemently. 'He may say he's not, but he's a Catholic through and through. I told him I'd had a termination – you remember? ...when we were students? – and he was really shocked. I'm just scared of his reaction when I tell him, and I'm going to have to tell him soon. If I start getting sick, he'll guess anyway. He's not a fool. But he'll think I'm trying to blackmail him into marrying me. He'll think dreadful things. And he'll leave me for good. I know he will. If he believes he can't cope, he'll just go.' Laura looked away from Vicky but her friend could still feel her shuddering as she struggled to hold back her tears.

'He's a fool if he reacts like that,' Vicky said.

'You don't know everything that happened when he and his wife lost the baby. I've never told you the half of it,' Laura muttered. 'He's terrified of making himself that vulnerable again.'

'Then if you want this baby, and he really can't cope with it, you have to choose,' Vicky said.

'I can't,' Laura cried.

'You can,' Vicky said. 'I know it's desperate, but you can if you have to. You're strong and independent and you can do what's right. It's not the end of the world these days to bring a child up on your own. And David and I will always be here for you. But I think you're being too pessimistic. It won't come to that, I'm sure it won't. I'm sure when you tell him what's happened, and how much you want the baby, he'll come round. He won't abandon his own child. And if he does, then he's not the man I think he is, or the man you should be committing yourself to. He's not good enough for you.'

'You make it sound so simple,' Laura said.

Vicky got up and went over to a side table and poured two glasses of gin and tonic.

'We'll drink to your baby,' she said. 'He or she will be loved and wanted by you and that's a lot more than some babies can expect. Congratulations, Laura, I'm delighted for you. I really am.'

CHAPTER SIX

The phone rang on DCI Thackeray's desk the next morning just as he was about to summon Kevin Mower to give him an update on the Karen Bastable case. He realised straight away that the news from the forensics lab took them a significant step forward, and he walked down to the main CID office himself to share it.

'Karen Bastable's mobile phone,' he said, taking Mower unawares.

'Guv?' he said. 'It was in her car, wasn't it?'

'It was, and forensics have been analysing it. They've not come up with any useful leads from the phone book or from the text messages: family and female friends, a few unregistered pay phones we'll never trace, all innocuous stuff. It's the photographs which are much more interesting. I've never seen the point of phones that take photographs myself, but it looks as if we should be thankful some people like to record their every move.'

'She took pictures in the forest?' Mower asked, feeling the surge of excitement that always came with a breakthrough.'

'They're emailing them to us,' Thackeray said. 'Can you get them up on your computer?' Mower turned to his screen and pressed a few keys, smiling slightly to himself. Thackeray was just old enough not to have grown up with computers as an everyday fact of life, and still stumbled occasionally with new technology. Within seconds, Mower had a folder of photographs on his screen and began to bring them up individually.

'She took a chance keeping these on her phone,' he said, as they looked at half a dozen blurred images of people wearing very little and engaged in activities that would not have seemed out of place in a porn movie. 'Her husband might have got hold of them.'

'Perhaps he's as inept as I am with these things,' Thackeray muttered. 'But are any of the participants recognisable?'

'Not really,' Mower said. 'One or two of them are wearing things across their faces, look – a scarf there, a mask, even. Wasn't there a famous case once involving a man in a mask? People tried to identify him by his willy?' He grinned but Thackeray did not respond and Mower turned back to the screen with a slight shrug and flicked through more images.

'They're all a bit blurred, guv,' he said.

'I can see that,' Thackeray said, sounding tetchy. 'Keep going.'

'Mobiles don't give you high-quality images, on the whole, especially if they're being waved around pretty much at random like this one seems to have been,' Mower explained. 'Forensics may be able to enhance them a bit, but I doubt if any of these would stand up in court as a clear identification of anyone.'

'Wait, look at that one again,' Thackeray said. 'There's a couple of cars in the background. Ask them if they can get a

better image of the registration plates. We might pin someone
down that way.'

'Here's a couple she's taken of cars arriving,' Mower said.
'It's almost as if she wanted a record of what was going on.
Perhaps she didn't feel very secure going up there on her own.
These were all taken the night she disappeared, apparently.
There's nothing any further back, unless she's downloaded
them onto a computer.'

'Did the Bastables have a computer in the house?'
Thackeray asked.

'I don't think so, guv, but I'll check.'

'And has someone picked up Bastable's shoes and clothes?'

'He wasn't best pleased about that, apparently,' Mower
said. 'They came away with his only pair of proper shoes – a
well-polished black pair, apparently, no doubt for weddings
and funerals – plus a bag full of trainers, and several pairs of
muddy tracksuit bottoms and trousers. The shoe size is about
right, apparently. He takes an eleven.'

'So we're in the hands of forensics?'

''Fraid so,' Mower said. 'I'll print off these pictures and
take them with me when I go to talk to Charlene and her
boyfriend again. Maybe they'll jog her memory a bit further.
But I don't hold out high hopes.'

'The best bet is a car registration,' Thackeray said. 'So push
the lab on that, will you?'

'Right, guv,' Mower said. 'Will do.'

The Murgatroyd Academy glittered in the pale morning
sunshine as Laura approached it by car the next morning. It lay
on flat land at the top of a long, gentle gradient above Leeds
town centre, offering a panoramic view of the city with its

domed town hall and sparkling modern blocks below. But its immediate surroundings were much more grim. Rows of tightly packed terrace houses had given way to more spacious semi-detached brick council houses, as she drove up the hill. But the signs of neglect and vandalism were the first thing which took the eye. Many of the gardens were overgrown and unkempt, here and there properties had been completely boarded up, and groups of teenagers hung about on street corners. The area was deeply depressing and in sharp contrast to the bustling, booming city below and to the new building that announced itself as the academy in letters a foot high on a board behind steel fencing and a firmly closed gate, which allowed passers-by only a glimpse of its glamorous modern facade.

Laura had never before visited a school with this level of security and she stopped outside the main gate and got out of her car. There was an answerphone system beside the gate and a notice which announced that entry was strictly by appointment only. Laura pushed the buzzer and when she explained who she was the gate swung silently open, reminding her of the similar security at Sibden House. David Murgatroyd's obsession with all things high-tech obviously extended across the whole of his empire.

Once inside, she parked in one of the spaces designated for visitors and sat for a moment gazing in astonishment at the architectural wonders that lay beyond the concealing fences: plate glass and metal soared four storeys high, dwarfing the surrounding community, the main entrance led into a glass atrium which would have graced a five-star hotel, and beyond that the school itself, its playing fields and tennis courts, dozed surprisingly silently in the sunshine. Of students there was no overt sign.

She locked the car and made her way to reception, where a young woman was clearly waiting for her arrival.

'The head will see you straight away,' she said, shaking hands perfunctorily. 'He has a short slot, as I think he explained. There's a meeting of the management committee at eleven and Sir David is coming in for that.'

Laura's pulse quickened. Perhaps at last she might get a glimpse of the elusive David Murgatroyd, even get a quick word with him. That was a bonus she had not been expecting on this trip to see exactly how one of his burgeoning chain of academies functioned, and she knew that Ted Grant would be pleased. But first there was the head teacher to see.

Gordon Masefield was an energetic man, small and plump but full of an almost childlike enthusiasm. He bounded across his office to meet Laura, shook her hand vigorously and offered her a chair, a cup of tea, which she declined, and a glossy prospectus, all within the space of thirty seconds.

'I'm so glad to meet you,' he said, as Laura glanced briefly at the photograph of Sir David Murgatroyd and Masefield himself that graced the first page of the brochure. 'I'm sure we can help convince Bradfield that a school like this can only be an asset from which their young people can benefit enormously.' Murgatroyd, Laura noted, was not at all as she had imagined him: he was obviously a tall man, dwarfing the head teacher in the photograph, and he seemed to be enjoying a well-preserved middle age, dark-haired, firm-jawed and not unattractive. Masefield, on the other hand, confident enough in person, was gazing up at his boss in the picture with an expression which could only be described as adoring. What was it, Laura wondered, that Murgatroyd did to ensure that men like Masefield, and his own assistant Sanderson, extremely competent men themselves, ate out of his hand? Was this what people called charisma, and if so, was it entirely a good thing, she wondered?

She realised that she had not really been listening to Masefield, who was still talking fast and furiously.

'I thought a quick tour of the academy first, and then we can deal with any questions you may still have at the end. Does that suit you, Miss Ackroyd?'

'Yes, that will be fine,' Laura said, and she obediently followed Masefield out of his office again. The tour was a whirlwind one, with Laura barely conscious of whom she was being introduced to, and what subjects were being taught in the rows of identical classrooms where ranks of neatly uniformed children stood up when the head opened the door in a way which recalled her own school days but which she knew was unusual in the current day and age. Here good order and industry were evidently imposed and she wondered quite how that worked in an area outside the school gates which was so obviously run-down and impoverished.

'Can I speak to some of the students?' Laura asked, after surveying a science class where young people in safety glasses experimented over flasks and Bunsen burners. 'One or two of the sixth form, perhaps?'

'That wouldn't be possible without their parents' permission,' Masefield said blandly, waving her out of the lab and along yet another corridor. 'Not that our parents are not uniquely supportive, of course, but I think press interviews would be an intrusion.'

'It must be difficult to keep parents on board in an area like this, with all its social problems,' Laura objected. 'This is the local school for the whole estate, I take it?'

'Well, in theory it is, but we have the advantage of having five applicants for every place,' Masefield said. 'We don't select on ability, of course; we're a comprehensive school, after all, and we take all the talents, but we do expect our parents to support the school's ethos.'

'Which is?'

'Oh, a Christian ethos, of course. We make no secret of that. Sir David runs his academies on biblical precepts. Everyone knows that. What they don't seem to appreciate is how successful that is in educational terms.'

'So who might not be welcome here?' Laura pressed. 'Muslims?'

'No, no, we find Muslim parents very often appreciate our approach to discipline and morality. We have a number of Muslim students here. As we do West Indians from more traditional families. So far, they are doing very well. Very well indeed.'

'But not the children of drug dealers?' Laura asked evenly. 'Or members of local gangs? Or single parents on benefits who can't afford the school uniform?'

'Their parents would be unlikely to be able to meet our expectations, I fear,' Masefield said. 'Some of the local children choose to go elsewhere.' I bet they do, Laura thought, recognising the evidence here of what Bradfield parents feared would happen there: the price of a gleaming new school would be the exclusion of 'difficult' pupils to ensure that exam results looked good.

'So what happens if a few of the less desirable students slip through the net?' she asked, not disguising her scepticism.

'We have a very firm policy on school rules. Three strikes

and you are out, basically, with no exceptions.' Masefield's expression had hardened now.

'So you filter the children coming in, and then keep on filtering the difficult ones out again as they go up the school?'

'We feel no particular obligation to families who find it impossible to commit to our objectives,' Masefield said flatly. 'We don't apologise for making demands. That is the price of a successful education. It requires effort on both sides.'

Laura did not feel she could argue with that, but she wondered at a head teacher who saw no merit in going the extra mile for children who had no support from home, punishing them twice, in effect, for factors over which they had no control. Then she remembered the Bradfield head Debbie Stapleton's other objection to David Murgatroyd's approach to education.

'And what about the curriculum, Mr Masefield? You mention biblical precepts. What does that amount to? Creationism in the science lessons?'

'Intelligent design is a valid means of looking at the world,' Masefield said, slightly defensively. 'In many American schools that is completely accepted now.'

'But not part of the National Curriculum here yet,' Laura said mildly. 'And what about sex education?'

'Like all schools, the governors discuss this with parents. So far we have had no objections to our conservative approach, which is based on biblical precepts.'

'No sex outside marriage?'

'Precisely. Many of our girls are part of the silver-ring movement, promising to remain pure until marriage.'

'You promote that?' Laura asked.

'One of our female staff members is very keen. She is responsible for sex education.'

'So you've cracked the problem of teenage pregnancy?' Masefield glanced away, suddenly embarrassed.

'Not quite yet, it has to be said,' he admitted.

'So, tell me, what happens if one of your teenagers concludes that he or she is gay? What is the school's reaction to that?' Laura knew she was being provocative but Masefield's bland certainties were beginning to annoy her.

'It is not a lifestyle choice which we would in any way condone,' Masefield said. 'Our general view of sexual activity within marriage would obviously not include same-sex relationships. Fortunately, praise the Lord, it's not a problem which we have met during the time we have been open.' They had by now come full circle and were outside the head teacher's office door where he consulted his watch ostentatiously.

'I'm afraid that's all I have time for today, Miss Ackroyd,' he said. 'I hope that has given you some idea of the sort of school we are running here. You will find the first set of GCSE examination results in the brochure I've given you. We were very pleased with them. They far outstrip anything which has been achieved in this area before. I'm sure, with Sir David's sponsorship, Bradfield could be just as successful, just as quickly. You can reassure your readers of that.'

Dismissed like a naughty school pupil, Laura walked thoughtfully out through reception, but at the top of the steps she stopped and watched a sleek Jag manoeuvre through the electronic gates and park next to her own dusty VW Golf. Even before the door opened, she guessed that this was the school's millionaire sponsor come to visit his fiefdom like a viceroy his colony. Taking a deep breath, she waylaid Sir David Murgatroyd as he strode towards the front door.

'Excuse me,' she said. 'I'm Laura Ackroyd from the *Bradfield Gazette,* and I wondered if we could have a word about your plans for Sutton Park School in Bradfield?' She thought for a second Murgatroyd was going to brush past her, swatting her away like an irritating fly, but for a moment he hesitated, looked her up and down, with an appraisal which Laura found disconcerting, and then stopped.

'Miss Ackroyd?' he said. 'I thought you had been told that I don't normally give interviews to the press.'

'But this isn't normal, is it, Sir David? There's quite a head of steam building up in Bradfield against your plan. I wondered if you had any comment on that, at all?'

'There's always a groundswell of opinion amongst people who are prepared to settle for the mediocre when they could have the excellent,' Murgatroyd said. 'Bradfield won't be any different. But in the end they will see the light.'

'Do you mean that in a religious sense?' Laura jumped in. 'Is that what you expect in the long run – to convert whole neighbourhoods to your own views, the views I've just been hearing about from Mr Masefield?'

'Yes,' Murgatroyd said flatly. 'I believe that is precisely what the Lord expects me to do.' He glanced at his watch and hesitated.

'Call Winston Sanderson,' he said. 'Come up to Sibden and I'll give you that interview you're so determined to have. You look like an intelligent young woman, not like so many of your colleagues. I'm sure you'll understand that what I am doing is a noble cause.' And he turned on his heel and strode up the steps to the doors of the academy, leaving Laura feeling gobsmacked in his wake.

As she drove away from the academy, her mobile rang and she stopped to take the call. It was the teacher who had agreed to meet her in the local coffee bar.

'I'm sorry,' the young woman said. 'I saw you leaving, but I don't think I can meet you, you know. It'd be more than my job's worth if anyone found out. I'm really sorry.'

'Me too,' Laura said. 'Call me again if you change your mind.' She was about to start the car again when she noticed two young boys, obviously of secondary-school age, kicking their heels on the corner of one of the neighbouring streets. She wondered why they were not in school, or even in school uniform, but was reluctant to stop and ask them given the spate of juvenile violent crime that had recently convulsed the country. But as she hesitated, two women joined the boys, one with a pushchair, and she could see, even from a cautious distance, that some sort of argument had broken out.

She pulled up at the kerb and wound down her window.

'Excuse me,' she said to the older of the two women. 'I'm from the *Gazette* in Bradfield. I was wondering what local people think about the new academy.' The woman looked at her for a moment and then laughed harshly.

'Mystic Meg, are you?' she asked. 'Why d'you think these little beggars are hanging around here getting into bother?'

Laura switched off the engine and got out of the car to join the group on the pavement.

'What do you mean?' she asked, looking at the two boys, who could not have been much older than twelve and who flushed under her scrutiny.

'They got bloody chucked out, didn't they? Hadn't been

there five minutes before they were in trouble.'

'What sort of trouble?' Laura asked.

'Owt and nowt, weren't it?' the older woman said, obviously the mother of one of the boys and clearly furious. 'Jackie here never had that sort of trouble with Darren at t'old school, did you?' The younger woman with the pushchair shook her head.

'They told us at primary he were a bright lad, should do well,' Darren's mother muttered.

'Different place altogether, that were,' the older woman went on. 'These two were late once or twice, didn't have their ties on once or twice, rubbish stuff, but there were nowt we could do about it. I went up there and spoke to t'new head but he weren't listening. Summat about three strikes, that's all he were interested in. Not just suspended, neither. Expelled. And when I complained to the council, they said there were nowt they could do about it. It weren't their school anymore. They're not the only ones, neither. There's ten or a dozen of them around the estate been chucked out, roaming around wi'nowt to do. The council's not come up wi'owt for them, neither. They offered our Craig a place at some school right over Beeston way. How's he supposed to get over there? This were our local school before these God-botherers got hold of it. It's been bloody hijacked.'

'Are you doing anything about it?' Laura asked.

'What can you do? There's some sort of parents' group getting set up at the community centre, but I don't reckon they'll get anywhere,' the woman said. She waved her arm in the general direction of the half-boarded-up shopping parade that lay at the heart of the estate.

'It's not as if these are bad kids,' she said. 'They're not in gangs or owt like that. I've just told Craig he's to come home wi' me now I've finished work. I'll not have him roaming around getting into all sorts, the way some do. He's not a bad lad, he did well enough in t'primary. I want him back in class but I reckon that lot up there are more keen on pulling kids in from other parts o't'town. Posher parts. The long and short of it is, they don't want kids from round here and they make any old excuse to get rid of them.'

'Can I quote you on that?' Laura asked.

'Don't put us name in t'paper,' Craig's mother said. 'We've got some sort of appeal coming up. Governors or summat. I don't want to muck up his chances wi' that, do I? Though they're all in Murgatroyd's bloody pocket, as far as I can see.'

And with that Laura had to be content. When she got back to the office she found Ted Grant in unusually ebullient form when she reported back to him on her trip.

'Excellent,' he said, after she'd sketched in her interview with the head teacher and the promise of more from David Murgatroyd. 'That should give these bloody naysayers in Bradfield summat to think about. It's always the same in this country. You get someone who makes a success of their life, who's full of good ideas, and there's always some bleeding heart making a bloody commotion about how whatever it is can't possibly work, won't be good for us if it does, offends "'ealth and safety", or could be trampling on someone's bloody human rights. It's no wonder we never make any progress. There's too many begrudgers trying to maintain the status quo. If the only objection's coming from the mothers of a couple of little tearaways, there can't be much wrong, can there?'

'It might be a tad soon to write your editorial,' Laura

suggested mildly. 'Let me interview the man first. And talk to this group that's trying to get the expelled kids reinstated. I got a number to call from the community centre.'

'Get that fixed up pronto,' Ted said. 'We can go with your stuff at the end of the week, maybe. We've a good story from Bob Baker which will run for a day or so anyway. This woman who's vanished turns out to be a right little slapper, according to her friends and neighbours.'

Laura drew a sharp breath.

'Her family will love us for that,' she said. 'Has Bob Baker talked to the police about it?'

'I don't need their permission to run some interviews with her mates,' Grant said, his colour rising, a warning to Laura that she had once again gone too far for her irascible boss. 'You should remember what I pay you for,' he bellowed suddenly. 'And it's not for representing your bloody boyfriend at editorial conferences. Just think about that.'

'Fine,' Laura snapped. 'I'll fix an appointment with Murgatroyd, then.'

'And make it snappy. You can't have the whole week for this school stuff, you know. In fact, I wonder now whether it won't just encourage the dinosaurs up at Sutton Park. Maybe the whole bloody thing's a mistake.'

Laura turned on her heel without any more argument. She knew from long experience that Ted Grant reacted badly to anything he regarded as contradiction, and she had too many other things on her mind to rush into a conflict which she knew she could not win. But on her way back to her own desk she stopped behind Bob Baker, who was pounding his computer keyboard as if he had a hot tip on the date of the Apocalypse.

'What did Karen Bastable do to you?' she asked, as she took in the viciousness of the character assassination which Baker seemed to have gleaned from her anonymous 'friends' in the neighbourhood.

'Well, it confirms what I said from the off,' Baker said. 'Hubby had plenty of reason to see her off, judging by what her mates say.'

'You need to watch out for the libel lawyers,' Laura said.

'You can't libel the dead,' Baker said. 'And I reckon this girlie's dead and buried. Only question is where, and how long it's going to take DCI Plod to find her.'

'So tell her kids she's a slag, why don't you? You're on the wrong paper, Bob. You should be down in London with the *Globe*.'

'And you'd do well on the *Lady's Home Journal*,' Baker came back quickly. 'They'd give you time off when you're on the rag. Get out of my hair, will you? You wouldn't recognise a good story if it jumped up and hit you between the eyes.'

Laura turned away, her face flushed, and her eyes suddenly filling with tears. She hurried to the cloakroom where she spent some time gazing at herself in the mirror. If she had wanted any confirmation that the pregnancy test had been only too accurate she knew that her emotional reaction provided it. But as she combed her hair, repaired her make-up and tried to compose herself enough to make it back to her desk, she knew that her problems were only just beginning.

CHAPTER SEVEN

Sergeant Kevin Mower had found Charlene Brough still in her dressing gown – a frayed woollen affair buttoned up to the neck – rather than the silky negligee they had disturbed her in the last time the police called. He accepted her cursory invitation to follow her into the living room, where she slumped into an armchair. The morning sunlight streaming in through the grubby windows revealed just how pale and washed out she looked as she drew hard on her cigarette and pushed her lank blond hair away from her face.

'What do you want now?' she asked.

'Boyfriend not here last night, then, Charlene?' Mower shot back and was rewarded with a scowl.

'He's buggered off, hasn't he?' she said. 'He couldn't be doing with all this bother over Karen, could he? When all she's probably done is gone off for a fling with someone she's met up in t'forest. She'll go spare when she finds out what a fuss it's caused.'

'You don't really believe that, do you?' Mower asked more gently. 'It's been three days now since her car was seen abandoned up there. That's a long time to leave your family without a word.'

Charlene nodded dumbly and lit another cigarette from the butt of the previous one.

'Have you any reason to believe that she's run off with anyone?' Mower persisted. 'Anyone she talked about? Anyone she thought was special, the way you did with Paul Logan?'

Charlene shook her head, and glanced away to hide the tears in her eyes.

'Terry's a bit of a boring beggar, and seriously weird with his politics, but she worshipped her kids,' she said very quietly. 'She'd not have gone off and left them without a word. She wanted a bit of fun, OK? Who doesn't? But she never said owt to me about it being any more than that.'

'Right,' Mower said. 'So I want you to look at some photographs which we took off her mobile phone...'

'You've got her mobile?' Charlene broke in, obviously surprised.

'She left it in the car,' Mower said.

'She'd never have done that normal, like,' Charlene said. 'She were wedded to that bloody mobile. She'd just got a new one, all singing, all dancing, pictures, music, the lot. I thought it were right daft myself. Who wants a phone to do all that stuff? But she did. She bloody loved it.'

'D'you know if she ever used it to contact anyone she'd met up there?'

'I shouldn't think so,' Charlene said. 'The whole point was you didn't know anyone. No names, no numbers, nowt. I only met Paul properly because he followed us home.'

'But Karen never left the forest in her own car that night, as far as we can tell, so that's not what happened to her,' Mower said. 'She's either still up there or left in someone else's vehicle, which is exactly why we need to find out who was there. Either way, she's probably come to some harm. Someone must have seen her at the end of the session. I want you to look at the photographs she took that night when she went up to the forest on her own, perhaps because she was a bit nervous.' Mower pulled his sheaf of enlarged pictures out and handed them to Charlene. 'Take a good look and see if there's anyone there you've seen before, or whether you can link any of the people in the pictures to the cars. Anything at all you can think of.'

Charlene thumbed her way through the photographs slowly without saying anything and then went back to the beginning and started again.

'A couple of the cars look familiar. They've been there before,' she said, pointing to the blurred images of a couple of vehicles parked under the trees. 'But I don't know who they belonged to. Some of the blokes take good care they're not going to be recognised, use masks and that – look, there, that one with the funny Tony Blair mask. He's there most times. A right goer he is, too. I think he drives a Volvo, as it happens, but that's not in t'pictures, is it?'

'You wouldn't have noticed any registration numbers?'

Charlene looked at him as if he was an idiot.

'Give over,' she said. 'There's one or two I could describe with their pants down, but I don't suppose that's any good to you. There's one bloke hung…'

'Yes, right,' Mower said quickly. 'Unless you can describe his face…?' But Charlene shook her head with a faint grin and turned back to the photographs. But in the end she shrugged and handed them back to Mower.

'There's nowt there I can help you with,' she said. 'I'm sorry. I really am. I liked Karen. She doesn't deserve summat like this happening to her. Does Terry know why she went up there?'

Mower glanced at his watch.

'Well, if he didn't already, he should do by now,' he said. 'My boss was going to tell him this morning.'

'Bloody hell,' Charlene said with a shudder. 'I don't think I want to be around when he finds out about all that. He's bound to blame me and he can be a violent beggar when he chooses. I'll give Paul a bell and see if I can stay with him for a while.'

'He's not married, then?'

'Separated,' Charlene said. 'And I might as well be, for all I see of my husband, with all his long-distance trips.'

'Let us know where you're going,' Mower said. 'We may need to talk to you again. There's just one more thing. The ads in the *Gazette* telling you when the meet was to take place. We've had them traced and the paper's come up with half a dozen, at intervals of a couple of weeks. Did the wording ever vary?'

'Not as far as I can remember,' Charlene said. 'A lad at work I was joshing around with one day showed me one first off. He'd been up there once or twice and thought it were a right laugh. It sounded as if it were worth a go.'

'Who was this lad?' Mower said quickly.

'John, he were called. I can't recall his last name. He were only casual. He left about six months ago any road, went to live in Birmingham, I think. But he introduced us, and then I took Karen later.'

'But no names.'

'Not proper names, no,' she said, glancing away. 'Just silly stuff, like Diamond Lil, and Mean Machine – he were, too. I didn't like *him* much. He were too rough for my taste.'

'OK, OK, I get the picture,' Mower said, slightly wearily. 'We'll talk to your work people about John who went to Birmingham. In the meantime, keep in touch, you and Paul. We need to trace some of these people and you're the only contact we've got.'

Back at police HQ he met DCI Michael Thackeray coming out of the CID office looking grim.

'How did you get on with Bastable, guv?' he asked.

'He took it relatively calmly,' Thackeray said. 'As if it was no more than he expected, I'd say. Or as if he'd known why she went up to the forest all along. He swears he had no idea, of course, but I'm not sure I believe him. What about you?' Mower recounted the gist of his inconclusive interview with Charlene Brough as he made his way to his desk. Thackeray followed and picked up a copy of that afternoon's *Gazette* from a table.

'Have you seen this?' he asked. 'Our friend Bob Baker's really excelled himself on this one.' Mower took the paper and quickly read through the front page story.

'As nasty a bit of character assassination as I've seen for a long time,' he said. 'Just as well you spoke to Bastable when you did, before he saw the *Gazette*.'

Thackeray read over his shoulder in silence for a moment.

'He may have done us a favour if it infuriates her husband as much as it's likely to do,' he said at length. 'Anything which rattles him is all to the good. That's the point at which he'll do something stupid.'

'You still reckon it was him?'

'It's usually the husband, isn't it?' Thackeray said. 'It's just as well all these so-called friends and neighbours stayed anonymous, though. Bastable would be round kicking their doors down if he knew who they were.'

Mower finished reading Baker's story and shrugged.

'There's not really anything there for us to follow up directly, is there? And you can be certain Bob Baker won't tell us who his informants are – if they're not all figments of his imagination, anyway. I can just imagine Ted Grant self-righteously protecting his sources.'

'I wouldn't want to put any credence in Baker's sources, anyway,' Thackeray said. 'It gives us a good reason for another house-to-house up on the Heights, though. And not too carefully concealed from the husband, either. Get Nasreem Mirza up there with some other female officers. See if they can flush out the same sort of gossip about Karen and her friend, Charlene, and what they've been getting up to in their spare time. It looks as if some of it was fairly general knowledge amongst some of the women. They say the husband's always the last to know.'

'Until some good friend decides to enlighten him,' Mower said. 'I wonder if someone actually did that in this case. Certainly worth asking. That could have been the catalyst that sparked him off.'

'Anything from forensics?' Thackeray asked.

'Nothing on the photographs yet, but Bastable's shoes don't fit the prints they found up there, I'm afraid. If someone was standing in the shadows watching what was going on, it wasn't him.'

'We're going to look very stupid if this wretched woman turns up safe and well and shacked up with some boyfriend in Skegness or Blackpool,' Thackeray said morosely.

'I don't think that's very likely, guv,' Mower said. 'The whole thing's got a nasty smell about it.'

'Well, leave it with forensics for now,' Thackeray said. 'They may come up with something. In the meantime, get a team up there to talk to the friends and neighbours. Karen Bastable's a striking-looking woman with that red hair. I've no doubt her comings and goings were noted by the local gossips with nothing better to do.'

'They're practically breathing down each others' necks on that new estate,' Mower said. 'It must be almost impossible to have any sort of a private life.'

'Who has a private life these days?' Thackeray asked himself as much as Mower. 'The whole concept's obsolete.'

Laura had tried several times to follow David Murgatroyd's advice and contact his assistant to make an appointment, but so far without success. She knew Ted Grant wanted to run her feature before the end of the week and the deadline was getting tight. But messages left on the Sibden House answerphone had so far elicited no response and she had failed to track Sanderson down at Murgatroyd's London HQ. When a receptionist advised disdainfully that she should try his mobile phone and Laura had asked for the number, she had refused to divulge it, saying she was forbidden to hand out numbers to anyone at all.

Laura sighed, and was wondering whether to try her luck at Sibden House in person again, when her phone rang and she unexpectedly found herself connected to Debbie Stapleton, the head of Sutton Park School.

'I just thought you'd like to know,' she said, her voice shaking slightly. 'It's this afternoon that the council has decided to bring David Murgatroyd and his cohorts to look round the school after we finish at three-thirty. All at very short notice. I had no idea until an hour ago. But as soon as the news got out, some of the staff and governors seem to have organised some sort of demonstration outside the gates. I guess the kids will get wind of it, and maybe even some parents, so we could have a bit of a confrontation going on. I thought the *Gazette* would like to know.'

'I'm sure we would,' Laura said, glancing towards the editor's glassed-off cubicle at the other side of the newsroom and meeting his less than friendly eye for a moment. 'I'll make sure someone comes down with a photographer. Thanks very much, Debbie. I take it you're not going to be at the demo yourself.' The head teacher laughed but without much mirth in the sound.

'I'm still planning to apply for my own job if this thing goes ahead, though I don't have high hopes,' she said. 'I don't think waving a placard at the school gates would do me much good, though, do you? I'll have to be there to show them round with a smile on my face.'

'Hard luck,' Laura said. 'I'll see if I can get there myself. I've had a half-promise of an interview with Sir David, so maybe I can catch him and firm it up.'

By half past three, with Ted Grant's grumpy acquiescence, Laura found herself outside the gates of Sutton Park School, where a handful of people had already assembled although school had clearly not yet finished for the day. She introduced herself to one or two of the demonstrators and was pushed in the direction of a stocky, dark-haired man in working clothes, who turned out to be the parent governor, Steve O'Mara, the man her grandmother had recommended she speak to.

'You're Joyce's granddaughter?' he asked, revealing a slight Irish brogue. 'She's a top lady, is your grandmother. I knew her when she was still a councillor.'

'She'd still like to be,' Laura said. 'It's only her arthritis slows her down.'

'She's still in touch, sharp as a knife,' O'Mara said. 'She's been very helpful with this bloody hijacker Murgatroyd.'

'I went to the academy in Leeds this morning,' Laura said. 'It seems to me that they achieve what they achieve simply by keeping out the most difficult children.'

'While our Debbie has been pushing up the results without keeping anyone out,' O'Mara said. 'You'll never crack the problems on the estates if you don't tackle the really difficult kids. I know. I live on the Heights. It'll be a bloody tragedy for Wuthering if Debbie loses her job.'

'Do you think that's likely?' Laura asked.

'I'd bet on it,' O'Mara said. 'It seems to be what he's done everywhere else. She's not exactly "born again", isn't our Debbie, and I doubt she'll go down well at all with them that are.' At that moment they heard a bell ring inside the school buildings and within minutes a flood of pupils burst out of the doors and through the gates, where a jostling crowd of them soon began to congregate, demanding to know what the demonstration was about. O'Mara did not hesitate to explain and, while some drifted off with many a teenage shrug, a significant number listened more carefully to what the gathered adults had to say, and decided to stay, some of them pulling sheets of paper out of their bags and improvising anti-academy posters which they attached to the school railings. Sir David Murgatroyd, Laura thought grimly, would not be best pleased at his reception.

And so it turned out. The dark, chauffeur-driven Jaguar, which brought him to the school, closely followed by two other cars, stopped some distance from the now considerable crowd and they could see the chauffeur using a mobile phone. Almost immediately, a police car appeared and four uniformed officers approached the school gates, clearing a path for the visitors' cars. This move was greeted with a few catcalls and whistles, which Steve O'Mara himself tried to silence.

'We don't want to get a reputation as hooligans,' he said to Laura. 'That won't do us any good at all.' As he spoke the three cars, led by the Jag, swept through the now open gates, which swung closed again immediately, and a police sergeant approached O'Mara with a notebook in his hand.

'Are you responsible for this demonstration, sir?' he asked.

'Not really,' O'Mara said. 'A few of us wanted to speak to David Murgatroyd before he visited the school. The rest was just spontaneous when the students came out.'

'And you are?' the sergeant asked, before writing down O'Mara's details in his notebook.

'You should be aware that you need police permission for a demonstration, sir,' the sergeant said.

'I told you it wasn't intended to be a demonstration, more a sort of lobby,' O'Mara said. 'I suppose you'll be telling me that's illegal next?'

'No, sir,' the sergeant said. 'But I have to say that this looks very much like a demonstration to me.'

'It wasn't until the youngsters came out of school and decided to join in,' Laura broke in. 'Perhaps you'd better talk to them, if you can pin them down.' She glanced at the milling crowd of teenagers and watched the sergeant's eyes follow hers and come to a conclusion which he did not appear very happy with. He turned to one of the constables standing close behind him.

'Get these kids on their way home,' he said stonily before turning back to Laura, as all three PCs began chivvying the students away from the school entrance.

'And you are?' he asked. Laura told him, wondering if the name meant anything to him. Michael Thackeray would not be best pleased to discover that she had clashed with a uniformed officer, however over-officious she might claim he had been. Their incompatible professions had brought them into enough conflict over the years for her to be in no doubt about that.

'And the photographer's with you?'

Laura nodded.

'I'm sure you don't think we need police permission to be here as well,' she said with her most engaging smile. But she doubted that her charm had achieved anything as the sergeant turned on his heel and set about clearing the crowd with a singular lack of charm of his own. Laura shrugged and turned back to O'Mara.

'Come and have a drink,' she said, nodding towards the pub on the opposite side of the road. 'Tell me all about your worries about the academy. I'll have to catch up with David Murgatroyd some other time.'

'Gotcha!' Sergeant Kevin Mower said with satisfaction as he put the phone down on the technical examiner who had been trying to enhance the photographs from Karen Bastable's phone. The good news was that the forensic team thought they had succeeded in deciphering two registration numbers from the blurred photographs of cars. The even better news he relayed to DCI Thackeray ten minutes later was that both cars had registered owners in Bradfield and that one lived just a stone's throw from the Bastables' home.

'You reckon they must know each other?' Thackeray asked mildly.

'I'd put money on it, guv.'

'Right, let's go and see what they've got to say for themselves,' Thackeray said, pushing the files on his desk to one side and stubbing out his cigarette. 'I need some fresh air, and depending on what they say, we may need Bastable in here again. This could be the breakthrough we've been waiting for.'

Their first call, in the leafy suburb of Southfield, led nowhere. The car with the registration number they had been given was an entirely different colour and model from the one in Karen Bastable's photograph and with a vital digit's difference in the licence plate. The perturbed owner assured the officers that he had just returned from a holiday in Scotland. Which left one possibility, and they soon had more than enough evidence to be knocking on Terry Bastable's door. They had spent the previous half-hour with his self-professed best friend, Les Duckworth, who lived in the next street and admitted immediately that he owned the red Astra parked in front of his house and identified from Karen's photographs. But Duckworth had denied all knowledge of even the rough location of Bently Forest, or ever taking part in even the mildest and most innocent of outdoor sexual adventures. And given his gross size, a beer belly of huge proportions hanging over his baggy tracksuit bottoms, which stretched almost to splitting point over enormous thighs and buttocks, Mower was inclined to believe him. No one even remotely like Les had appeared in Karen's photograghs and he must have known himself, if he had taken part, that he would be extremely easy to identify, however many masks he had used to conceal his face.

'Is that what they were at?' he had said, in what appeared to be genuine astonishment. 'Mucky beggars. Terry told me he wanted to borrow t'car because his was in dock and he needed to take Karen to work. She works late shift and there's no buses back. But I thought it were a bit odd when I read in t'*Gazette* that her car were found right up there. I were going to ask Terry about it.'

'I suppose it never entered your head to tell us that Terry Bastable had borrowed your car that night,' Thackeray said angrily.

'I were going to ask Terry about that an'all, as it goes,' Duckworth said, immediately on the defensive. 'But I've not been right well this week. I've had the flu. That's why I weren't bothered about giving him t'car t'other night. I went to bed early. I were wheezing like a bloody blocked drain.' Mower glanced at the empty lager cans and the sports pages strewn around the living room and wondered whether either had acquired therapeutic properties he had not heard about.

'And you've never been to Bently Forest any other time?' Thackeray snapped.

'I told you, I've never heard o't'bloody place,' Duckworth almost shouted, and immediately started a breathless coughing fit, as if to prove the veracity of his story. They left him to his flu and his lager, and walked round to Bastable's house where Bastable eventually opened the door, looking grey and unshaven.

'Have you found her?' he asked and his shoulders slumped convincingly enough when Thackeray shook his head.

'We need to ask you some more questions about your movements on the night Karen disappeared,' Thackeray said. 'You can either do it here or down at the station...'

'What movements?' Bastable came back quickly, still holding the door firmly half closed. 'I told you, I were here all night, looking after t'kids.'

'Can we come in, Mr Bastable,' Thackeray asked, 'or would you really prefer to come to the station?' Scowling heavily, Bastable opened the door for them and pointed them in the direction of his untidy sitting room, where plates of half-eaten pizza were still left from the previous evening's meal. The Bastables' home was obviously seriously missing a woman's touch, Thackeray thought. He chose an upright chair, leaving Bastable to flop onto the sofa while Mower took out a notebook and stationed himself near the door.

'There seem to be some things you didn't tell us about the night Karen went missing,' Thackeray said, mildly enough to be disarming. But Bastable responded with aggression.

'Like what?' he snapped.

'Like the fact that you had borrowed Les Duckworth's car that afternoon.' Bastable's face, already an unhealthy colour, drained to a dirty white.

'So what? I needed it to fetch some stuff from t'supermarket after Karen went out. I took kids wi'me. Nowt wrong wi'that, is there?'

'So you took the car back after that?'

Bastable hesitated.

'He said I could keep it till morning,' he said. 'He weren't well. He weren't going out. Said leave it till t'morning.'

'So you had the car all evening?'

'I told you. I went to t'bloody supermarket.'

'Your children will remember that then?' Mower intervened, but Bastable just shrugged.

'Happen,' he said.

'So how do you explain that the car was seen at Bently Forest after Karen got there?' Thackeray asked.

'It weren't. That's a lie,' Bastable said. 'I never went anywhere near t'bloody forest. I don't even know the way.'

'It's easy to find if you followed her there,' Thackeray asked. 'So what happened? Did she recognise the car? Did she recognise you in the car?'

'I weren't there,' Bastable said. 'I bloody told you. I weren't there.'

'But we know the car was there. We're certain of that,' Thackeray said. Bastable's eyes roamed uneasily around the room.

'Must be a mistake,' he muttered.

'No mistake,' Thackeray said. 'We'll be examining the car in detail, of course. There will be forensic evidence of who's been in it – you, or the children – and quite possibly traces of where it's been.' He paused, leaving Bastable looking sick.

'Traces of Karen,' Thackeray spelt it out. 'Or even Karen's body. Everyone and everything leaves traces.'

Bastable ran a hand over his stubbled head and face before nodding, his shoulders slumped, and Thackeray pressed home his advantage.

'I think it's time you were a bit more honest with us about what exactly happened that night,' he said. Bastable groaned and sat in silence for a full minute, hands clasped, staring down at his dirty trainers.

'I knew she were up to summat,' he muttered eventually. 'I'd reckoned for a while that she had a boyfriend. She suddenly started going out wi'that cow Charlene from her work. That were new. And her clothes. She started buying stuff that were more sexy, more revealing, you know? She said there were nowt going on but I didn't believe her. So I borrowed Les's car, left the kids here and followed her. I never reckoned she'd drive so far. I thought she'd be going to a pub or a club, local like. I couldn't believe it when she drove right up there into t'hills. I were beginning to get panicky about leaving t'kids. Matty can be a little devil when he chooses...'

'So she saw you?' Thackeray said. 'Down the track into the woods, she spotted the car and saw you driving it?'

'No, no, she never,' Bastable protested. 'I stopped for five minutes, no more. Watched what were going on, saw Karen get out o't'car and join in...wearing next to nowt...I were right choked. But there were so many people there, I couldn't do owt, could I? I left her to it. Came back home in a right state but the kids were OK. No probs. Planned to have it out wi'Karen when she got back, but she never did, did she? She never did get back. One of them bastards...' He broke off, too distraught to continue. Or else a very good actor, Thackeray thought.

'Let's get this completely clear, Mr Bastable,' he said. 'You're telling us that you followed your wife in a borrowed car, a car which she was likely to recognise, but she didn't see you and you didn't make any attempt to speak to her when you realised what was going on?'

'Right,' Bastable said, his expression sullen now.

'You simply turned around and came home?'

'Right,' Bastable said again. 'I couldn't deal with it wi'all them beggars there, could I? I'd have bloody dealt wi'it when she got back, though. I'd have given her a right thrashing.'

'That's your usual answer to problems, is it, Mr Bastable? Violence?'

'If it's called for,' Bastable said, without hesitation. 'Two-timing cow!'

'You realise that we'll check out your version of events with anyone else who may have been in Bently Forest at the same time you were there,' Thackeray said. 'We will undoubtedly want to question you again and take a full statement.'

'Check away,' Bastable said, defiant now. 'That's what happened.'

But when the two officers went back to their car, Kevin Mower laughed.

'Does he really expect us to believe all that?' he said.

'I want Duckworth's car searched for DNA, hair, blood, anything at all,' Thackeray said. 'If Karen was ever in that car, dead or alive, I want to know about it. And we need to know who else was up there that night.'

'And that's going to be the hard part,' Mower said as he slid the car into gear. 'I can't see any one of them rushing forward as a witness to anything that happened there. Judging by what Charlene said, they'll be keeping their masks very firmly in place.'

CHAPTER EIGHT

When Laura got back to the office, she found the newsroom already half empty, though Ted Grant was still in his office, the door ajar, and as soon as she had taken off her coat and settled back at her computer, his half-expected roar of a summons reached her.

'Did you get hold of Murgatroyd?' he asked without preamble, and before she opened her mouth to reply he stormed on regardless.

'I've had Peter Maxwell from the council bending my ear,' he said. 'He's apparently had Murgatroyd's PA on the phone complaining that we're running some sort of anti-academy campaign. What the hell's all that about?'

Laura shrugged.

'Considering I haven't written a word yet, I don't see how he can have jumped to that conclusion.'

'Did you get an interview with Murgatroyd?'

'No, I couldn't get near him. There was a minor protest going on outside the school – governors and a few parents. They'd got wind of his visit somehow. And then when the kids started coming out they thought it was a good idea to join in. I don't imagine any of the students have the foggiest notion what becoming an academy means, but they joined in the fun anyway. Then the police turned up and it all got a bit heavy.'

'Aye, well you can write that up for tomorrow morning anyway,' Grant said. 'Did we get pictures?'

'Yes, Tony was with me. They should be on your screen by now.' Grant clicked into Photoshop and cast a cursory eye over the photographer's offerings.

'Owt and nowt there,' he said. 'Now, are you going to finish this piece for Friday or do I need to pencil summat else in instead?'

'Murgatroyd promised me an appointment, but his sidekick, Sanderson, seems to be avoiding me. He's the one who must have spoken to Maxwell. He seems to be the main obstruction, though I've no idea why. I don't know whether it's deliberate. Seems a bit odd, if it is. I'll keep trying, but if I can't pin him down tomorrow I think you'd better hold it until next week. We can't really run without some sort of comment from Murgatroyd himself. I need to ask him why he's ploughing all his money into inner-city schools, what he thinks he'll get out of it, or whether it really is for some sort of higher religious cause. Perhaps he just likes kids, although I don't think he's got any of his own. I've not found any record that he's even been married.'

'Sounds to me you don't have even the beginning of a profile of this beggar,' Grant said dismissively. 'Well, if you want more time, you'd better come up with something tasty. I'm not sure we shouldn't ditch the whole thing. Just run news stories as and when they happen and let the protesters fight it out in the letters column.'

'If he's this elusive, he must have something to hide,' Laura said, not entirely convincing herself. 'There's trouble brewing at the school in any case, so we'll have a good story one way or another. The head seems convinced she's going to lose her job and some of the governors are going to be furious about that. They'll all lose their positions, too. Murgatroyd gets to appoint all the governors and make the policy, in exchange for what is actually a very small financial contribution.'

'Peter Maxwell reckons it's just the usual suspects at the school, troublemakers of one sort or another, trades unionists, lefties and liberals, looking a gold-plated gift horse in the mouth.'

'He would think that, being a dyed-in-the-wool Tory himself,' Laura said. 'I get the impression that there's more to it than that. Give me a couple more days.'

Grant nodded reluctantly.

'It had better be good,' he said.

Taking Grant at his word, Laura glanced at her watch and reckoned that she had time for one more assault on Sibden House before she went home. It was a long shot, she knew, but gave her another excuse to avoid the conversation she needed increasingly urgently with Michael Thackeray. She shivered slightly as she accelerated out of town along the valley of the Maze. There had been a time when she would have expected to be delighted at the prospect of becoming a mother, but she had been entangled in the aftermath of her partner's tragedies for so long that she barely remembered what a straightforward emotional reaction was like. She had buried herself in her work, but now that was no longer an option for very long. Some sort of decision would have to be taken and very soon, and the prospect filled her with foreboding.

To her surprise, when she parked outside Sibden House, the answerphone on the gates got an immediate response, and she recognised the voice of Winston Sanderson.

'Is Sir David Murgatroyd at home?' she asked. 'He did ask me to contact him.'

'He's not here,' Sanderson said, his voice brusque and clearly, on this occasion, not willing to unlock the gates. 'And I don't know when he will be. He was not best pleased to find demonstrators outside Sutton Park this afternoon. I spotted you there, too. That's not the sort of publicity he wants when he's trying to do people a favour.'

'Well, if he won't explain his motives it will be difficult to persuade people to his point of view,' Laura said.

'I hear what you're saying,' Sanderson said. 'But he won't give interviews. We've been through all this, Miss Ackroyd. You're wasting your time here. I'll talk to him about some sort of press release in the near future. That's the best I can do for you.'

'He said he'd talk to me, personally, when I bumped into him in Leeds,' Laura persisted, though she guessed she was wasting her time.

'He hasn't mentioned it to me, and I keep his diary,' Sanderson said, and cut the connection.

Was that the truth, she wondered as she turned the car round in the narrow lane and set off back down the hill again? As she turned onto the main Bradfield road, she saw a dark-coloured Jaguar making the turn up to Sibden and recognised David Murgatroyd's car. If she had been just five minutes later, she thought angrily, she might have been able to waylay him at the gates to the house. Winston Sanderson was a liar, she thought, although whether it was on his boss's or his own behalf was impossible to know.

Sergeant Kevin Mower knocked on Thackeray's office door towards the end of the afternoon with a gleam in his eye. He found Thackeray wreathed in cigarette smoke as usual, in defiance of all the rules, and not apparently taking much interest in the piles of files on his desk.

'I had an idea, guv,' Mower said cautiously, not sure what sort of a reception he was about to get. Thackeray seemed visibly to haul himself out of whatever deep pit he had been visiting.

'What was that?'

'These meetings up in the woods,' Mower said. 'They're arranged through the small ads in the *Gazette,* right? So why don't we put an ad in ourselves, with a date. With a bit of luck, at least a few of them will turn up looking for fun and games and, hey presto, we've got our witnesses, if not our abductor.'

'If we're talking murder we're hardly likely to get a result. A killer won't be rushing back up there in a hurry.'

'And whoever puts in the ad normally will know it's a fake and likely won't turn up,' Mower said. 'But if they really don't know each others' identities it would be difficult for the organiser to stop it happening once the ad appeared.'

'You'll only get the people who are unaware that Karen went missing in that exact spot, and there can't be many of them around,' Thackeray objected.

'Not everyone reads the *Gazette,* in spite of what Laura might think. And they won't recognise Karen's name either.

All anonymous, Charlene said. And we've not released details of what she was doing up there yet. They may not connect her with their activities.'

'It's a long shot, but it might be worth a try,' Thackeray conceded. 'See what you can do to set it up in the morning. But check with Charlene to make sure you get the wording right, otherwise you'll blow it.'

'Right, guv,' Mower said. 'I'll get off home then.' But as Thackeray watched him go he knew it was not home which was putting that gleam in the sergeant's eye. It had not escaped his notice that Mower had been unusually cheerful lately, nor much detective skill to work out why. He sighed, half wishing he could share his enthusiastic acceptance of no-strings involvement with the opposite sex, but knowing that he had been programmed too early and too thoroughly ever to go down that road. He piled the files on his desk into an untidy heap in his in tray and put on his coat. But when he had picked up his car and eased his way into the early evening rush in the town centre he turned north instead of south and took the road up the Maze valley towards Arnedale, the small market town where he had been at school, and not far from where his father had worked a small hill farm until ill health forced him into a frustrated and lonely retirement.

Thackeray did not often visit his father. It had never been a comfortable relationship, soured by Joe's unforgiving puritanism and Thackeray's own determination to go his own way and eventually abandon his father's religion and the farm, which the old man had hoped he would take over when he retired. Even the slow decline of both their wives had brought no glimmer of fellow feeling. His mother's descent into MS when he was still only a boy had killed Thackeray's faith as

surely as it eventually killed her, while his own wife's mental
illness and its consequences had drawn no sympathy from Joe,
who blamed that family tragedy squarely and implacably on
his son. Even so, Thackeray felt duty-bound to visit Joe in his
retirement bungalow from time to time, and this evening,
driven by the deep uneasiness in his relationship with Laura,
which he knew had its roots in his own failed marriage, he felt
drawn to Arnedale almost in spite of himself.

When he reached his father's home, he almost drove past,
recognising the car that was parked outside the bungalow at
an odd angle, half on and half off the pavement. But then he
shrugged resignedly. Perhaps, he thought, the presence of
Father Francis Rafferty would ease the visit along, leaving less
opportunity for father and son to tear open old wounds. In
spite of having abandoned his church and his faith, Thackeray
still regarded the old parish priest, who had known him since
he was a child, as a friend, and a good one, who had
unexpectedly stood by him with support and sympathy at a
time when few in his family or in the town had offered
anything but rancorous condemnation.

Joe must have seen Thackeray's car pull up in front of the
priest's because he had the door open even before his son had
closed the garden gate behind him, but there was little warmth
in the old man's eyes and Thackeray was shocked by how
much he seemed to have physically shrunk since he had last
seen him a few months before.

'Nah then,' Joe said, leading the way into his crowded
living room, still stuffed with some of the heavy, old furniture
he had brought from the farmhouse when it was finally sold.
Rafferty stood up when the younger Thackeray came in and
held out a hand in greeting.

'I'm glad to see you, Michael,' he said. 'I heard you'd been having a rough time. A shooting, was it? You've made a full recovery?'

'More or less,' Thackeray said. 'One of the risks of the job.'

'Not quite what the papers said,' Rafferty objected quietly.

'They had their own take on it,' Thackeray conceded. 'But my bosses weren't happy. I didn't go by the book.'

'You were always a chancer,' Joe said, flinging himself down in his favourite chair by the meagre gas fire which had substituted inadequately for the massive stone fireplace in the farmhouse.

'Not really,' Thackeray responded, amused by his father's gross misunderstanding of his nature, and Rafferty, who had also aged since he had last seen him, flashed him the sympathetic smile of a man who knew him better.

'Have you married again, after going through all that for the young woman?' the priest asked, aware, as he would be, that the death of Thackeray's long-divorced wife had removed any obstacle a priest could raise to such a course.

'Not yet,' Thackeray said, and his frozen expression warned Rafferty off any pursuit of that topic. 'So how have you been, Dad?' he asked Joe, who scowled and pulled his thick woollen cardigan closer around him.

'Much you care,' he muttered, glancing at Rafferty, as if for approval. 'I don't see you from one month's end t'bloody next.'

'Come on, Joseph,' the priest exclaimed. 'You've got a host of people from the parish coming to take you out, taking you to Mass, bringing you meals. How can you complain? I'm here so much my housekeeper reckons she never sees me.' But Rafferty's joviality made no impression on Joe.

'I once had a family,' Joe said, staring steadfastly at the fire.

The anger rose quickly in Thackeray's throat at his father's self-pity and the sudden sharp memory of the family he himself had lost, and he got up and went to the window where he choked back the bitterness of years. He felt, rather than heard, someone move to stand beside him.

'Leave it, Michael,' Rafferty said quietly. 'He doesn't know what he's saying.'

'He knows exactly what he's saying,' Thackeray said, moving blindly towards the door. 'And how to twist the knife. I have to be going, Dad,' he muttered, without looking back.

Rafferty followed him out and put a hand on his shoulder.

'It gets no easier, does it, for either of you? I'm supposed to offer consolation, but I get nowhere with Joe. And you?' He shrugged, looking desolate himself, beneath the halo of snow-white hair. 'Can you find no happiness with this young woman of yours, Michael? You've been together a long while now.' Thackeray shrugged.

'She wants a child,' he said flatly. 'And I can't face it.'

'Ah,' Rafferty said. They stood for a moment side by side, gazing bleakly along the row of retirement bungalows which seemed to have provided no respite for Joe Thackeray, before the old priest put a gentle hand on Thackeray's arm again. 'You're a brave man, Michael, from what I read about you in the newspapers, but that's merely physical courage, a welcome thing but not enough. Maybe what you need now is a different sort of courage to put the past behind you and make a new start. I know you don't believe it will do you a mite of good, but I'll pray for you anyway. As I do for Joe, that he will learn forgiveness. I'll pray that neither of you's a lost cause.'

Thackeray turned to Rafferty and smiled.

'You never give up,' he said.

'Why would I?' Rafferty said, his brogue more pronounced. 'The good Lord never gives up.'

Thackeray hardly remembered the drive home when he finally parked outside the flat he shared with Laura Ackroyd in a converted Victorian house. He sat for a moment clutching the steering wheel after he had switched the engine off as if it were some sort of lifebelt which could save him from drowning. He was aware that the lights were on in the flat and that Laura must be there, no doubt cooking a meal which would somehow bridge the gap between his ingrained country taste for simple food, which he had never cast off, and her more adventurous preferences. They were, he thought, an ill-matched couple and he doubted that they could remain a couple much longer.

He opened the front door and took off his coat before going to find Laura, as he expected in the kitchen, and felt cheered by the simple domesticity of the scene. He kissed the back of her neck, where her unruly copper hair escaped from a casual ponytail, and felt the stirrings of desire. He sensed her respond to his exploratory roaming hands, but she pulled away and turned to him, wooden spoon in hand, her eyes troubled.

'Not now,' she said, giving him a chaste kiss on the cheek. 'This will spoil. And I need to talk to you.' She had been steeling herself for hours and was not to be put off now.

'What is it?' he asked, sniffing suspiciously at the garlicky aroma and peering at the conglomeration of vegetables she had been stirring in a large pan.

'Ratatouille,' she said. 'Mixed veg, Mediterranean style, to go with the lamb cutlets. Compromise?'

'Huh,' he said, turning away with a smile. 'More foreign muck.' He poured a vodka and tonic for her and a tonic for himself, and went into the living room to watch the television news, but he switched the set off when she came in to join him.

'So, why so serious?' he asked as she sat down beside him, dodging his outstretched arm. She took a deep breath before she spoke.

'I've something to tell you,' she said, seeking some reassurance in his eyes but finding only sudden anxiety. 'There's no easy way to say it,' she said, her voice jerky and slightly harsh. 'I'm going to have a baby, Michael, and I hope you can be happy about it. I didn't do it deliberately, in fact I'm not sure how it happened, but I'm pregnant.'

Thackeray shot to his feet as if he had been physically struck, and went to the window where the curtains were not yet drawn. He stood for a long time staring out into the gathering darkness where a solitary blackbird was singing its heart out in one of the still-dormant trees. He felt physically frozen and began to shiver uncontrollably, the almost constant pain in his back, where he had been shot over a year ago, beginning to stab. He was aware of Laura coming to stand close to him, but he pulled away from her and went to brace himself with his back to the door, his expression a mixture of bewilderment and outrage.

'How?' he asked. 'How could you let that happen?'

'I don't know, honestly I don't. I must have missed a pill. I just don't know.'

Thackeray shook his head and closed his eyes briefly, and Laura watched him with tears filling her eyes.

'Just tell me,' she said. 'Tell me what you're thinking. If you can't handle it...' She paused, for a long moment, obviously hoping he would speak, and when he didn't she shrugged and continued faintly. 'Well, *if* you can't handle it, I'll have to decide what to do.'

Thackeray turned away without a word and went out of the room. Laura heard the outside door slam and, within seconds, Thackeray's car start up in the street outside and drive away. She sat for a long time by the fireplace, gazing into space as the light faded, until a smell of burning brought her back to the world and she rushed into the kitchen to switch off the gas under the ruined meal. She cursed under her breath as she scraped the pans into the rubbish bin. Then she picked up her own coat and bag and left the flat.

Vicky Mendelson opened the door to Laura at the first ring on the bell, her face full of concern, and ushered her into the sitting room.

'I've just chased the boys to bed,' she said. 'And David's out, so it's just us. Do you want a drink?'

Laura shook her head.

'If I start drinking, I might not stop,' she said.

'Oh hell. So tell me what happened,' Vicky demanded, so Laura did.

'I think it's all over,' she said finally. 'He won't forgive me if I have the baby, and he certainly won't forgive me if I don't. It's a lose-lose situation.'

'The man's impossible,' Vicky said angrily. 'I'm surprised you've stuck with him so long.'

'When he nearly died last year, when he got shot, I realised I couldn't live without him,' Laura said. 'So what can I do now? It's my fault. I was careless, stupid even. When I found out, I thought I could persuade him to go along with it. But he wouldn't even talk to me. Not a word…' Laura wiped the tears from her eyes angrily. 'This baby needs a father. I'm not sure I can bring it up on my own.'

'I'm sure you can,' Vicky said. 'Lots of mothers do. But I think you're writing Michael off too quickly. It must have been a shock to him. Give him time, and he'll come round. Didn't he say that he thought he could cope once?'

'Once,' Laura said bitterly. 'But he soon seemed to lose heart, thought better of it, whatever.'

'Oh Laura, I'm so sorry. I don't know what to say.'

'He went off without a word. I'm so afraid he'll do something desperate. He's been so down lately, mainly because of the shooting last year, but I'm sure it's partly to do with the fact that he knows I want a child.'

'Not suicidal, surely?' Vicky said, unable to hide her horror.

'There are lots of ways to commit suicide,' Laura said. 'Michael once tried very hard with bottles of booze. I know that.'

'You've no idea where he's gone?'

'He's still got his own flat on Manchester Road. He's always refused to sell it. He uses that as a bolt-hole sometimes.'

'Do you want to go round there? Should we both go? David will be home soon, so I could leave the children with him.'

'I don't think so,' Laura said wearily. 'He'd hate you getting involved.'

'Of course,' Vicky agreed. 'It's just that I feel I want to do something. He makes me so furious. This should be the start of the happiest time of your life – his too, for God's sake – and look at the mess you're both in. I feel guilty for ever having introduced you to each other.'

'Don't be silly,' Laura said with a faint smile, taking Vicky's hand and squeezing it. 'It's not your fault. And as you say, lots of people bring children up on their own. If that's what I have to do, then that's what I'll have to do. We have had some good times together, you know, in spite of everything. And this is Michael's baby, mine and Michael's, so perhaps he'll decide that he can be a father again, somehow, when it arrives, if not before.' She did not sound as if she was convincing herself and Vicky gave her a long hug.

'Let's hope so,' she said. 'So sod him, and start looking forward, why don't you? Your life is about to change big time. You have absolutely no idea what you're letting yourself in for.'

Michael Thackeray sat for a long time in his car watching the crowds of young people swirl around the town centre in cheerful groups, dodging in and out of pubs and clubs. It was still early and they had not yet reached the pitch where fights would break out and a handful of staggering girls would be sick in the gutter or fall down shrieking with laughter, half in and half out of their skimpy clothes and apparently never feeling the cold. What was wrong with him, he wondered, that he had never ever enjoyed life in that uninhibited way, never, even as a student in Oxford, with an apparently brilliant future in front of him, felt really carefree? There had always been this weight on his shoulders that he had once tried to lift with the help of the sort of temporary cheerfulness and eventual oblivion alcohol brought, but that had become a demon which destroyed his family and almost destroyed him as his brilliant future receded.

Tempting as some of the pubs he had just driven past had

seemed, holding out their comforting embrace of bright lights and cheerful clatter, and promising forgetfulness, he had resisted them without even slowing the car. More than anything, the thought of the new life he had created, even unknowingly, stayed like a single bright star at the centre of his mind, guiding him away from the worst of his temptations. But that did not ease the mental turmoil that had overwhelmed him as soon as Laura had broken the news that she was pregnant. He had not trusted himself to speak, fearing either an outpouring of anger for which she would never forgive him, or a scream of pain which she would never understand. Her words had ricochetted round his mind and he had been unable to do anything but turn and run.

He sighed and pulled away from the kerb and headed up the hill out of town towards his own flat. He needed to be alone, he thought, and he feared that in the end he might always need to be alone.

CHAPTER NINE

It was surprising, DCI Michael Thackeray thought, through the fog of a sleepless night, that the foxes had gained access to this unholy parcel, but they had scraped through a light covering of dark peaty soil and chewed through the plastic wrapping and exposed a naked foot, which they had gnawed to the bone, leaving the unlucky early morning jogger no doubt as to what was inside when he stumbled over it on his regular run. He was sitting now, half in and half out of a police car, still visibly shaken even though it had taken more than half an hour for the forces of law and order to reach him after he had phoned in on his mobile to report his discovery, and another quarter for the forensic teams to arrive and begin photographing the scene, before erecting a white plastic tent over the body and its immediate surroundings. The cars and vans were awkwardly parked now on boggy ground from which it might be difficult to extricate them when their jobs were done.

They were eight miles or so beyond the edge of Bradfield and more than a thousand feet higher, on a windswept plateau of wiry moorland grass dotted with boggy patches where browning sedge struggled for survival and the occasional stand of spiny gorse leant away from the prevailing westerlies. Whoever had left this parcel here in a shallow grave had been unlucky to have anyone stumble over it so soon that, as far as he could judge, decomposition had not yet seriously set in. Up here, on the high tops, it could have been several weeks or even months before anyone else had stumbled across it, Thackeray thought.

'Take a statement from our lad over there, Kevin, will you?' he said. 'Then he can get off home. He looks half frozen already.'

'Right, guv,' Mower said, hoping that even though he had been roused too soon from the companionable warmth of a shared bed, he did not look half as shattered as his boss appeared to be. Thackeray's haggard look and the dark circles under his eyes suggested to the sergeant a night without any sleep at all.

'Here's Amos,' Mower said as he turned away and noticed a car pull up cautiously at the edge of the road on the moor top. The pathologist, Amos Atherton, was clearly not willing to risk his Beamer in the mud, and he began a slow trudge along the rough track which took off at right angles from a quiet back route to Lancashire. It was an isolated spot, especially at this time of the year, when the local sheep had been taken to lower ground for lambing, leaving the area to only the hardiest birds and wild animals.

Amos Atherton, breathing heavily, eventually reached Thackeray and slapped him on the back, at his most jovial in spite of the bitter wind whipping over the moors from a sky of scudding grey clouds and spattering rain.

'What's this? A late Christmas present?' he asked.

Thackeray did not respond and Atherton looked at him sharply, before turning to the task in hand inside the flapping tent.

'Have you got photographs?' he asked, eyeing the half-buried plastic. 'Can I open it up?'

'Go ahead,' Thackeray said. The layers of what looked like black dustbin liners from which the foot protruded at an awkward angle were secured with bands of brown duct tape, almost like a mummy, and when Atherton gently slit the parcel from the exposed foot to what appeared to be the top of the head, it fell away to each side like a pod.

'Christ,' Atherton said, with unaccustomed profanity as the cold light revealed what appeared at first glance to be little more than the contents of a butcher's slab. Thackeray's face turned to stone and one of the younger officers close behind him turned away, pale and retching.

'Human remains, no doubt,' Atherton said quietly. 'Fairly recent, too.'

'Male or female?' Thackeray asked. The body was naked but had been so savagely mutilated that its gender was not immediately apparent.

'Female, at a guess, but as you can see the sexual characteristics have been pretty much obliterated.' He sighed heavily and lifted a stray piece of black plastic from what was left of the head, where little of the face was distinguishable.'

'And why the hell would he cut all her hair off?' he asked, peering closely at the tufted remains clinging to a torn and bloodied scalp. 'What the hell is that all about?'

'Cause of death?' Thackeray asked, but Atherton just shrugged.

'No idea,' he said. 'We'd better get her down to the mortuary, as soon as I've finished this examination and your SOCOs are through. You've got a serious problem here, Michael. Whoever did this has gone totally berserk, and I wouldn't bet a brass farthing on him not doing it again.'

Superintendent Jack Longley gazed at his DCI gloomily, and not merely because of the gruesome post-mortem details Thackeray had just relayed to him. Michael Thackeray, he thought, looked seriously ill but he knew from long experience that the younger man would confide nothing and admit nothing about his private life, or even his health, if it did not suit him to do so. Longley had gone out on a limb when he had insisted on Thackeray's suitability for the job in Bradfield, given the ample evidence of a chequered previous career, and he still felt, in spite of some near catastrophes, that his confidence had been well placed. Which did not stop him frequently wishing that Thackeray would sort out his relationship with Laura Ackroyd instead of apparently lurching from one emotional crisis to another.

He had thought, after Thackeray had been shot in the back, that his career might be over, had gone so far as to suggest that he retire early. But the DCI had insisted on coming back to work after what most of his colleagues thought was far too short a convalescence, and had so far seemed to function much as normal even if, to judge by appearances, that was far from what he was feeling. More than one colleague had reported noticing the painkillers on his desk, that he appeared to be taking as routine, and Longley had more than once wondered if he should not order him to take more sick leave.

This morning Thackeray looked like death and Longley

was sure that it was not simply because of the discovery of the bloodied, burnt, mutilated and so far unidentified body on Staveley Moor that had now been picked over and dissected on Amos Atherton's slab and consigned to a numbered drawer in the mortuary refrigerator.

'No chance of an ID then?' Longley asked.

'No chance of facial recognition,' Thackeray said. 'Certainly no distinguishing features. No jewellery. We'll have to go for DNA. But given what was left of her red hair, I'd put money on it being Karen Bastable. It has to be, hasn't it?'

Thackeray's mind zeroed back to the slab where Atherton had shown him what was left of the woman – at least, he said, he could be sure of that much – who had been found on the moors. But the examination of the body had been even more appalling than usual and Atherton's conclusions so unbelievable that Thackeray felt that he himself had been torn apart by wolves in much the way that the woman's body had been ravaged.

'Most of the injuries seem to have been inflicted before she died,' Atherton had said, his expression unreadable, after detailing the external and internal state of the body for his report. 'Slashing rather than stabbing wounds to most parts of the face and body, burns…if the object was to inflict the maximum pain then this would have done it.'

'He tortured her to death?' Thackeray had asked, almost unable to grasp the enormity of it.

'Not quite,' Atherton said. 'The *coup de grace* is a single deep stab wound to the heart. A large, sharp instrument, quite possibly the same one that inflicted many of the other slashing injuries. But she must have been half dead from loss of blood and shock by the time the final blow was struck. I reckon he was just making sure at that stage.'

'Dear God,' Thackeray said, stepping away from the table and untying his gown, reluctant to let Atherton see how deeply he was shaken.

'Was she raped?' he asked, over his shoulder.

'Almost certainly. I've taken samples as far as I can, but as you can see, that area is in a mess. I'll let you know about the possibilities for DNA analysis. Apart from her own, of course.'

Thackeray swallowed hard and shook himself back to the present and found Longley watching him closely.

'It's one thing to go out for a night of illicit sex, quite another to fall into the hands of a psychopath,' he said.

'Are you sure you can handle this, Michael?' Longley asked.

'Of course I can,' the DCI replied sharply. 'I need to get this bastard for my own satisfaction. And quickly, before he strikes again.'

'You don't reckon it's the husband then?'

'I did have him down as prime suspect,' Thackeray admitted. 'And I'm certainly not ruling him out. We'll question him again as soon as we get a positive ID. And we're still waiting for the forensics from the car he borrowed to follow Karen up to the forest. But this seems too extreme for a domestic, to be honest, too calculated. She'd been tied up with duct tape before the final attack. There were traces left on the arms, legs and round the mouth. That takes considerable premeditation. Bastable is a bit of a thug but I don't think he's a psycho. And I don't really think he's bright enough to have planned this. Or mad enough to have carried it out.'

'Have you checked out with Holmes for any similar cases?

If this is as extreme as you say, it might not be the first time and there'll be a record on the computer.'

'That's in hand,' Thackeray said. 'And we're going ahead with the ad in the *Gazette,* to see if we can flush out any more of Karen's playmates from the forest. Although if one of them was responsible for this, he's not likely to show his face again. But basically this is dependent on forensics at the moment. The SOCOs say that they've lifted some partial fingerprints from the black plastic she was wrapped in, which is a bit of a miracle given that she's been buried for at least a couple of days, Amos says, and it had been raining heavily. And Amos is looking for DNA, of course – the victim's and the killer's. He's also found some fibres in her mouth which look interesting. But all this will take time, of course.'

'There's absolutely no way we can physically identify the body?'

'No clothes, no jewellery, not even a wedding ring,' Thackeray said. 'She had red hair, which the killer has hacked off, but that's about all I could offer Bastable for ID purposes. Karen had red hair. But you've got to assume that, if he did it, he won't want the body identified anyway. He could deny it's her simply to give himself more time. We'll have to wait for the DNA before we can possibly consider a charge. We've already taken samples from the house, of course, to check out this car Bastable borrowed. I'll see if I can put pressure on the lab to get a quick result, but you know what they're like. They're rushed off their feet these days.'

'What are you going to tell the press?'

Thackeray shrugged wearily.

'Whatever we tell them – and we've little enough to give them – Bob Baker at the *Gazette* will add two and two and make five. There's bound to be speculation. What I'm planning is to get Bastable in here again this morning to give him another going over, and then put a statement out about the discovery of a body after that.'

'Leave a press conference until after we've got an ID, you mean?'

'I think so, don't you?'

'Keep the press office at county informed,' Longley said. 'I'll handle a press conference when you're ready.'

'Fine,' Thackeray said.

Laura Ackroyd sat at her computer that morning feeling stunned, mouth dry, eyes gritty and brain feeling too numb to respond to anything less than an earthquake. She had stayed late with Vicky Mendelson, guessing that she would not sleep if she went back to the empty flat. She had no hope that Michael Thackeray might have returned. In fact, she had very little hope that he would ever return, though the thought of bringing up a child alone was one which she still shied away from, barely able to contemplate the enormity of it, in spite of Vicky's optimism. But eventually, realising that Vicky and David were becoming increasingly anxious to go to bed, she had torn herself away from her friends' house and driven home, knocked back a couple of V and Ts and fallen into a doze on the sofa, before finally crawling into bed at three in the morning. But she had hardly slept, wakened at seven by the alarm from a fitful sleep from which even a deliberately chilly shower did not entirely rouse her. She got to work late, earning a filthy glance from Ted Grant, who missed very little that happened in his newsroom, and had since then alternated between gazing dead-eyed at her screen and making a few telephone calls to try to track down David Murgatroyd, without success. The man was elusive, she thought, and deliberately so. But the more elusive he proved to be, the more determined she became to find him and get the interview she wanted and which had been half promised.

But before she could call Winston Sanderson again on his London number to press her case, her phone rang with an incoming call. At the other end her grandmother sounded both angry and unusually hesitant.

'What is it, Nan?' Laura said, surprised but barely able to keep the impatience out of her voice. 'Are you in Portugal? Was the journey OK?' Joyce Ackroyd hesitated for a moment and then began to speak very quickly.

'I'm sorry to bother you at work, pet, but it's Debbie Stapleton,' she said. 'I've just had a call from Steve O'Mara, the parent governor, you know? He got me all the way out here on my mobile. It's amazing, isn't it? He says she's been told to stop opposing the academy plan if she wants to be considered for the headship. And it's a really nasty threat. You probably didn't know. Not many people do.'

'Know what, Nan?' Laura broke in, not especially surprised at Joyce's news. She already had the impression, after Ted Grant's comments about pressure from the local council, that the supporters of the school plan would use any means open to them to push their proposal through.

'She's wide open to this sort of blackmail,' Joyce said, her voice sinking to an embarrassed mumble.

'Why?' Laura asked, intrigued now, wondering what dark secret the apparently dedicated and squeaky-clean Debbie Stapleton might be concealing.

'She's gay, as you call it these days,' Joyce said flatly. 'She lives with a woman friend out in the country somewhere. She's very discreet but obviously someone's found out and is spreading the word. And you know what these born-again Christians feel about that. And the Muslims, come to that. She has a lot of Muslim parents at the school. They'll kick up as well, if they find out.'

'Ah,' Laura said quietly. 'And there was I thinking all this bigoted nonsense was over and done with, in this country at least. Does Steve think David Murgatroyd has found out about this?'

'No, no, the pressure seems to be coming from some of the governors and possibly from the council. You know how keen they are to get their hands on the cash to rebuild. They don't want anything standing in the way of that, never mind who gets trampled underfoot. The threat seems to be that they'll tell Murgatroyd about her sexuality if she doesn't keep quiet about her opposition to the scheme. And to think this is supported by the party I worked for for all those years. You can understand the Tories going for it, but the Labour councillors? Huh?' Joyce broke off with an angry grunt and Laura could imagine the pain of her disillusion and her bitter frustration at no longer wielding any influence at the town hall. Joyce Ackroyd was not growing old contentedly. Far from it.

'I'll make some inquiries,' Laura said. 'I think there's a lot of lobbying going on, but that sounds several steps too far. Let me see what I can find out.'

'You sound a bit down yourself, pet,' Joyce came back. 'Are you all right?'

'Yes, I'm fine,' Laura lied. 'How are you? How's the hip? Was it all right on the plane?'

'Oh, you know. It comes and goes,' Joyce said. 'It's not going to get any better, is it, at my age?'

'And mum and dad? I'll call you all at the weekend for a proper chat, but I must get back to work now.'

'You work too hard, pet,' Joyce said quietly, before saying goodbye.

Laura sat for a moment trying to absorb the information her grandmother had passed on. She doubted that Peter Maxwell, the councillor in charge of schools policy, would ever admit to exerting that sort of pressure on Debbie Stapleton. Nor would Debbie herself be very likely to want to admit to being the victim of a particularly nasty form of blackmail if she had succeeded in keeping her sexuality under wraps for the whole of the time she had been at Sutton Park. If she felt she needed to be discreet in normal circumstances, she certainly would not want that sort of publicity in the middle of a furious battle for her school and her own professional future. The inescapable fact was that exposing this particular attempt at blackmail would also expose the victim and, given that Murgatroyd and his supporters almost certainly did not want Debbie Stapleton to retain her headship, covering the story at all would simply ease their way to getting rid of her.

Laura left her desk and went outside into the car park, where she called Sutton Park on her mobile, and to her surprise was put through to the head teacher almost straight away.

'This is a private call,' Laura said when Debbie Stapleton came on the line. 'Can you talk?' When the head teacher had assented, she went on, weighing her words carefully.

'I thought you ought to know that there are rumours circulating about your private life. I'm not interested in writing anything about it, but someone might be. It's not something I can control. And it sounds like something David Murgatroyd, with his views, would be very interested to hear about.'

Debbie Stapleton laughed, a curiously mirthless sound.

'Oh yes, don't worry, I know exactly what's going on. It's like something out of the 1950s. We thought these battles were over and done with and then these fundamentalists come along, Christians, Muslims, you name it, and suddenly we're back in the Dark Ages. Don't you worry. I've had it spelt out to me just how unsuitable being gay might make me as a candidate for my own job if Murgatroyd found out. And how easily he might find out if I go on being stroppy about the takeover of the school.'

'I wish I could expose these bastards,' Laura said.

'Yes, well, give me a bit of time to think,' Debbie said. 'I'm not sure that I might not just come clean and expose them myself. I don't really think I'll get the job anyway. Murgatroyd will be looking for some born-again clone to run his academy and I certainly don't fit that profile either. I'm not having children taught religious myths as if they're scientific fact in biology lessons. They can discuss Adam and Eve in religious studies as much as they like, but not in science. Maybe I'm a fool to even consider applying for the job.'

'Don't give up,' Laura said. 'The kids need teachers like you. Keep me in touch with what you're planning.'

'I will. And thanks for your concern,' Debbie said, and hung up.

Laura went back to the newsroom with a thoughtful expression and logged on to the Internet to check the list of academies that David Murgatroyd had already set up, against the local newspaper archives in the towns concerned. It was no surprise to discover, from their coverage at the time each of them had been set up, that there had been similar debates to the one now raging in Bradfield, and that the controversy did not always die down once the new school had opened. In one area parents complained bitterly within months that the school was weeding out the most difficult children by excluding them on what seemed like very flimsy grounds. In another, a religious studies teacher had resigned in a fury, complaining to the local paper that she had been asked to teach about the Bible as if every word of it were literally true. And in a third, the existing head of the previous school who had, unusually, been appointed to run the new academy, had taken the new governors, all appointed by Murgatroyd, to an industrial tribunal claiming he had been forced out soon after it opened because he refused to toe one of Murgatroyd's many hard lines.

There was more than enough evidence to suggest that, just as she had discovered in Leeds, Murgatroyd's academies were not proving universally popular and were not necessarily helping the difficult and deprived children they were supposed to benefit. In fact, Laura began to wonder if David Murgatroyd's agenda was even remotely in touch with that of the Government, which was supporting him to the tune of millions of pounds. She had enough ammunition, she thought, to tackle Peter Maxwell at the local council, to ask him just how and why he thought this particular wealthy philanthropist would benefit the struggling children of Bradfield's poorest areas. And incidentally, she might tease out whether or not he saw a future for Debbie Stapleton in Bradfield, or whether she was already down simply as collateral damage.

CHAPTER TEN

It had taken three officers and a set of handcuffs to bring Terry Bastable to police headquarters this time, and even after the trip into the centre of town in the back of a police van, he was still slumped in a chair, with his hands secured behind his back, breathing heavily and cursing the two officers who were struggling to hold him down when DCI Michael Thackeray and DS Kevin Mower came into the room.

'Calm down, Mr Bastable,' Thackeray said, his voice cracking across the small room like a whip. 'You'll do yourself no good behaving like that. I'll wait all day and all night to talk to you if I have to.' Bastable looked at him with naked hatred in his eyes but eventually the stream of obscenities dried up and he sat panting like a dog, his shaved head glistening with sweat, until the uniformed officers cautiously let go of his shoulders and allowed him to sit more comfortably in his chair.

'You understand why you've been brought here?' Thackeray asked. 'You've been arrested on suspicion of the murder of your wife, Karen.'

'Who says she's been murdered?' Bastable spat back. 'You've not shown me a body. I've not identified her. What the hell's going on?'

'If you keep calm, I'll tell you exactly what's happened,' Thackeray said, glancing at one of the uniformed constables who was standing poised to grab the angry man again, with what might seem unwarranted forbearance, given the black eye he had evidently incurred during the arrest. 'You can take the cuffs off now,' Thackeray said to the uniformed officers when Bastable appeared to have accepted the situation he found himself in. 'We'll be fine. Get that eye seen to, Jim.' He turned back to Terry Bastable.

'I understand you've been cautioned. Do you want a solicitor present?' Thackeray asked.

Bastable shook his head and suddenly slumped awkwardly forward across the table, his shoulders shaking and his head in his hands. Thackeray took one of the chairs facing Bastable and Mower sat next to him.

'Then we'll tape-record this interview,' Thackeray said, nodding at the sergeant who set up the equipment and identified the three people left in the stuffy, claustrophobic room.

'Is she dead, then?' Bastable mumbled. 'Have you found her dead? Why didn't you tell me? Why didn't you let me see her?'

'Right, Mr Bastable. Let's start at the beginning, which we could have done some time ago if you hadn't decided to assault my officers when they asked you to come to the station. We have found a body. Unfortunately, it's been so severely treated that it would have been impossible to identify the person for certain, visually.' Thackeray watched Bastable closely as he spoke but could see nothing but bemused horror in his eyes. 'We will have to identify Karen by comparing her DNA, taken from your house – you remember, we took some clothes and her hairbrush? – with DNA taken from the body. But we are satisfied the dead woman is almost certainly your wife. The hair is identical. We had that confirmed about an hour ago and I immediately sent officers to bring you here for questioning.'

Bastable groaned theatrically.

'What happened to her?' he asked. His eyes were red now but he smeared the tears away angrily and Thackeray could not tell how much of his reaction was play-acting and how much was genuine.

'We're hoping that you will be able to help us find that out,' he said. 'You're under arrest, so we will be taking your fingerprints and a DNA sample, and it will be quite clear whether you had any contact with Karen at the time of her death or immediately afterwards when the body was disposed of. What I advise you to do now is tell us everything that happened on the night you say she went missing. You should be aware that now we know she's dead, and how she died, I already have forensic officers going over your house to see whether or not there is any evidence at all that the murder took place there. The car you borrowed from your friend is also being examined, as you know. If Karen, or Karen's body, was in that car there will inevitably be traces left behind. If, as you claimed earlier, the children were in it to go to the supermarket, they will have left traces too. We will find out where that car went that night, and who was in it.'

'You're setting me up for this, aren't you?' Bastable said, suddenly furious again, eyes popping. 'You're bloody well setting me up. I knew as soon as I set eyes on that little Paki bint you'd have it in for me. It's persecution, that's what it is.'

'My interest is in finding out the truth about Karen's death,' Thackeray said, ignoring this tirade. 'And so far you've been telling me a pack of lies. First you were at home all evening. Then you admit you borrowed a car to go to the supermarket. Then you admit you followed Karen and saw what she was up to but she didn't see you. Where's it going to end, Mr Bastable? Just where does the truth lie?'

Bastable shrugged and did not respond.

'What you need to understand, Terry,' Mower broke in, 'is that all of this can be checked scientifically and if your wife was in that car that night, dead or alive, we'll find out. So you might as well tell us the truth now, and make it the whole truth while you're about it.'

'She weren't in the car,' Bastable said. 'I swear to God, she weren't. I never even spoke to her. I saw what she was up to and then I came back home and got stinking drunk and went to sleep, and it weren't till next morning that I realised she hadn't come back at all.'

'Didn't it strike you that if she had seen Les Duckworth's car up there she would have realised the game was up and she might be better off staying away? She'd stay out of the way of your fists if she had any sense.' Thackeray said. 'Why bother reporting her missing? The only reason I can think of is that you wanted to establish yourself as the anxious husband because you knew very well she was dead, because you'd killed her yourself and dumped the body.'

'No,' Bastable said. 'That's not how it was. I waited for her to come home, right? OK, I was going to have it out with her, but she never came, and I fell asleep, didn't I? Woke up in t'morning early on t'sofa, still in my clothes, and realised summat bad must have happened. I didn't know if she'd seen me and run off or if she'd come to some harm wi'that gang of sex maniacs up there. Of course I reported her missing. Wouldn't you?'

'But you didn't tell us where she'd gone, or what you knew she'd been doing. Why not? If you genuinely feared for her safety, you would have told us the whole truth from the start.'

'Because I bloody knew that this is what would happen,' Bastable spat out. 'I bloody knew you'd think I'd harmed her, and I knew I bloody hadn't. I just wanted her found. There, does that satisfy you?'

'Not really,' Mower said. 'It sounds like a load of rubbish to me.'

'Did you see who she was with in the forest?' Thackeray asked, suddenly changing tack. 'Would you recognise her partner if you saw him again?'

Bastable shook his head like a tormented bull at the corrida.

'It were difficult to see right to t'centre of the ring,' he said. 'And most of the men had their faces covered. Some had them silly masks on – Tony Blair and them politicians. You know?' Thackeray nodded as Bastable confirmed what he already knew about the meetings at Bently Forest.

'Did it turn you on, Terry?' Mower asked suddenly. 'Watching all that stuff? We know you had a lot of porn at home. Did you get worked up watching all that?'

The question seemed to touch a raw nerve as Bastable flushed.

'Bitch,' he said explosively. 'She's not slept wi'me for months and now I know why. She were getting more than enough, weren't she?'

'So what did you do? You must have been very angry. Did

you wait for Karen to drive out of that forest track and drag her into your mate's car?' Thackeray pressed on while Bastable's eyes roamed around the small room as if seeking the smallest crack in the tiles to hide himself in.

'No, I didn't,' Bastable said. 'I didn't. I didn't. I don't say I weren't fucking furious, but I went straight home.'

Thackeray shook his head implacably.

'No,' he said. 'I think that's exactly what happened. You lay in wait for her and stopped her car somehow. You had a furious row and ended up killing her. You've already told me you wanted to give her a good thrashing. Then you drove her car back into the woods to hide it for as long as possible to make it look as if she'd driven off in it herself, and then you put her body in Les Duckworth's car and dumped her somewhere else entirely so it looked like a random attack by a stranger when she was eventually found. Isn't that what happened, Mr Bastable? Isn't that what the scientific evidence will tell us when we get it? You killed her, dumped her body and only then went home to drink yourself to sleep.'

Bastable shook his head from side to side and groaned.

'No,' he said again.

'Did you rape her as well, Terry?' Mower asked. 'That's something else we'll be checking with your DNA sample. You can't escape the science these days, Terry. You should know that.'

'I didn't touch her. I told you. I haven't slept with her for months.'

'So you say,' Mower said. 'Anyway, we'll soon know, one way or the other, so you're wasting your time lying.'

'You were unlucky that the car and the body were found so quickly, weren't you, Terry?' Thackeray resumed. 'You must have hoped for more time. Maybe hoped the body would never be found, dumping it in a remote spot like that. Had you been up there before?'

'I don't know where she was found, do I? You haven't told me. So you're not going to catch me that way. I didn't bloody do it,' Bastable said, half rising from his seat and then slumping back again as Mower, too, got to his feet and leant over the table threateningly.

'You might not have intended to kill her,' Mower conceded. 'Maybe it was just a thrashing you intended. But you're a big man, Terry, and we've seen today how easily you lose control. Is that what happened? Did you lose it? Someone certainly did and you're the obvious suspect.'

'No,' Bastable said. 'No, no, no. I'm not answering any more of your questions, you bastards. I want a solicitor before I say another word.'

'Right,' Thackeray said. 'You can wait in a cell while we contact the duty solicitor for you.'

When Bastable had been taken away, and the recorder switched off, Thackeray ran a hand wearily through his hair.

'What do you think?' he asked Mower but the sergeant shrugged.

'He's not going to crack without more for us to go on,' he said. 'It's all down to the forensics on the cars, isn't it? It's ten miles or more from Bently Forest, where she was last seen, to the moor where she was found. She must have made that journey by car, alive or dead. And if she was dead, there has to be blood, probably a lot of blood. There was no blood in her own car so if Bastable's our man, he must have used the one he borrowed. I'll get on to the lab and see if they can give us any preliminary findings at all.'

'Do that,' Thackeray said. 'Otherwise we're going to run out of time with him. I'm still not totally convinced that he's our man, and I'd like it settled before we start putting a huge effort into looking for some other psychopath, with all that entails.'

Halfway through the morning Laura Ackroyd's phone rang and she recognised the voice of Winston Sanderson, Sir David Murgatroyd's personal assistant.

'Has he agreed to an interview at last?' she said, still smarting from the pressure Ted Grant had put on her at that morning's editorial meeting to get hold of Murgatroyd or give up the chase. The implication was that failure would be down to her incompetence rather than Murgatroyd's recalcitrance and she left the meeting with cheeks aflame with anger at Grant's routine unfairness.

'Meet me for lunch,' Sanderson said. 'I can tell you more then.'

Laura hesitated, curbing irritated thoughts of monkeys and organ-grinders.

'Can you really help me with this profile?' she asked, her voice sharp with anxiety. Suddenly a life with which she had felt almost content seemed to be disintegrating around her.

'Of course I can,' Sanderson said. 'Be my guest. One o'clock in the Clarendon lounge. That suit you?'

A couple of hours later Laura walked into the Clarendon Hotel bar, deep-carpeted and as quiet as she always imagined a London club might be. The Clarendon was the haunt of Bradfield's ageing and most affluent burghers, including Laura's own father in his days as a local entrepreneur, before he retired to play golf in Portugal, and the grey men enjoying their lunchtime tipple were clearly more than a little disconcerted by the appearance of a young and elegantly suited black man relaxing in their inner sanctum. Sanderson got to his feet with almost exaggerated politeness as Laura approached, every inch of her progress followed by calculating blue eyes, as she took the armchair on the other side of his table.

'What can I get you?' he asked and raised a hand to the expectant waiter on the other side of the room when she asked for a vodka and tonic.

'So, am I going to get my interview?' Laura asked after taking a sip of her drink. She glanced around and raised a hand at one of the rotund men whom she recalled was an old friend of her father's, who glanced away, embarrassed to be caught watching her so closely. Sanderson followed her eyes and raised an eyebrow.

'I gathered you were a native of these parts,' he said.

'Born and bred, just like Sir David,' Laura said. 'I used to come here with my father, although my parents have retired to live in the sun now.'

'Which I suppose explains why you take such an interest in this wretched failing school at Sutton Park.'

'According to the inspectors, it's no longer a failing school,' Laura said. 'Which is why so many of the governors and parents seem to resent what they see as a takeover by an outsider, and an outsider with views which don't necessarily fit with their own. But this is a conversation I need to have with Sir David. With all due respect, you're not the prime mover in all this. He is. And I have to say that the opponents of this scheme are getting pretty fed up that Sir David is not willing to talk to them privately or give any public interviews to the press or TV. Why so secretive, Mr Sanderson? Has he got something to hide?'

'That sort of intrusive question may be the reason why Sir David is so wary of the press,' Sanderson said, his voice silky but his eyes angry. 'I told you last time we met what Sir David's objectives are in setting up a faith academy in Bradfield. He doesn't make any secret of the fact that this is to be a biblical, Christian school.'

'A fundamentalist school, then,' Laura said. 'I've been talking to some people who are afraid that the school will take a hard line on issues like homosexuality and abortion, which are legal in this country, whatever some religious groups choose to believe. And a hard line can easily lead to bullying of young people, and even of staff if, maybe, they're gay, or if the girls become pregnant and choose a termination. Is there any guarantee that won't happen? That young people won't be bullied by other children, or even by the school staff?'

'There is good and evil in the world, right and wrong, Miss Ackroyd, and you can be sure that any school Sir David is involved in will make sure that young people know the difference. If parents don't like that approach they can take their children away.'

'And the staff? What would the school's attitude be if it discovered that a member of staff was gay? Or was living in an unmarried relationship?'

'I think it unlikely that the school would appoint anyone of that sort,' Sanderson said, his own distaste very clear.

'So you would discriminate, in other words?'

'We would seek staff in sympathy with the ethos of the school. That's not unlawful,' Sanderson said. 'It's what Sir David does in all his academies.'

'So what happens to existing staff whose faces don't fit?'

'They leave. We're not ungenerous about that.'

Laura took a deep breath and decided that pursuing this avenue might do Debbie Stapleton more harm than good.

'So what's the timetable now? When will a new head be appointed?' she asked.

'The new governors are now in place, as a sort of shadow administration,' Sanderson said. 'They've drawn up a shortlist of candidates for the headship.'

'Before the scheme is even formally approved?'

'There is a lot of planning to be done. The timetable's not unusual, which is something you would know if you'd done your research properly, Miss Ackroyd.'

'And is Debbie Stapleton on the shortlist?' Laura asked.

'No,' Sanderson said. 'I'm afraid she isn't.' He hesitated for a moment and then steepled his long fingers under his chin.

'You know I'm surprised you're so hostile to this project,' he said. 'I would have thought that anyone born and bred here would be delighted to see a dilapidated old school renewed and given new life. Your councillors certainly are. Although I suppose with your grandmother so involved in left-wing politics, it's only to be expected. We didn't realise the connection until quite recently.'

Laura took a sharp breath.

'My grandmother's politics are nothing to do with me, Mr Sanderson,' she said. 'And mine are nothing to do with you. Anyway, this is a community issue, not a political one. And in any case, I give both sides of the argument. That's my job,' Laura said, draining her glass.

'I do hope so, Miss Ackroyd,' Sanderson said.

'Even so, I still feel that Sir David should be prepared to

make the argument himself, especially as he's a local man. His reticence will puzzle people. They will wonder what he has to hide.'

'He has nothing to hide, Miss Ackroyd, and if you suggest anything of that sort in your article, I think he may be inclined to consult his lawyers. And your editor certainly would not like that.'

The threat was overt, but Laura merely smiled thinly.

'He may be a powerful man, Mr Sanderson, but he should remember that Yorkshire people don't like being pushed around. He will have to fight his corner, one way or another, and I hope he'll still come round to the idea that putting his own case in an interview might actually help him. Will you relay that message to him, please?'

'The answer will be the same. And I seriously suggest that you give up this pointless pursuit now. It really won't do your future any good.'

Laura suddenly felt a wave of anger threaten to overwhelm her. She took a deep breath.

'If that's a threat, which is what it sounds like, I think you'll find I'm not easily intimidated,' she said.

'I don't think your policeman is going to help you with this,' Sanderson said, his voice silky. 'Sir David has much more powerful contacts than that.'

Laura flushed angrily.

'What's that supposed to mean?' she asked.

'Whatever you take it to mean, Miss Ackroyd,' Sanderson said. 'No more, no less. But if you felt like a little chat with your boss, I wouldn't blame you.' He got to his feet, leaving Laura, for once in her life, lost for words. 'Take Ted Grant's advice and don't push your luck,' he said, and spun on his well-shod heel and left her staring at her empty vodka-and-tonic glass in disbelief, still with her audience of now goggle-eyed suits.

She walked back to the office slowly, gazing into the shop windows but only half taking in the arrays of spring fashion which she would normally have studied with interest, even though the weather was still distinctly wintry. How had Sanderson uncovered so many details of her private life, she wondered? And even more worryingly, why had he bothered? And why take the trouble to discount the influence of Michael Thackeray who, even in normal circumstances, would be hugely reluctant to involve himself in inquiries by the *Gazette*? At present, he would be more furious than usual to be dragged into her affairs, although it was some faint comfort to know that the all-seeing eye of Sir David Murgatroyd had not penetrated so far into her private life to know that their relationship was teetering on the brink. Not yet, anyway, she thought grimly. If he or Sanderson poked their puritanical noses into her private life and uncovered the bleak options she was facing just at the moment, things could get very nasty indeed.

On an impulse, she called the town hall on her mobile and struck lucky with Peter Maxwell, the councillor in charge of the town's schools. He was just coming out of a meeting and could give her ten minutes. She raced up the broad stone steps two at a time to the ceremonial floor, presided over by the ranks of Victorian aldermen in portraits notable for their self-satisfaction rather than artistic merit. Maxwell, a stocky man wearing a blue suit and tetchy expression on his pasty face, clutched a pile of files that threatened to spill over the floor as he went into his office and nodded to Laura without much enthusiasm.

'What can I do for you?' he asked. 'I've another meeting in fifteen minutes.'

'I won't keep you,' Laura said. 'I'm still working on my piece about the new academy at Sutton Park, and I wanted to check a few details with you.'

Maxwell let her precede him into the office before dumping his files on his desk and sinking into his swivel chair.

'You know, this new school is the best thing that's happened to this benighted town for years. Even this government comes up with one or two good ideas occasionally. I hope you're not going to knock it.'

Laura grinned.

'Well, I'm not sure David Murgatroyd's the person I'd want in charge of my kids, if I had any,' she said. 'His views are so far out they're over the horizon.'

'But he comes clutching two million pounds, and with a lot more Government cash to follow,' Maxwell said. 'Where else would we get that sort of money for a brand new school? The council taxpayers? You must be dreaming.'

'Did you know that they haven't put Debbie Stapleton on the shortlist for the headship?'

Maxwell looked at her sharply.

'They've told you that, have they? Well, I'm not really surprised. They'll want to make a clean start.'

'Is that clean as in virtuous, according to their lights?' Laura's tone was waspish but Maxwell did not rise to the challenge.

'Clean as in a new beginning,' he said, and Laura could not tell if he knew what she was talking about and thought it better not to enlighten him.

'So basically the council will push the scheme through,

however much the governors and parents protest?'

'Absolutely,' Maxwell said. 'And now I really have to get ready for my next meeting. Don't let your grandmother work you up on this one. Believe me. It's in everyone's best interests.'

'Except Debbie Stapleton's,' Laura said getting to her feet.

'Yes, well, you know what they say about making omelettes. I'm afraid in this case Debbie's just one of the eggs.'

CHAPTER ELEVEN

DCI Michael Thackeray drummed his fingers on his desk in frustration as he scanned the forensic report which Sergeant Kevin Mower had just handed him.

'They're still examining traces of human hair and other fibres and various unidentified smears they found in the passenger compartment of Duckworth's car, guv,' Mower said, summarising the document which he had already scanned for half an hour looking for anything which could remotely be used to charge Terry Bastable with his wife's murder, and finding nothing. 'It was in a fairly scruffy state. No one had tried to clean it out, that's for sure. There were hairs in the boot, which got them a bit excited apparently, but they turned out to be animal. Duckworth apparently had a dog until recently, so that explains that. The bad news is that they've found nothing that looks even remotely like blood. Karen could have been in the car, but it doesn't look as if she was killed in it, and her body wasn't transported in it. You couldn't have done either of those things without getting a speck of blood inside. The state she was in, I don't think it's remotely possible.'

'So we're left with the possibility that she went in the car willingly, if she went at all? That doesn't seem very likely, does it?' Thackeray sounded as tetchy as he looked, and Mower wondered what was going on in his private life to make him look as frayed as he had seen him since his near-fatal shooting.

'The only other possibility is that he knocked her unconscious and took her off somewhere else to kill her. But the PM report didn't suggest a blow to the head, did it? The damage was caused by a sharp instrument; there were burns, but not much in the way of major bruising.' Mower shrugged. 'We've not got much choice but to wait for the DNA tests on the traces they've found. That's the only thing that's going to give us a clear picture of whether she'd ever been in that car or not.'

'So we've no choice but to let Bastable go for the time being,' Thackeray said wearily. 'There's nowhere near enough evidence to charge him. Bail him to report back here in two weeks, by which time we should have got the DNA results back from the lab and we'll have a clearer idea where we stand.'

'Right, guv,' Mower said.

'What about the ad in the *Gazette*? Are we making any progress with that?'

'Went in last night, guv, setting up a meet for Friday. Charlene Brough says they never got much notice. A few days at most. But the gap between events was usually about two weeks, sometimes more, so some people may get suspicious and not turn up.'

'Probably exhausted,' Thackeray said drily. Mower grinned, thinking how much stamina he could find in the right circumstances, but he said nothing. Furtive sex with strangers was not his scene, he thought. And he was surprised at how many people seemed ready to indulge in it.

'We've set the meet for eight o'clock, which is apparently the usual time. I've warned uniform that we'll need some bodies that night to bring people back here. We can't sensibly interview them out in that wilderness, so I'll lay on vans. I don't suppose they'll be best pleased but we've got grounds to arrest them for public order offences, I think, if they get stroppy. It may be a remote spot but it's still a public place, if we need it to be.'

'Don't provoke them too much,' Thackeray said. 'We need some cooperative witnesses on this one, or we'll never crack it. I want chapter and verse on what went on up there that night.'

'Right,' Mower said. 'But if we're looking for someone who was just hiding in the trees watching the proceedings, they may not even have been seen.'

'Someone must have seen something,' Thackeray said. 'We know they won't come forward voluntarily so we'll just have to go out and fetch them in. Once they know we know they were there, they'll cooperate, for fear of something worse.'

'I'll sign Bastable out, though it grieves me to do it,' Mower said. 'He's one of those punters you just know's done something gross, even if you don't know what and haven't a cat in hell's chance of proving it.'

'In the bad old days they just used to fit blokes like that up and feel justified in doing it,' Thackeray said. 'But we live in different times – unless you're a suspected terrorist, of course. Bring me some evidence, Kevin, or some cast-iron witnesses, and it'll give me great pleasure to lock Terry Bastable up and throw away the key.'

*　*　*

Laura headed south out of Bradfield, down the link road to the M62 and then, foot down, to the M1 and the south. She had been astonished, and then elated, to receive a call during the afternoon from a woman she had never spoken to before but who claimed to be Sir David Murgatroyd's PA in his London office, inviting her to meet him at a country-house hotel just outside Sheffield, where he could give her a brief interview. After her edgy meeting with Winston Sanderson only hours earlier, she had double-checked what was being suggested, hardly able to believe her luck.

'Are you sure?' she asked. 'I was told earlier today that there was no way he would see me.'

'Sir David has been known to change his mind,' the woman said drily. 'You must have been very persuasive when you met him. Anyway, he's staying the night in Sheffield and then coming back to London first thing, so this is your only chance for a while. Can you get there?'

'Yes, fine,' Laura said. 'Give me the directions.' She knew that the trip would take up most of the evening, but as the alternative was to sit at home alone and brood she had no hesitation in devoting the time to work. She left the office at four, hoping to beat the thickening traffic which would soon choke Yorkshire's major arteries, but soon found herself crawling around the outskirts of Leeds behind a stream of heavy lorries, and becoming anxious about her appointment. But to the south the traffic eased slightly and within an hour she was on country roads beyond Sheffield and heading towards the Peak National Park. The hotel, when she got there just as a misty dusk was closing down the view of the hills that surrounded the city, lay back from the road heading west into the high country, a solid stone mansion surrounded by parkland and ancient trees where a few bedraggled sheep grazed.

She made herself known at reception and within a few minutes Murgatroyd himself came down the broad staircase, dressed in a dark business suit, with a file of paperwork in his hand. He crossed the reception lounge with long vigorous strides and held out a hand to Laura. His grasp was firm, his touch warm and to her surprise his smile seemed genuine, as it had been when she had accosted him at his academy in Leeds. She found herself reluctantly smiling back.

'I'm sorry if Winston Sanderson has been obstructive. He oversteps the mark sometimes. He's very loyal. Too loyal, maybe. He didn't know that I promised you an interview,' he said. 'Winston sometimes misinterprets my intentions. Come and have a drink.'

He led the way into a comfortable lounge bar and ordered her the V and T she requested.

'Have you got time to stay for dinner?' he asked as he settled himself in the deep armchair on the opposite side of the table, putting his own Scotch down after a single sip.

'Not really,' Laura demurred, hiding her surprise, although the sight of the dining room beyond the bar, with its gleaming glass and silver, was enticing. 'I have to be at work early tomorrow.'

'Me too,' Murgatroyd said. 'But in London, which is why I couldn't get back to Sibden House tonight. I have to leave here at crack of dawn. Perhaps I can show you round the old place next time I come up.'

'I think that would be too late for the feature I'm writing,' Laura said, still surprised by his friendliness. 'I have been there, you know. Winston Sanderson invited me in. It's a wonderful old house. I'm surprised you don't live there full-time.' But she knew immediately that was a comment too far.

'It has very mixed memories for me,' Murgatroyd said, his face darkening. 'But I really don't want to talk about my personal life. Ask anything you like about the academy programme. I've brought you some brochures about the schools that are up and running. I'm sure Sutton Park is going to be just as successful as the rest are proving to be.'

Laura glanced down at the table and sampled one of the olives the waiter had put down with the drinks.

'I've already done a lot of research on all that,' she said. 'The reason I wanted to meet you personally was to talk a bit more widely. I understand you don't want a lot of intrusive questions about your past, but what about your motivation? What makes a successful man like you want to become involved in education in a quite hands-on way? Is the motivation entirely religious or is it more personal? Do you have children of your own?'

Murgatroyd sipped his Scotch and looked at Laura with an expression which she could not interpret. In spite of his greying hair, he was still a good-looking man, Laura thought, and he evidently kept himself in trim, but it was his eyes which fascinated her. They were deep set and of an unusually dark blue, flecked with gold, and he tended to hold her own with slightly unnerving intensity for a fraction longer than was comfortable. She glanced away, while he appeared to be considering his reply.

'I came to religion relatively late,' he said. 'My family were not churchgoers and I gave God no thought at all while I was at school and at Oxford. In fact, after everything that happened to me as a child, the idea of a loving God was somewhat alien to me. It wasn't until I was in my thirties that I found Jesus, and I have tried to live my life according to His precepts ever since. It seems to me that if you have discovered the truth, you are duty-bound to pass it on if you have the opportunity and, put at its simplest, my wealth gives me that opportunity. I will be very pleased if the children who attend my academies pass their exams and make a success of their lives in secular terms. I will be much more pleased if they come to know Our Lord and are saved.'

'But this implies that the school will proselytise in a way that the law does not really allow, if you use public money,' Laura said. 'And one that will make it very difficult for parents who don't share your beliefs to send their children to your schools. It means your schools inevitably choose the families they want, rather than the other way round.'

'Not at all,' Murgatroyd said. 'We find families of all religions – and sometimes of none – appreciate the firm discipline and moral teaching that we offer. If they are willing to abide by our rules, they are all welcome.'

'But if the students themselves find that difficult, you throw them out?' Laura pressed.

'If they won't follow our rules, we will suspend them, yes. Any good school will do that.'

'So although your schools are supposed to be offering something better for young people who come from deprived backgrounds, if they prove too difficult, they're kicked out? That's not really solving their problems, is it?'

'It's a pity in many ways that this scheme only deals with older children. What I would really like to do is have them from five, or even from nursery-school age. Then I think we could make an even more significant difference. We would reach them before the temptations of sex and drugs and violence get anywhere near them.'

'And if their parents are drug addicts? Or father's in prison? Or mother's on the game?' Laura asked sceptically. 'Or the parents themselves are little more than children? You know the problems on some of the worst housing estates.'

'I do, and that's why I think a boarding school for such children would be good,' Murgatroyd said. 'In the long term, that is something I would like to pursue. I've been in tentative talks with the Government about that. I see no reason why boarding education should be restricted to families who can pay fees. There are other children who could benefit, from a much younger age.'

'Give me the child before he's seven? You almost sound like a Jesuit.'

'I think that sort of approach has a lot to recommend it.' The intense eyes were colder now, and it was obvious to Laura that Murgatroyd was beginning to regret his decision to see her. He clearly was not used to being challenged in any way and found her questions irritating.

'You didn't say whether you had children of your own or not,' she said.

An expression flashed across Murgatroyd's face which she could not interpret.

'No children,' he said. 'I've never married.' Laura wondered if that meant that he observed his own draconian precepts on chastity but she did not have the nerve to ask that question. Murgatroyd's eyes were fixed on hers again now, still with that slightly unnerving intensity.

'You haven't really given me very much for the personal part of my profile of you,' she said, throwing caution to the wind. 'You've obviously pursued a very single-minded course in business and, I suspect, in your private life. Do you think that what happened in your own childhood has inspired you – or even driven you – in the direction you've taken?'

Murgatroyd picked up his drink and took a gulp, his eyes turning opaque.

'There are a lot of things which have happened in my life that I wish had never happened,' he said. 'But contrary to modern expectations, I don't find that baring my breast to all and sundry – sharing my pain, as they say – helps me at all. Quite the reverse. I prefer the past to remain firmly where it is, in the past. So I think, Miss Ackroyd, we should call it a day now. When I get back to Yorkshire I would be very happy to show you Sibden House, if you think that will help with your article. I'll give you a call, if I may.'

Murgatroyd got to his feet and Laura had no choice but to follow suit, feeling oddly that she had been sized up in some way and not necessarily found wanting, in spite of his brusque dismissal. She suspected that very few people were ever invited to Sibden House.

'Thank you,' she said. 'It would help to meet again, if it can be fairly soon.' On his own home turf, where he had lived with his parents, she was sure that she could tease out some more personal revelations from this deeply reticent man. But for now, they shook hands formally, and Murgatroyd turned back to the stairs, leaving Laura to make her way back to the car. It was a long way to come, she thought, for not very much. She would have to do better next time or Ted Grant would pull the plug on the whole investigation, and that would be a pity.

* * *

Thackeray was still in his office long after most of his detectives had gone home. He had not bothered to switch on the lights as the dusk closed in and the room was illuminated only by the flicker of headlights as the traffic swung around the town hall square a couple of stories below, cutting across the hanging fug of tobacco smoke with which he regularly filled his office, in defiance of the rules. What he really wanted, he thought, as he lit up a fresh cigarette, was a drink, and that was the one thing he knew he must not have. If he went down that path he feared that he would never come back this time. It would be the end of his career, and the end of his relationship with Laura, and although he might live with the former he knew he could not survive life on his own.

And yet, he thought, for the first time in more than a decade there were now three people in this equation, and every time he thought about that possibility the panic took his breath away and he lurched back to the day that still haunted him, when he had found his baby son dead in his bath and his wife sprawled on the bed like a rag doll, mouth open, unconscious, almost asking him to put a pillow over her face and end her life as well. He had been tempted. He had never denied that, to himself at least, but in the end, blinded by tears and almost unable to speak, he had called the ambulance and she had survived, though only in a sort of half-life which had lasted years. The catastrophe had almost killed him then, and would always torment him, and he still could not see a way to open himself to that terrifying vulnerability again.

He jumped as someone opened the door and peered into the room. Kevin Mower looked startled to find him there in the gloom and switched on the light to find his boss blinking in the sudden illumination.

'Are you OK, guv?' he asked. 'I thought you'd gone home.'

'I'm fine,' Thackeray said, though he knew he sounded far from it. 'I thought you'd gone, too.'

He tried to jerk his mind back to the murder investigation, on which progress was still painfully slow. If they didn't make some sort of a breakthrough soon, he thought, the powers that be would call in some outsider to review progress and that was a humiliation he did not want to put himself and his team through.

'Are we all set for tomorrow?' he asked.

'I was just downstairs finalising everything with uniform. We've enough people and vans to bring anyone who turned up for their little orgy back down here for questioning,' Mower said. 'I was just wondering how far we let them go before we jump them. Psychologically speaking, it might be a good idea to let them get their kit off. Being arrested in your underwear is always humiliating.' He grinned wickedly at Thackeray, who shook his head in distaste.

'Stop them in their cars as they arrive,' he said. 'If this has leaked out and we get the press up there, we don't want to be accused of anything ourselves. Keep it cool and clinical. They can hardly claim to be out for a ramble through the woods at that time of night in the pitch dark, can they? Hopefully we'll be able to match enough of them, or their cars, to the photographs on Karen's camera to persuade them that it's useless to deny having been there before. But remember: they're being invited to the station to help us with our inquiries. They're witnesses, not suspects, until we tell the bastards differently.'

'Right, guv,' Mower said soothingly. He was surprised at Thackeray's vehemence. He did not often give vent to his puritanism so openly, especially not to Mower, whose own lifestyle was distinctly more cavalier. Something, he thought, and it had to be Laura Ackroyd, was getting to him big time.

When Mower had closed the door behind him, Thackeray stood up and put on his coat. But then he sat down at his desk again, unsure where to go. As he gazed unseeingly at the papers on his desk, wondering whether to try to bury himself in work again, his mobile rang and he was not entirely surprised to see that it was Vicky Mendelson calling.

'Hello, Vicky,' he said cautiously. 'This is a pleasant surprise.'

'You may not think so when I've finished with you,' Vicky said, and Thackeray could hear the suppressed anger in her voice. There was a long pause before she went on. 'You'll probably complain that I'm interfering where I've no right to interfere, but someone has to. You're putting Laura in an impossible position. And it is driving her crazy. Surely you, of all people, don't want her to have a termination. She might think your relationship could survive that, but it wouldn't, would it? It couldn't. You'd hate yourself even more than you do now, and in the end she would hate you for pushing her into a corner and persuading her to get rid of a child she really, really wants. Come on, Michael. We've been friends a long time now. You can't do this to Laura. You really can't.'

Thackeray sat in his chair feeling as if he had been kicked in the stomach. The phone was still clamped to his ear but he found it impossible to speak.

'Are you still there, Michael?' Vicky asked. He took a deep breath.

'I'm here,' he said.

'Am I right?'

'You're right. Of course, you're right. Which doesn't mean anything. It's not as simple as that.'

'If you love Laura, it's as simple as that,' Vicky said, more quietly. 'This is your baby, too.' Thackeray felt his jumbled emotions beginning to overwhelm him.

'I'll think about it,' he mumbled, as if he had not been thinking about it night and day since Laura had broken the news to him. He cut the connection, buried his head in his arms on the desk and wept, as he had not done for a very long time, for what he had lost, and might lose again.

CHAPTER TWELVE

Laura Ackroyd gazed at the front page of the next day's *Bradfield Gazette* with a sick sense of disbelief. Above Bob Baker, the crime reporter's sixteen-point byline, the headline shouted what looked like the end of head teacher Debbie Stapleton's career in the town. 'Academy hopeful's gay love nest', it said. 'Parents object to gay head staying on in new school'.

The story underneath this unsubtle denunciation claimed that a group of fundamentalist parents at Sutton Park School – some Christian and some Muslim – had discovered that Debbie was gay, and lived with her partner in a country cottage in the Dales. While other parents were campaigning against the academy plan, this group had set itself up to support David Murgatroyd's scheme and more specifically to make sure that Debbie did not get the headship of the new school.

Laura walked across the office and dropped the first edition on Bob Baker's desk in front of him.

'Where did you get hold of this nasty little bit of gossip

then?' she asked. Baker looked at her with a triumphant smirk on his face.

'Can't really claim credit for it,' he said. 'Fell into my lap, didn't it? The parents group rang me up to fill me in. I've no idea how they found out, but it stands up. I went out to the cottage and chatted up the girlfriend.'

'You don't out her as well, do you?' Laura asked, glancing down again at Bob's story, which she had not finished reading to its conclusion.

'No, no, she asked me not to and she's not really relevant, is she? Though I dare say her name will come out in the end. But the parents aren't bothered about her, are they? It's the Stapleton woman's job application that's annoying them. Doesn't fit the "ethos" of the new school, whatever an ethos is when it's at home. What it comes down to is that they don't like gays, full stop. It's against their religion.'

'It's a lot of homophobic rubbish,' Laura said angrily. 'I thought we'd moved on from this nonsense. Isn't it illegal now?'

'Well, whether it's illegal or not, this lot haven't budged an inch, and that's a good story, whichever way you look at it,' Baker said. 'The lawyer looked at my piece anyway. Ted insisted. But if they're making a song and dance about it, that's a story, whether you personally like their views or not. I sometimes wonder about you, Laura, I really do. You get too close to the people you're writing about. It's not a good idea. Anyway, you can talk to Ted about it if you like, but I can tell you for nothing, you won't get far. He's the one who decided to make it the front-page splash.'

'He would,' Laura said through gritted teeth. How much longer, she wondered, could she put up with Ted Grant's misguided ambition to turn a local newspaper into a clone of the worst of the London red tops, where he had briefly and, his Bradfield colleagues suspected, unsuccessfully, worked years ago? She sighed. If it had not been for Michael Thackeray, she would have moved on from the *Gazette* long ago. And now? The prospect looked increasingly unlikely as her thoughts turned more and more insistently towards what she was beginning to think of as her child.

She turned back to her desk and struggled to get to grips with her morning's work. She kept going, sustained by several cups of strong coffee, until a decent time to slip out of the office for lunch, and took refuge in her car where she could talk on her mobile in privacy. When she got through to Sutton Park School she was put through to Debbie Stapleton without question.

'I take it you've seen the *Gazette?*' Laura said. 'I'm sorry. I really am.'

'It's a bit late for that, isn't it?' Debbie shot back. 'I thought I could trust you.'

'You could...you can,' Laura said. 'You have to believe me. I had nothing to do with Bob Baker's story. I didn't even know it was going into the paper until I saw the first edition this morning.'

There was a long silence at the other end, and Laura began to think the head teacher had cut the connection, until eventually she spoke again.

'It's too late now,' she said. 'My job's down the tube, isn't it? And my partner's less than happy. She's scared she'll be splashed all over the front pages as well. Do you think the London papers will follow this up?'

'They could do,' Laura said. 'You should be ready for them

if they do. If they pick it up from the *Gazette* they'll descend like a swarm of locusts, wanting quotes, pictures, what the parents think, what the neighbours think, the lot. If you and your partner can arrange to go away for a bit, I'd recommend it. It's not much fun being at the centre of a paparazzi feeding frenzy.'

'I thought this was the twenty-first century,' Debbie said, the bitterness in her voice almost scalding Laura's ear. 'It feels more like a bloody witch-hunt in the thirteenth.'

'Some of these religious nuts want us to go back to that,' Laura said. 'I really believe they do. I sometimes feel as if I'm having to refight battles that my grandmother thought she'd won. I'm sorry, Debbie, I really am. If there's anything I can do to help, let me know.'

'Thank you,' Debbie said. 'But I doubt it. It's all right for you media people, isn't it? You move in and move on. Those of us left in your wake have to put our lives back together as best we can.'

'I'm so sorry,' Laura said softly.

'So am I,' Debbie said, and this time she did end the call, leaving Laura feeling deflated and weary in her car. She leant back and closed her eyes and wondered where this particular witch-hunt would end.

By seven that evening, as darkness fell, three police vans and a dozen officers were concealed in Bently Forest waiting for the first of the doggers to arrive. The plan, Mower thought, was pretty foolproof. They would allow cars to enter the narrow track leading to the clearing before stopping them, to avoid any possibility that a panicked driver would try to get away. If anyone tried to reverse out, there was another police car on standby a little further up the road, which could be summoned quickly to block the track entrance to make sure that no one escaped. Mower was very clear in his briefing that the DCI would not tolerate any fish wriggling out of this net, even if it meant arresting them as suspects for the murder of Karen Bastable if they refused to come to the station voluntarily. But he had little doubt that most of them would accept the voluntary option.

By seven-thirty, the time Karen's friend Charlene had assured them the doggers met during the dark nights of winter, the officers manning the ambush were becoming restless and ribald, and there was more than one suggestion that they should allow the doggers through and let them get on with whatever it was they wanted to get on with before accosting them *in flagrante*. It was not until ten to eight that the first headlights could be seen approaching through the trees and the sergeant in charge of the uniformed officers stationed himself in the middle of the track with a powerful torch to flag down the approaching car. A heavy four-by-four lumbered to a standstill and a fierce exchange followed before the driver consented to take one of the seats in the police van that would ferry him, and eventually twelve other men and a handful of women, to police headquarters. It was a couple of hours later that Mower dropped a list of names onto Thackeray's desk, where the DCI had been anxiously waiting developments.

'They all came more or less willingly in the end,' Mower said. 'And quite a haul it turned out we'd netted. One minister of religion, a couple of company directors and one senior councillor, all of them furious at being stopped, all of them claiming to be out for an innocent late-night drive until they realised that we already had most of their mates in the vans. Then they went very quiet. You could have heard a pin drop on the way back to HQ.'

'If you've taken statements from them all, make it very clear that we may want to talk to them again, then send them home to bed.'

Mower laughed.

'I'd be surprised if any of them get a good night's sleep,' he said, with no hint of sympathy in his voice. 'And it won't be the fact that they missed out on their nooky that's bugging them.'

'They should have thought of that earlier,' Thackeray said, his expression chilly.

'D'you want to talk to any of them yourself, guv? Councillor Maxwell's doing his nut. Demanding to talk to the chief constable. Going on about his human rights, no less.'

'Well, he'll have to make do with me,' Thackeray said. 'I'll come down in ten. Let him sweat for a bit. It might concentrate his mind.'

'Oh, I think his mind's well concentrated,' Mower said with a grin. 'Not least on what the *Gazette*'s going to make of all this once it leaks out. And that won't take long, I reckon.'

'What are they saying?' Thackeray asked. 'The general gist?'

'That it's an innocent bit of fun. No money changes hands. They don't know the names of the people involved, as most of the men, at least, went to some trouble to disguise themselves – anything from Tony Blair and George Bush to Mickey Mouse and Marge Simpson, apparently. And the women were all more than willing. Most of them made a big thing of that. Most of them admit to seeing Karen there that night she disappeared. And on other nights previously. She didn't hide her face. But I've not found one who'll admit to having sex with her. We'll have to cross-check who admits to wearing which mask – or take DNA samples from the lot of them.'

'We'll do that if we have to,' Thackeray said, his face grim. 'Do they know who's been organising it? Who's been putting the ads in the *Gazette*?'

'They all say not – and they all claim it certainly wasn't them,' Mower said sceptically. 'They pretty well all say that they heard about it from someone who already took part. Given time, I expect we can work right back through the chain to the source.'

'Right, I'll come down and talk to Councillor Maxwell, and you can send the rest of them home for now. But don't give any of them the impression that they're off the hook. I don't want any of them sleeping easy in their beds.'

'Their cars are still up at Bently,' Mower said.

'Some taxi firm's going to do well out of their jaunt tonight, then, isn't it?' Thackeray said unsympathetically. 'Let them find their own way home.'

Thackeray found Peter Maxwell pacing uneasily about an interview room. He spun towards the DCI as he came through the door, clearly furious.

'Mr Thackeray, isn't it? What the hell are you doing bringing us all down here and keeping us for hours?' he said. 'It's quite unnecessary. We could all have come in tomorrow to answer any questions you might have. It's little short of harassment. I've a good mind to talk to the chief constable about it. He happens to be a personal friend of mine.'

'I'm sorry you feel like that, sir, but when a woman who

belonged to your group has been found murdered, I would have thought you would want us to take it very seriously,' Thackeray said. 'And I'm sure my superiors will agree.'

'She didn't 'belong' in the sense you're implying,' Maxwell said. 'No one did. People just turned up. No one knew anyone in any real sense of the word. Just as well, as it turns out, as we seem to have attracted some right little slags.'

'If the women were slags, what does that make you, sir?' Thackeray asked sharply. 'It was all casual sex, wasn't it, on both sides? Did you have sex with Karen Bastable the night she went missing?'

'No, I did not,' Maxwell said.

'According to DS Mower, one of the women has said that she thought you did. What sort of a mask were you wearing that night?'

Maxwell flushed.

'The Lion King,' he muttered.

Thackeray raised an eyebrow at that.

'Did you use the same mask on every occasion?'

'Yes,' Maxwell said, then hesitated. 'Usually. Not always. Sometimes we swapped around – for fun, as it were.'

'Or to confuse anyone who might want to identify you?' Thackeray hesitated. 'Although I gather, from some of the women's statements, they had other ways of identifying you. Certain epithets that amused them.'

'Dear God,' Maxwell said, sinking suddenly into one of the chairs and burying his head in his hands for a moment. 'What have I let myself in for?'

'I'm not sure, Mr Maxwell,' Thackeray said, his voice like ice. 'You should be aware that we may need a DNA sample from you. From your point of view, it's probably preferable that you volunteer one. If we arrest you, of course, we have the power to take one anyway. We'll let you know.'

'We haven't committed a crime,' Maxwell said, regaining some of his belligerence. 'What crime have we committed?'

'Oh, I'm sure we can come up with something along the lines of outraging public decency,' Thackeray said. 'Unless we need to arrest you on suspicion of murder.'

Maxwell paled and swallowed hard.

'Can I go now?' he asked, with the faintest trace of a whine in his voice.

'Of course,' Thackeray said. 'We'll let you know when we need to speak to you again.'

As the interview rooms gradually cleared, Thackeray sent his team home, with instructions to be in early the next morning when the real task of cross-referencing and analysing the collection of statements they had made would begin. He walked slowly back to his office, and sat down again at his desk, deliberately switching his mind away from the doggers and gazing at his mobile phone for a long time before eventually picking it up and punching in the number that he knew almost better than his own. Laura picked up straight away, but her tone was cool.

'Can we talk?' Thackeray asked quietly, aware of his heart thumping.

'Is there anything to talk about?'

'Vicky called me and read me the riot act,' he said, his voice thick with emotion. 'I am trying to come to terms with this, Laura. You must believe me.'

'Call me again when you've come to terms with it, then,' Laura said angrily. 'But you don't have much time. There are decisions I have to take, plans I have to make. There's only a certain length of time you can let the past bugger up the future, and you're well over the limit. This is now and there's a baby on the way. You can't stop the clock. So let me know – soon.'

The silence after she had cut the connection rang in Thackeray's ears like a death knell. He sat for a long time at his desk before eventually getting to his feet and putting on his coat. But before he could switch out the light his mobile rang. He scanned the screen quickly, hoping it was Laura again, and almost cut the call off when he saw it was not. But Superintendent Longley was already in full flood.

'I've just had Peter Maxwell bending my ear,' he said. 'What the hell have we landed ourselves in with these bloody people? Do you have a suspect you've got any chance of charging, or what? I need to clear my lines before they all get on the phone to the chief constable and make my life a misery.'

'They were brought in as witnesses,' Thackeray said. 'I can't believe you're suggesting we soft-pedal because half of them are Freemasons and the other half belong to your golf club. Sir?'

'You know that's not what I'm saying, Michael. Don't be so bloody offensive. But I need to know what's going on with these beggars. They can't all be murderers and those who are not can make our lives very difficult if they choose. How long do you think it'll be before the *Gazette* gets a whisper? You'd better be very careful about the pillow talk yourself. That young woman of yours is as sharp as a barrowload of porcupines.'

'There'll be no pillow talk,' Thackeray said between gritted teeth. Longley hesitated, as if wondering if he could follow up that remark, and decided against it.

'Let me have a full report first thing in the morning,' he said. 'This could get very nasty.'

'It's already very nasty,' Thackeray said, thinking of the post-mortem report which had listed the forty-nine injuries Karen Bastable had been left with, most of them inflicted painfully before she had died. The mental image of that carefully constructed parcel of human remains still flashed vividly in front of his eyes whenever he thought about the murdered woman and filled him with fury. So, she was a slapper, as several of this evening's witnesses had contemptuously complained. She was, as her friend Charlene cheerfully admitted, out for a bit of fun. But no shortcomings on Karen's part could even begin to justify her fate.

'I'll see you first thing, then,' Longley said.

'Sir,' Thackeray agreed wearily. He buttoned up his coat, switched off the office light and locked the door. Nothing awaited him but a small and slightly bleak flat where he still stored some of his possessions. It had been a bolt-hole which he had seldom used as his relationship with Laura lengthened and deepened, but one he had never quite summoned up enough courage to dispose of. It increasingly looked, he thought, as if that was all he could now call home.

CHAPTER THIRTEEN

Sergeant Kevin Mower had worked in Bradfield long enough to have almost obliterated the memories of his inglorious and brief career with the Metropolitan police. And least welcome of all was any reminder of his spell at Paddington Green, where his involvement with the wife of a senior officer had led to his rapid departure from his job and a hasty relocation to the north of England. But the information that had landed on his desk that morning took him unwillingly back to his unruly youth and a quick trawl through his surviving contacts in London to discover who might be willing to help with his inquiries.

The catalyst for his phone-bashing was a brief report which identified the fingerprint that had been found on the plastic wrapping around the remains of Karen Bastable. According to the database, it matched the prints of a convicted drug dealer and suspected pimp, who had last been recorded ten years previously, living in a bedsit amongst the warren of run-down houses which had until then defied creeping gentrification between Paddington Station and Notting Hill. Mower very much doubted that traces of Leroy Jason Green would remain in West London, especially as he had good evidence that he had very recently been in West Yorkshire, but he had to be sure, especially as the last official contact with Green had been on his release from prison eleven years earlier. The criminal records photograph revealed a young, good-looking Afro-Caribbean man who had succeeded in retaining a faint smile in the face of the police photographer.

Mower eventually got through to a Detective Sergeant Doug Mackintosh at Paddington Green, a name he vaguely recognised, but who seemed to have no recollection of his own brief sojourn at the station, which was probably just as well.

'Doug,' he said more cheerfully than he felt. 'They tell me you're the man for intelligence on your manor. I wonder if you can help me? I've got a good fingerprint lead on a murder suspect up here and he turns out to have been one of your bad lads some time back.' He passed on the name the fingerprint records office had given him, and Green's record of intermittent fines and imprisonment for drug offences from the Police National Computer, and waited, without much optimism, for anything further the Met could come up with. But to his surprise, it turned out that he had struck gold with Doug Mackintosh, who had the sort of encyclopaedic memory that was invaluable to police intelligence. Mower heard the computer keys rattling at the other end of the line and then Mackintosh came back to him with a note of quiet triumph in his voice.

'He's still on file here, though we haven't had any official contact with him for more than ten years. He did a three-year stretch for dealing, not the first time he'd been nicked, and we assumed not the last. But then he went very quiet. I've got a couple of later reports on his activities locally, and then he seems to have vanished. Maybe that's when he graced you up there with his presence, but I would have expected him to have been more than a blip on your radar before now, given his record.'

'We've got nothing up here,' Mower said.

'Well, he'd been in and out of trouble since he was thirteen, according to our information, though he was never charged as a juvenile. That came later. But he kept cropping up as a known associate of various undesirables over a period of years. And again, after he came out of the nick, for a year or so. But we never managed to pin anything else on him. Either he got a lot more careful or, more unlikely, he gave up dealing. He certainly didn't seem to change his associates much. There's one odd note, though. One of his mates apparently told one of our informers that Green had "got religion". Maybe in gaol? Who knows? It happens sometimes. After that little nugget of info was recorded, he seems to have dropped out of sight completely and my predecessor in this job seems to have reckoned he left the area about nine years ago. No information about where he went. Simply dropped out of sight.'

'That fits with his criminal record,' Mower said. 'He's had no convictions in the last ten years, as far as I can discover. Which means the photo we have of him is years out of date.'

'But you reckon he's in the frame for murder?' Mackintosh asked. 'He must have moved into the big time and kept a very low profile. Maybe someone up your way made him an offer he couldn't refuse. But I must say, we never had him down as more than a relatively minor player.'

'Could be he moved up a league, I suppose.' Mower said. 'But this isn't gangland stuff, drugs, gun crime, the usual. This is sexual and very nasty.' Mackintosh whistled down the line.

'Serial killer?' he asked.

'No evidence of that yet, but we're asking other forces to check for similar cases.'

'Right,' Mackintosh said. The computer keys tapped away again at the other end of the line. 'I've got no current information about family, though there's mention of a mother and a sister in some of the early references. I'll put the word out and let you know if we get a sniff about where he's gone, if you like, anyone still around who might know. If it's that serious. Though it's a long time since he moved on, by the look of it.'

'I'd be grateful,' Mower said. 'We need to find him fast. It's the sort of case where it could happen again. If it hasn't already.'

'Keep me posted,' Mackintosh said. 'It's always interesting to know where our graduates end up. And help make sure they're still getting their just desserts.'

Superintendent Jack Longley sent for his DCI halfway through that morning, and Thackeray found him in a foul mood.

'I've just spent an hour with the chief trying to work out how to handle the press over this,' Longley said. 'We'll have all the hounds of hell up from London as soon as it leaks out. I'm surprised that little toerag Bob Baker hasn't got onto it already, but the press office says not. I suppose the people you interviewed are keeping a very low profile themselves in the circumstances, but we'll have to say something sometime today. I can't imagine all that activity up at Bently Forest went entirely unnoticed, remote as it is. Someone from the Forestry Commission will see the signs left by all those vehicles and begin to wonder what was going on.'

'I should imagine there are some frantic phone calls going on this morning,' Thackeray said. 'Kevin Mower says that it was obvious some of the men knew each other when they were put into the vans. We're working out the links between them all. It's a moot point whether they had recognised each other at the gatherings, as most of them claimed to have worn masks while they were playing games up there, but we're analysing their statements to try to work out how they heard about what they seem to call their 'little club'. Someone out there launched this thing and I want to know who that was. It's only been going about six months, according to some of them, but I'm not sure I believe that. They say it started up in the summer, when the weather was warm, and there was some talk about whether they could keep going as it got colder, but apparently they worked out ways of keeping warm enough.' Thackeray's face was dead-pan but Longley allowed himself a small smile.

'Banging away a bit more vigorously, maybe,' he suggested. 'Anyway, the chief's told the press office to prepare a statement for later today, which he'll approve personally. If we leave it until after the *Gazette*'s gone to press, we might gain ourselves a bit more time to think, but the proverbial will undoubtedly hit the fan tomorrow.'

'No doubt,' Thackeray said.

'What about forensics?' Longley asked.

'Mower's not had much joy with the fingerprint on the plastic Karen Bastable was wrapped in. It's on record but belongs to a black lad, a Londoner with a record, who seems to have disappeared from the radar about ten years ago. How he comes to be up here, God only knows. Anyway, we're pursuing that, and they think they may possibly get DNA from it, but that will take time. DNA results on the body itself are not through yet. When we get those we can ask the men we picked up in the forest to supply DNA samples for elimination purposes. If they won't volunteer, we may have to arrest them. I've no doubt one or more of them had sex with Karen that night, though that doesn't mean they necessarily killed her.'

'What a nightmare,' Longley said. 'Peter Maxwell swears he never touched her, but no doubt someone did.' He glanced down at the list of names which lay on the desk in front of him and permitted himself a grim smile. 'I know most of these beggars socially,' he said. 'They must be going spare. If – or when – their wives find out there'll be an army of bloody Amazons on the warpath. Any other leads?'

'We've circulated other forces to see if there've been any similar cases, but I don't hold out high hopes,' Thackeray said. 'With that level of brutality, any similar killing would have been all over the tabloids and we'd have been well aware. But it's worth a trawl. I asked for details of unsolved disappearances as well. If our man has made a habit of burying bodies on the moors, he could have got away with it until now. It was sheer chance Karen's body turned up so quickly. It could have lain up there for years before anyone stumbled on it.'

'Like the Moors murder lad who's never been found?'

'Exactly,' Thackeray said.

Longley sighed.

'You never get used to it, do you? The level of depravity. I can't say I'm not looking forward to my retirement, you know, Michael, and a rest from all this blood and mayhem. Old Huddleston, your predecessor, seems to spend most of his time at Headingley watching cricket. That wouldn't suit me. I've got my eye on a little place up the Dales, not too far from a good golf course, of course. And maybe I'll take up fishing. They say that's very soothing...' Thackeray was surprised to see the dreamy look that came over Longley's face as he contemplated this idyllic future. His own retirement was much further away than the superintendent's, and he had to admit that it filled him with a sort of panic, particularly if, as seemed likely, he had to face it without Laura. He shuddered slightly.

'If that's all...?' he suggested.

'Aye, get on with it, Michael,' Longley said, with a heavy sigh. 'I'll send you a copy of the press release when it's finalised. Keep me up to speed on developments, though. I want no special favours for these beggars you brought in last night. They brought it on themselves. So play it by the book. But I want no cock-ups either, no excuses for complaints. One of them may be as guilty as hell, but the rest are likely innocent, legally any road, and we'll have to live with them when it's all over. So tread carefully.'

'Sir,' Thackeray said, and turned to go. 'Though you can be sure the papers won't find any of them innocent when they get a handle on them.'

'Just don't let the handle come from us,' Longley said.

Laura Ackroyd sat at her computer feeling faintly nauseous. It was, she supposed, only what should be expected, although as far as she knew Vicky Mendelson had never suffered much in that way. She had seemed to sail through her pregnancies in an enviable glow of euphoria. But then she had wanted her babies, Laura thought, and she was doubting, in the sleepless watches of the night, that she really wanted hers, at least without Michael at her side. She was finding it difficult to concentrate on the first draft of her feature about Sutton Park School and she was faintly relieved when her mobile rang. But when she pulled it out of her bag and saw who the caller was she hesitated for a long time before finally answering.

'What the hell do you want, Vince?' she asked angrily before her former boyfriend, ex-colleague and more recent tormentor, had time to draw breath.

'That's not very friendly, doll,' Vince Newsom said. 'Especially as I'm halfway up the M1 to cover this lezzy headmistress you've outed up there. Bradfield doesn't half pick 'em, don't you reckon? And I suppose you're all for her exercising her human rights with the little darlings in Year seven.'

'If you're just going to be vile, we may as well stop there,' Laura said.

'OK, OK,' Vince said, laughing. 'I know all about your liberal sensibilities. I just wondered if you knew whether darling Debbie's been suspended or not. The school's not taking calls from the press, and the council press office is playing dumb as well, so I don't know whether to head for the school or this village where she lives. What do you reckon?'

'I've no idea,' Laura said. 'I don't see any reason why she should have been. But Bob Baker broke the story and he's following it up.' She glanced across the newsroom at Baker's desk, which stood empty, the computer screen blank. 'He's not here at the moment, so I can't pass you over,' she added with some satisfaction.

'Do you have his mobile number?'

'No,' Laura said truthfully. 'I can't help you, I'm afraid.'

'Huh,' Newsom muttered, from which Laura gathered that
he did not altogether believe her, and knew she would not
make the slightest effort to find it for him, but she merely
smiled at that. 'I think I'll head out to the love nest and then
come back into town if she's not there,' Newsom concluded.
'What about lunch, doll? For old times' sake.'

'No thanks,' Laura said firmly. 'I've not forgotten the last
time you were up here. Or forgiven you.'

'Water under the bridge, sunshine,' Newsom said airily.
'Lighten up, why don't you? Go with the flow. How's the love
life, by the way? Still with your gloomy copper? You could do
better than that, you know.'

Furious, Laura cut the connection. When she was a very
young and, she admitted to herself, impressionable reporter,
she had been seduced by Newsom's good looks and
undoubted charm, and had lived with him for more than two
years before throwing him out of her flat when she finally
realised just how unscrupulous he was prepared to be to
further his career. It was a judgement which was only
confirmed in spades later when he helped himself to
information she had been given to pass on to Michael
Thackeray, putting them in a position that threatened both
their careers. There were still unanswered questions in Laura's
mind about exactly what had happened that night, when she
had stupidly drowned her sorrows to the extent that she had
not really known what she was doing, and had allowed
Newsom to take her home and rummage in her bag for her
keys, and more. Dislike and distrust had turned, she realised
now, into something very close to hatred, and it was not an

emotion she had previously thought herself capable of. She sighed, and turned back to her computer screen. But she could not concentrate, and when the words on the screen misted over in front of her, she eventually went outside to her car to call Debbie Stapleton's home number. The phone was answered quickly and a slightly relieved voice replied.

'Oh, it's you,' Debbie said. 'I've had a dozen calls this morning already from newspapers and TV.'

'Have they suspended you from the school or something?' Laura asked.

'Not formally. The governors are meeting as we speak. They really have no grounds for suspending me, though that doesn't mean that Peter Maxwell won't put pressure on them to try their best. In the meantime, the chair has advised me to stay at home, ostensibly so he can deal with the press. Fat chance. My phone number's in the book and the phone's never stopped ringing since the *Gazette* story appeared. Even my neighbours are looking at me a bit oddly. They've never seemed the least bit bothered by us before.'

'Unplug the phone,' Laura advised. 'You'll get no peace otherwise.'

'I need to keep the line open for the school,' Debbie objected.

'Let them use your mobile.'

'Of course, silly me. You can tell I'm a novice in this sort of crisis. And my head's all over the place.'

'Are you all right? I thought you might have taken my advice and gone away,' Laura said.

'My partner has, and to be honest I'm beginning to wonder if she'll ever come back. She was even less prepared for this sort of campaign than I was. She's appalled, terrified even, though no one's even arrived on the doorstep yet.'

'They will,' Laura said. 'I know for a fact that Vince Newsom of the *Globe* is heading in your direction. Take my advice. Don't let him over the threshold. He's all charm on the surface, can do sympathy like a born-again agony aunt, but he's a snake. Don't trust him an inch, or you'll find yourself on the front page of every red top in the country tomorrow morning. Once one gets its teeth in, the rest will follow like night follows day.'

'Oh God,' Debbie said, and Laura could tell that she was on the verge of tears, but she knew she had to tell her the truth. Nothing less would prepare her for what might follow.

'Do you know who outed you to these radical parents?' Laura asked.

'I have no idea,' Debbie said. 'Not many people knew I was gay – we were very discreet – and those who did have always seemed completely supportive. I knew we had a few Christian fundamentalists around as well as some Muslims, but they've never given us any trouble until now. I can only think that someone mentioned it innocently to someone who was shocked.'

'Or someone who was looking for a weapon to use against you in the school row. Did Peter Maxwell know? He could easily have told David Murgatroyd. He certainly has issues with homosexuality, being the sort of born-again Christian he is.'

'I don't think Peter Maxwell knew. He was on the panel at my interview for the job, but your sexuality is not something decent employers ask about these days. It's very much off limits.'

'But it won't be with Murgatroyd,' Laura said. 'One way or another, he'll make sure it's on the agenda. And the tabloids will go along with it given half a chance. They still enjoy a bit of queer-bashing if they think they can get away with it. And a real live row gives them the chance.'

'With so many Muslims in the school it's the perfect issue for Murgatroyd, isn't it?' Debbie said.

'Perfect for anyone who wants to keep you out of the academy headship,' Laura agreed. 'This leak is no accident, Debbie. Someone has told Bob Baker deliberately to scupper your chances of the job.'

'I didn't know I had enemies like that,' Debbie said, her voice forlorn.

But before she could respond, Laura heard a slight gasp at the other end of the phone.

'There's a car pulling up outside and a guy getting out, a blue BMW, I think,' Debbie said.

'What does he look like?' Laura asked.

'Tall, blond, that floppy hair public schoolboys have, good looking...'

'Sounds like Vince Newsom,' Laura said, realising that Newsom might have lied to her about how far up the M1 he had actually driven when he had called her. 'Batten down the hatches, and unplug the phone,' she said.

'Give me your mobile number, quickly, in case I need some advice,' Debbie said, and gave Laura her own number in exchange.

'Good luck,' Laura said before they cut off. 'You'll need it.'

Laura went back up to the newsroom feeling seriously depressed. She could not help feeling responsible in some way for Debbie Stapleton's predicament although she had done nothing wrong. Bob Baker was still not at his desk and she realised that Debbie's description of her visitor could have just as easily described Bob as Vince Newsom, and that made her feel slightly better. She disliked Bob and some of his methods, but he was not in the *Globe*'s league of intrusive unpleasantness yet, although she guessed he harboured serious ambitions in that direction.

She sat down at her desk again and called Councillor Peter Maxwell's office.

'What's it about?' his secretary asked with what Laura felt was unwarranted suspicion.

'We've been talking about Sutton Park,' she said. 'I've a few questions about the latest developments.'

'I'll see if he'll talk to you,' the secretary said, and eventually put her through.

'I wondered what your reaction was to this new parents' campaign,' Laura said. 'It all seems to be getting pretty nasty.'

'Oh, that,' Maxwell said, and Laura wondered why there seemed to be a note of relief in his voice. 'The governors are meeting this morning and my impression is that they're not best pleased. It's not my responsibility, but off the record, I should think the story in the *Gazette* has scuppered her chances with David Murgatroyd. He won't go for a gay head teacher. No chance.'

'Did you know she was gay before yesterday's story, as a matter of interest?' Laura asked, trying to keep her voice level.

'No, I didn't,' Maxwell said flatly. 'And don't you or Bob go suggesting I did. To be honest, I've no idea where Bob got the story from, but it wasn't from me or anyone in my office. You know what the council's policies are on sexism, racism and all the other isms.'

'And yet you'll hand over a school lock, stock and barrel to a known homophobe?'

'There's no evidence that Sir David Murgatroyd has ever discriminated against anyone,' Maxwell said. 'The Government would not have allowed him to set up so many academies if there was. So as far as the council is concerned, that's the end of it. So if that's all you wanted to ask me, I'll get on. I've a lot on my plate this morning, as it happens. Nice talking to you, Laura. Really nice.'

And with that Maxwell hung up, so quickly that Laura wondered what exactly he was trying to hide.

'Well, you seem to have all the symptoms of a pregnancy, as you seem to know already, and you missed your pills. I'll do the tests but I think you can take it that you definitely have a baby on the way,' the doctor said, peeling off her plastic gloves. Laura swung her legs off the examination couch and rearranged her clothes. The doctor looked at her sharply as she waved her into the chair by her desk and consulted the notes on her computer screen.

'You're not married?'

Laura shook her head.

'No, I'm not married. I have a partner – off and on.'

'Is he the father?'

'Oh yes,' Laura said, but she knew the dullness in her voice was betraying her.

'But there's a problem?' Dr Mariam Ali suggested. She was a comfortably plump middle-aged woman with her dark hair fastened back from a round face faintly lined by life, her dark eyes full of concern. Her consulting room was almost preternaturally tidy, and she dressed with elegant understatement in dark trouser suits and bright silk shirts, but Laura knew that she had faced difficulty in the practice because some patients still disliked a woman doctor and others took against anyone Asian, especially in the aftermath of terrorist outrages.

'He doesn't want the baby. He lost a child a long time ago and doesn't think he can do it all again.'

'And you? What do you want?' the doctor asked.

Laura shrugged dispiritedly.

'If my partner will stay with me, then I want the baby,' she said. 'Without him, I'm not sure I can do it alone. It's a huge responsibility.' Laura wondered what Dr Ali's position was on abortion. It was not a thought that had ever crossed her mind before, but now it might be crucial. But the doctor showed no sign of censoriousness.

'It is a very big responsibility, bringing up a child on your own,' she agreed. 'Two parents are better. Do you have family locally who could help?'

Laura shook her head.

'Only my grandmother who needs all the support she can get. My parents are abroad. I'm an only child.'

'I can't advise you, Laura,' the doctor said. 'If you decide to seek a termination, that has to be your decision and there will be some counselling we can offer. All I can say is that you need to come to a decision soon. Late terminations are not advisable, on health grounds.'

'Right,' Laura said, her eyes filling with tears.

'Can you really not reconcile your partner to the idea of being a father again?' the doctor asked. 'Why don't you talk to him again?'

'I'll try,' Laura said.

'Make an appointment to see me again in about a week,' Dr Ali said. 'We'll need to arrange antenatal care at the maternity unit if you are going ahead with the pregnancy, and other things if you're not.' She looked at Laura for a moment. 'I'm sorry. I like to see my expectant mothers happy, not depressed.'

'I'm sure you do,' Laura said, regaining some of her normal sharpness. 'But I'm not sure I can help you there. If I end up having to choose between the baby and my partner that will be the hardest decision I've ever had to make, and happy's not the likeliest outcome. Thanks for your time, Doctor. I'll see you in a week.'

CHAPTER FOURTEEN

'I need to go to London, guv,' DS Kevin Mower announced later that day when he presented himself in DCI Thackeray's office to report on progress. 'My contact at Paddington Green has tracked down Leroy Green's sister living in Archway and I reckon we need to see her face-to-face. He has to be our prime suspect, in spite of the other parties involved with Karen that night.'

'Do you need to take anyone with you?' Thackeray asked.

'Nope. Doug Mackintosh is happy to come with me, and as he's got all the background, that seems to make sense. If you could clear it with the Met I could get down there this evening and arrange to see her in the morning. I'd be back tomorrow afternoon, unless she pins him down to a location in London. But that seems unlikely as he was up here so recently.'

'Right, I'll talk to the Met,' Thackeray said. He sighed. 'I've just been going through these statements from the people we picked up in the forest. What a sleazy lot they are, exhibitionists gone rancid. But so far not one of them's admitting they had sex with Karen the night she went missing.'

'There's a lot of garbage in there,' Mower said. 'I wouldn't think you can believe more than a fraction of what any of them say. Particularly the blokes. The women don't seem to be so bothered about covering up. Most of them have less to lose, I guess. They seem to be living boring lives in pretty loveless relationships and just out for a bit of what they regard as fun. The blokes are a definite cut above that, and have a hell of a lot to lose if all this becomes public.'

Thackeray nodded.

'Quite a gathering of the great and the good, looking for a free brothel, effectively,' he said, not disguising his contempt. 'The perfect scenario for a predator, as it turns out.'

'Did you see where Sharif's tried to analyse who told who, what and when?' Mower asked. 'As far as I can see the word-of-mouth trail leads back to Peter Maxwell about eighteen months ago, and he claims he found a site on the Internet, first of all and didn't manage to get anything off the ground. I've got someone having a browse of sites for swingers and doggers, to see if we can track down what he claims he saw, but the chances of uncovering who's behind anything like that are pretty remote. It could originate anywhere.'

'We'll have to get them all in again. And I intend to start with Maxwell personally, whatever the chief constable thinks,' Thackeray said. 'I didn't believe half of what he was telling me last night. And this time we'll ask them all to volunteer a DNA sample and fingerprints – for elimination. If they refuse, we'll have to consider our options, but I don't believe none of them had sex with Karen. According to most statements there were only four women there that night and about ten men. Are they really trying to convince us that Karen was just a spectator? Has anything come in about similar cases elsewhere?' Since recent disasters concerning communication between police forces, big efforts had been made to ensure that similar cases could be tracked around the country through a national database, but both men knew that even now it was not foolproof.

'There are no cases with bodies tortured and mutilated like Karen's,' Mower said soberly. 'It would have been front-page news in any case, just as it will be here now we're releasing some of the details to the press. But I'm having missing persons cases looked at as well – young or middle-aged women who've gone AWOL and never been found, though there are hundreds of them. It's not uncommon, after all. A few cases have been regarded as potentially suspicious, husbands have been interviewed and then ruled out just as we've pretty well ruled out Terry Bastable, for the moment at least. But no bodies have ever been found. We're pulling out records for anyone who has anything in common with Karen, but there's not a lot to go on. Apart from an enthusiasm for outdoor sex, she seems to have led a pretty ordinary life.'

'But the sex is an obvious means for a predator to gain access to a victim, anonymous, secretive, either behind closed doors or in remote places. Perfect. We can't rule out the possibility that there are other cases, even without bodies. He may just have been unlucky with Karen's body being found so quickly. Anyway, we obviously need to talk to Leroy Green. He's been off the radar for the best part of ten years. Where's he been and what's he been doing during that time, before turning up in close proximity to Karen Bastable's dead body? Get yourself off to London and see if his family know where he is. We need to trace him – fast.'

'Right, guv,' Mower said, turning away to hide the flicker

of anticipation in his eyes. Even after years in the north, a night out in his native city was an attractive prospect. He would hit the night spots before pursuing his quarry in the morning, and just hope the hangover was not too dire.

Peter Maxwell's fury was obvious as soon as DCI Thackeray opened the door of the bleak interview room, with DC Mohammed Sharif close behind him. He had deliberately left Maxwell to stew for half an hour after he had accepted his request to present himself at police headquarters for a further chat. The executive councillor was obviously not used to being kept waiting and his face was flushed with annoyance.

'I only have a forty-five minute window,' he said. 'I've an executive committee meeting at two.'

'I'm afraid I'll have to intrude on your day for as long as it takes, Mr Maxwell,' Thackeray said, waving the councillor into a seat as he and Sharif took the two chairs opposite and the DC set up the tape recorder. 'There are several things we need to clarify with you about the group you and Karen Bastable were members of, and about what happened exactly on the night she disappeared.'

Maxwell scowled.

'Are you accusing me of something, Chief Inspector?'

'You mean apart from using what amounts to an outdoor brothel?'

'No money changed hands,' Maxwell said, evidently unabashed.

'Well, I'm not accusing you of anything else. Not yet, Mr Maxwell. We are still at the stage of getting the events clear, in some sort of chronological order, that's all.'

'Exactly what, for instance?' Maxwell challenged him.

'Well, we've now had a chance to analyse all the statements that were taken last night and it seems clear from those that the attention of several people was drawn to the dogging group by you. And they told other people, in a fairly clear chain. Two of the women, Karen herself and her friend Charlene, were told about it by a manager at their work. You are the only person who claimed not to remember who drew your attention to the activities in Bently Forest. Did you initiate them, Mr Maxwell? Was the whole thing your idea, after you picked the idea up from the Internet? Or did someone else introduce you to the group?'

'Of course it wasn't my idea,' Maxwell almost shouted. 'I just went out of curiosity once or twice, no more than that. Someone showed me an advertisement in the *Gazette* and said he knew where it was all happening. I can't even remember who it was now...' He trailed off, as if not expecting Thackeray to believe what he was saying. But Thackeray did not challenge him on that.

'How long ago was that, Mr Maxwell?' he asked. 'Can you remember that? We have a series of dates fixed by the ads in the newspaper, so we know roughly how many of these meetings there have been. How many have you been to exactly? Did you go to the first one last June?'

'I wasn't counting,' Maxwell said. 'It was just a casual thing, a couple of times.'

'Some of the group remember the Lion King as a more regular attender than that,' Thackeray said.

'No, no, not really. Not regular at all.' Maxwell glanced around the cramped interview room with its furniture bolted to the floor and its high window of opaque glass as if seeking an escape route that did not exist. The high colour in his cheeks had receded now and he looked increasingly pale and ill.

'So let's concentrate on the last meeting, the night Karen disappeared. We have two witnesses who say that the Lion King had sex with Karen that evening. Is that true?'

Maxwell swallowed hard and then shook his head.

'I don't know,' he muttered. 'I didn't know who the women were, what they were called. None of us did. It was intended to be anonymous. It was more enjoyable that way. You could do whatever you liked with no possibility of a comeback.'

Thackeray was aware of Sharif moving uneasily in his chair beside him and flashed him a warning look. He did not want Muslim sensibilities muddying the water.

'Some people knew who Karen was, not least the man she worked with, so it was not necessarily completely anonymous,' Thackeray said. 'I have a description of what Karen was wearing when she got out of her car – as far as that goes. Perhaps you would recognise...' he glanced down at his notes '...hot pants, no bra, but a loose semi-transparent top in a thin purple material. It didn't hide much, apparently. Does that ring any bells?'

Maxwell shook his head and said nothing.

'Mr Maxwell, we have Karen Bastable's body, and there may very well be traces of whoever she had sex with that night. A DNA sample from you will prove one way or the other whether you were intimate with her. There's really no point in prevaricating about it.'

'I didn't kill her,' Maxwell said so quietly that Thackeray could barely hear him. He glanced at the tape recorder.

'Could you repeat that for the tape, please.'

'I didn't kill her,' Maxwell said.

'We'll come to that later,' Thackeray snapped. 'Did you have sex with her?'

Maxwell nodded, wringing his hands together.

'I must have done. I told you I didn't know her name.'

'Did you use a condom?'

Maxwell nodded, and gazed around the room again in near desperation and embarrassment.

'And where exactly did you and Karen do this? In your car?' Thackeray persisted, with no trace of sympathy for the man across the table, who was beginning to shake slightly.

'No, in hers. It was a cold night. We used the back seat.'

'So if there are traces left by this activity, that's where we'll find them?'

'I suppose so,' Maxwell said.

'I ask that for a reason, Mr Maxwell,' Thackeray said. 'Karen didn't apparently leave the forest in her own vehicle. As you probably know, it was found there and it's now being examined for forensic evidence. But we would also like to know whose vehicle she did leave in, either alive or dead. If you have no objection, I would like to have my forensic team examine your car as well. If you're telling me the truth, you have nothing to worry about. Their examination will corroborate your story. As will the DNA sample and fingerprints that I am sure you are going to volunteer after we finish this interview.'

Thoroughly deflated now, Maxwell nodded helplessly.

'I need a solicitor,' he said dully.

'That's up to you,' Thackeray said. 'You're not under arrest and I only have one more question for now. I want you to think back very carefully to last summer and try to remember who drew your attention to the ad in the *Gazette* that first took you to Bently Forest. We know pretty well who you told, and who they told, right down the chain to Karen Bastable and Charlene Brough. But who told you, Mr Maxwell? You must remember. I'm sure an invitation to an orgy is not something which crops up every day in the corridors of local government. Somebody set this up, and if it wasn't you, then I need to know who it was.'

'I don't know,' Maxwell said. 'I really don't know. The newspaper was being passed around in the Clarendon bar, getting a lot of smutty comment, and someone said they thought it all went off up at Bently. I simply went up there out of curiosity. I don't know who placed the ads. I never have known. I don't know anyone who does know. And that's the truth.'

When they had delivered Maxwell downstairs to have his fingerprints and DNA swab taken, Omar Sharif followed the DCI back upstairs to the main CID office.

'Do you think he's telling the truth, sir?' he asked doubtfully.

'He's probably telling us part of the truth,' Thackeray said. 'Unfortunately, the ads in the *Gazette* were dropped in by hand, paid for in cash, and no one seems to remember anything about who placed them. One of the staff thinks she recalls speaking to a man but that's about all we've got.'

'Surely they keep a record of advertisers,' Sharif said.

'In theory, but they handle thousands every week. They're looking at their records but with the number of ads going through the system it's time-consuming, and I don't suppose the person gave his or her real name anyway,' Thackeray said. 'What I want you to do next is have a quiet look at Maxwell's background. Apart from the fact that he's one of the council's high-flyers, we know absolutely nothing about him. Is he married, divorced, cohabiting, has he a family, where does he live? If he's the mastermind behind this group I want to know everything there is to know about him. We may have to do the same checks for every single one of them, but he seems to be the end of the chain so we'll start with him.'

'The prime suspect then?'

'Well, that's a bit premature. We need the forensics, as always,' Thackeray said.

'You reckon whoever set it up did it with the express purpose of finding a victim?' Sharif asked. 'In which case it could be someone who's never revealed himself at all, couldn't it? Someone placed the ads and got the doggers up there and then waited his chance to abduct a woman.' Thackeray could see the distaste in Sharif's face and wondered how someone from such a puritanical tradition could cope with the excesses of modern Britain, but Sharif did seem to cope with some equanimity with the drink and drugs and sexual licence and inevitable violence that was every police officer's lot. He balanced on his cultural tightrope very effectively, Thackeray thought, and should go far.

'It could be,' Thackeray agreed. 'If the advertising people at the *Gazette* can just come up with a name or address or phone number for that first ad last June, that will give us a lead to explore. In the meantime we'll just have to follow up the ones we've got. Log this new task and then get on with it. You've met Maxwell, so that should give you a head start.'

'Sir,' Sharif said.

Ted Grant paced around his newsroom like Bligh on the *Bounty* seeking out slackers to flog, his face flushed and his eyes gleaming with excitement.

'Never mind lesbian headmistresses,' he roared in Laura's

ear. 'We could have a full-blown serial killer on the loose here with all the trimmings. Another Yorkshire Ripper. I want you to get up to the Heights and talk to the husband. Then do a trawl through the files and see if any other women have gone missing without trace in the last few years. Bob, let's go over this press release and see what we can read between the lines. Laura, you'd better sit in on this or you'll be out of the loop when you talk to Bastable. Come on. Let's get our backsides in gear. This is a biggie.'

Laura trailed after Bob Baker into Grant's pokey glass-walled office at the end of the newsroom, and leant slightly wearily against the door to listen to what Baker had brought back from the police press conference at county headquarters. She felt nauseous and knew she looked pale, and had found it difficult to concentrate since she had come back to the office after her doctor's appointment, where she had told the ever-sympathetic Dr Ali that she was determined to have her baby. She just hoped that Grant would be so fascinated by what Bob Baker was telling him that he would not notice her less than rapt expression. The younger man ran a hand across his floppy blond hair and Laura could see, even from her position behind him, that he was almost quivering with excitement.

'I don't think they're telling us the half of it,' he said. 'What I got out of my contacts was that Karen Bastable was one of a group of swingers who were getting together up in Bently Forest and that the cops did some sort of a round-up last night, pulled in more than a dozen people – God knows who – all of them suspects. This could be big, Ted, very big. A national story. There were telly cameras at the press conference – News 24, Sky, the local boys – the nationals will be on their way, if they're not here already for the other thing,

Lezzy Debbie's love nest. I heard that Vince Newsom's already on to that one. Bradfield's going to hit the big time, so we need to be right on our toes.'

Ted Grant cast a sharp eye in Laura's direction and looked slightly discomforted. 'Yes, well, let's leave the headmistress for the time being. She'll keep. Let's concentrate on the swingers in the woods...'

'Well, as I hear it, swingers isn't quite right,' Bob said. 'What they were actually up to was more in the nature of dogging.'

'Dogging, was it?' Grant said, and Laura could see that his normally acute antennae had failed to recognise the word.

'Public sex,' she said quietly. Ted nodded to himself, unwilling to admit his unfamiliarity with the concept.

'You reckon Karen Bastable brought it on herself then, do you?' Baker asked over his shoulder, knowing his question would provoke Laura.

'It's all down to consent, isn't it?' she said sweetly. 'And I doubt any woman actually consents to being chopped into little pieces, which from what you say is what happened to this poor woman.'

'So do we have any idea who they picked up last night?' Ted asked. 'Were they giving anything away on that score?'

'Not a lot,' Baker said. 'But I reckon I can winkle out a few names if I hit the phone. No probs. My impression was that there's a few local worthies been caught with their pants down. Jack Longley looked seriously miffed about something when I saw him. Perhaps it's members of his golf club putting their putters to unusual use.' Bob sniggered slightly but Laura was aware that Ted Grant was not looking amused. She knew that he fancied himself as one of the big fish in Bradfield's small and sometimes murky pond, and wondered if he was afraid he might be caught in any splashback from the dogging scandal when it became public knowledge.

'I'll have a word with Jack Longley myself,' he said to Baker. 'Leave him to me.'

Baker raised a sardonic eyebrow at that but did not argue.

'Right, let's get on with it then, before the lads and lasses from London start milling about and muddying the water. I want us two steps ahead of the nationals on this one. We've got the contacts, we know the ground, let's build on that.' And with that he dismissed them and picked up his phone, his face flushed with emotion that seemed to Laura to mix excitement and fear.

Laura drove slowly up towards the Heights, where four towering blocks of flats, which had dominated the western skyline of Bradfield since the Sixties, had recently been reduced to rubble. The site of the flats was surrounded by a high security fence but she could see how the streets around the estate had been liberated now that they were relieved of the shadow of what, over the years, had become high-rise slums: the haunt of drug dealers, prostitutes and a handful of families who had not been able to escape to anything better.

She slowed down by the old people's bungalows where her grandmother, Joyce Ackroyd, would normally have been eager to welcome her with a cup of tea and the latest gossip from the estate, but the old lady would not be able to offer her no doubt caustic views on the sexual scandal, which seemed about to engulf the town, from Portugal. As a town councillor a generation ago, Joyce had been largely responsible for the building of the Heights and had watched its disintegration with disbelief as money ran out for repairs and young people with no jobs, and eventually no hope, descended into despair and violence.

The Bastables' house was on the edge of the Heights, a tidy-looking road of semi-detached houses, many of which had obviously been bought by the tenants who had put in new front doors and windows, relaid the drives where they parked their cars, and tended the gardens with care. The Bastables were clearly one of the families who had signed up to property ownership, but when Terry Bastable answered her knock on his front door, it was obvious that things were going very wrong behind the white lace curtains that shielded his windows from the street. Bastable was unshaven, his eyes red-rimmed and his beer belly bulging over the waistband of his dirty tracksuit bottoms.

'Who are you?' he asked belligerently. 'Are you from t'police?' When she told him, his face and shaven pate became even more flushed and he made to close the door in her face.

'Piss off,' he said. 'I'm not talking to no effing newspapers. Don't you know when to leave folk alone? I've got two motherless kids in here crying their bleeding eyes out, and what am I supposed to tell them about how she died? Do you think I want them reading all this stuff on your front page?'

'You might be better talking to me than to some of the London reporters when they turn up, as I'm sure they will,' Laura said mildly.

Quite suddenly Terry Bastable seemed to fall in on himself, like a deflating Michelin man, his face crumpled and his eyes filled with tears as he stepped backwards and held the door open for Laura.

'You'd best come in,' he said. 'I'm going barmy here, with

the kids in bits and the bloody police still thinking I did it. It's a bloody nightmare, it's been a nightmare since Karen left, and I don't know what the hell to do.'

Cautiously, Laura followed the big man into the living room, where she found a blond boy playing a computer game on the huge flat TV screen, and a red-headed girl crumpled in a heap on the sofa, fast asleep beneath a grubby blanket. Both looked as pale as their father and had dark circles under their eyes. Bastable shrugged at the littered and dusty space the two children inhabited and waved a helpless fist.

'I don't know what to do with them.' he said. 'They won't go to school. They won't do owt I say. I've been laid off from work and I don't know where the next penny's coming from, do I? You'd best come in t'kitchen. I'll make us a cup of tea.'

Speechless, Laura followed him through into an equally cluttered and dirty kitchen, the sink piled high with washing-up and the debris from what looked like several recent meals cluttering the table. Bastable extricated a kettle from the clutter, filled it with water at the sink and put it on.

'Here, let me,' Laura said, picking out what appeared to be the cleanest mugs from the chaos and washing them at the tap. Then she waited while Bastable came up with tea bags from a cupboard and a bottle of milk from the fridge, which he sniffed suspiciously before adding it to the brew and handing her one of the mugs.

'You'd best sit down,' he said grudgingly, waving her onto one of the stools at the table and taking one himself. He looked at Laura, eyes startlingly blue within the red rims. 'I'm at the end of my bloody tether,' he said. 'No one round here'll gi'me the time o'day. They all think I killed her, don't they? The fuzz have more or less admitted that they haven't got any evidence against me, but there's not a single beggar on Wuthering believes that. The kids were being run ragged when they went back to school for a day or so, being teased and bullied, called killer's kids... In the end they ran off home, and t'school says they'll be better here for a bit while t'fuss dies down. But what am I supposed to do with 'em stuck here all day? And now all sorts of folk have started ringing up, newspapers, television, wanting my side of the story. I don't have a side of the story, do I? She went off one night and never came back. And now it looks like some bastard's killed her. And it weren't me!'

'Don't you have any family who could take the children for a while?' Laura asked, but Bastable shook his head.

'They don't speak to us, do they? They don't like my politics, do they? Too extreme for them. My sister married a bloody darkie, a n...' He hesitated and then let the word go. Laura had noticed the faded BNP sticker in the front window. 'They even send me bloody Paki policewomen,' he muttered half under his breath, and took a slurp of tea.

'Have the police told you you're no longer a suspect?' Laura asked.

'I'm still on police bail, aren't I?' Bastable said bitterly. 'But as far as I can see, all their prying and searching and tests've come up with nowt. Which is right, because there's nowt to find. I didn't kill Karen. All right, I followed her up there that night and saw what was going off, but that was it. I came home. I might have killed her if she'd come back, the cheating cow, but she never did, so I didn't, did I?' He pushed clenched fists into his eyes for a moment as if to keep not just tears, but a whole welter of pain inside his shaven head. Laura felt a surge of pity for him, as she would for a tormented bull in the

Spanish ring. She disliked the man, and hated his politics, but no one, she thought, deserved this.

'You had no idea that this sort of stuff was going on?' Laura asked. 'No rumours around the estate?'

'Well, it weren't blokes from round here, even if some of the lasses were,' Bastable said, his former belligerence flooding back. 'You could see that from the sort of cars that were going up there. A Volvo, a Beamer, an Audi Quattro – not the sort of motor you find on the Heights, are they, unless you're dealing drugs? Stands to reason, they wouldn't want their own women joining in. That'd never do. Just a few slags from the Heights that no one'll miss if owt nasty happens to them. Bastards!'

Thackeray would no doubt be matching up expensive cars to well-heeled owners, Laura thought, before the *Gazette* unleashed the information to an unsuspecting Bradfield public that he was seeking a brutal sexual killer amongst the town's great and evidently not so good. Terry Bastable, the most immediate victim, would not be the only person outraged by the news.

'If you give me an interview it'll probably keep the national reporters out of your hair,' she said. 'It's obvious the police don't consider you a serious suspect anymore, so the London press will be chasing up the new leads the police have announced this morning. But my news editor wants a short piece about how you and the kids are getting on. D'you think you could cope with that?'

Bastable stared at her, his eyes blank.

'It's a mucky job you've got there, lass,' he said. 'Aye, get on with it, then. It makes no odds to me. There's enough round here coming to have a good gawp at us. The whole town might as well join in.'

Laura pulled her tape recorder out of her bag and switched it on, feeling faintly sick.

'Talking might just help,' she murmured.

'Aye, and pigs might fly, an'all. So what do you want to know?'

CHAPTER FIFTEEN

Kevin Mower rolled over lazily in bed and reached out for the companion he had fallen asleep beside. When his inquiring arm found nothing but a crumpled sheet, he snapped fully awake and sat up, looking around his small hotel room in surprise. Had he dreamt the previous evening's pleasures? he wondered, and then realised that watery noises were coming from the en suite bathroom. Whether the cold morning light would be as kind to the improbably named Juniper as the semi-darkness of the nightclub had been eight hours previously he rather doubted, but at least he knew that she had not crept away at dawn with his wallet and credit cards in her bag. He was a fool, he thought, but it had been fun.

He rolled out of bed himself, pulled on boxer shorts and a T-shirt and tapped on the bathroom door.

'D'you eat breakfast, honey?' he asked, and when an answer came in the negative, he rang down to order himself a continental breakfast anyway.

Two hours later, showered, shaved and well satisfied after another brief session in bed, he found himself being driven through Kentish Town by DS Doug Mackintosh on their way to interview Leroy Jason Green's sister, Leanne.

'Did you tell her what it was about?' Mower asked.

'Just that we wanted to talk about her brother,' Mackintosh said as he negotiated a double-parked white van which was adding to the usual traffic chaos on the approach to the Archway junction, where the A1 debouched into the maelstrom of inner London. 'She didn't seem particularly surprised, just said she hadn't seen him for years.'

'No one seems to have seen him for years,' Mower said. 'But he was in Yorkshire ten days ago in close proximity to a mutilated body. We know that without any doubt.'

'So what's he been doing for nine or ten years?' Mackintosh wondered, as he negotiated the junction and turned into a side street and parked on a double yellow line, sticking a Metropolitan Police sticker on his dashboard.

'They clamp you as soon as look at you,' he said, by way of explanation, getting out of the car and heading towards one of the Victorian terraced houses that lined both sides of the street, leaving Mower to follow before he locked the car with his remote over his shoulder.

Leanne Parsons, formerly Green, opened the door to them almost as soon as they rang the bell. She was a tall, elegant woman with smooth straightened hair and non-committal eyes, who took her time to assess the two men on the doorstep and study their warrant cards.

'You'd better come in,' she said grudgingly, leading the way into a vibrantly decorated sitting room to the right of the front door and offering both men the chance to admire her back view in figure-hugging jeans and top. 'You were lucky I have a day off work today.'

'And you do what, exactly?' Mackintosh asked.

'I'm a social worker,' Leanne Parsons said as she waved her visitors into armchairs and sat opposite them on the other side of the fireplace, knees together and hands clasped demurely in front of her. Mower smiled faintly. In his experience, social workers did not generally look quite like this.

'Ah,' Mackintosh said. 'So your brother's record is a bit of an embarrassment, I suppose?'

'His record is old, Sergeant Mackintosh, as I think you must know if you've done your research properly. Like many young men he got into trouble as a teenager and then began to sort himself out later. It's not unusual. And in any case, as I told you on the phone, I haven't seen him for many years. Can you tell me exactly why there's this sudden interest in him?'

Mackintosh waved a hand in Mower's direction.

'My colleague here from Yorkshire would like to talk to him,' he said. 'I'll leave him to explain.'

'You'll appreciate that I can't go into detail,' Mower said quietly, wondering what effect it would have on this poised woman if her brother was eventually charged with a horrific murder. 'But we have evidence that connects Leroy Green to a very serious crime.'

'What evidence?' Leanne shot back, and Mower guessed that she would be fierce in defence of anyone she thought was being unjustly accused.

'Forensic evidence you can't argue with,' he said flatly. 'A fingerprint that matches your brother's that are still on file. We need to speak to him very urgently.'

Leanne's knuckles whitened as she clasped her hands together more tightly and dropped her head for a moment. She said nothing for a moment, and it was as if she was conducting a fierce dialogue in her own mind as various emotions seemed to flit across her face.

'Very serious?' she asked at last.

'Very serious,' Mower said.

'OK,' Leanne said. 'I'll tell you everything I know, but I don't think it's going to be much help. I honestly don't know where he is, and I haven't seen him for at least eight years. It was sometime around the millennium. He'd already moved on and I was quite surprised when he turned up on the doorstep to wish me a happy New Year. I was still living down Paddington way then. Once I got married and moved up here, he wouldn't have known where to find me even if he'd wanted to. He didn't leave a forwarding address so I couldn't let him know, and my mother died about that time. I couldn't even tell him that, so he didn't come to the funeral. It was as if he wanted to have a completely new life somewhere else, nothing to do with his past, or his family.'

'Your mother must have been upset by that,' Mower said.

'She was, yes,' Leanne said. 'He was the only boy, eight years younger than me, two sisters in between. But he ran wild in his teens. Broke my mother's heart. And then he cut off contact with us all.'

'Did he give you any idea what he was doing for a living, or where he was living?' Mower pressed.

Leanne shrugged.

'He seemed happy enough but he gave very little away.' She gazed out of the window for a moment before going on.

'I think he mentioned living in the Midlands but whether that was then or previously I don't remember. He was cagey, very cagey. But he never shared much with us girls. He was the youngest and my mother spoilt him rotten, and he more or less did as he pleased from being about ten or eleven. I was much less surprised by the fact that he fell into drugs and crime than I was by the possibility that he'd reformed himself somehow. If he'd told me that on that visit I probably wouldn't have believed him.'

'So could it have been a criminal lifestyle that he didn't want you to know about?'

'I don't think so,' Leanne said. 'Has he been in trouble since? You're more likely to know about that than I am.'

'Not as far as we're aware. Not under that name, anyway.'

'Why do you say that?' Leanne asked.

'Why do you ask?' Mower shot back. 'Do you think he could be using a different name?'

'Perhaps it wouldn't surprise me,' Leanne said thoughtfully. 'Before he disappeared he'd started going to an evangelical church in Bayswater. It really seemed to grab him. My mother was a churchgoer but the rest of us had given it up as we got older. But suddenly Leroy seemed to want all that old-time religion. He started reading the Bible morning, noon and night. He talked about a new start, a new birth even, getting baptised, all sorts of stuff. I took it all with a pinch of salt. And then suddenly he packed his bags and took off.'

'Do you recall which church it was?' Doug Mackintosh asked.

'Some creationist church off Queensway. I don't think it was all black, like a lot of them are. The pastor was a white man. I remember Leroy saying that.'

'I know the one you mean, and it's still there,' Mackintosh said. 'Perhaps we should take a look and see if anyone there remembers him, or knows where he ended up. What do you think, Kevin?'

Mower glanced at his watch and nodded. He felt that the wanted man's sister had proved a dead end. They knew little more now than they had when they arrived so another lead was welcome, and he did not have to report for work in Bradfield until the next morning.

'Fine,' he said. 'Let's do it.' He handed Leanne Parsons his card.

'If you think of anything else that might help us trace him, give me a call,' he said. Leanne studied the rectangle closely.

'Bradfield,' she said. 'I don't even know where that is.'

'Well, your brother evidently does,' Mower said. 'And believe me, when I say we need to talk to him, the need is urgent.' Leanne looked him straight in the eye for a moment.

'Is it murder?' she asked.

'I can't tell you that,' Mower prevaricated but Leanne nodded to herself, as if he had confirmed it.

'I'm just glad my parents have passed on,' she said. 'He was the apple of their eye when he was a little boy, but I always knew he was trouble.'

Three-quarters of an hour later, after passing Paddington Green police station, outside which Mower had declined the offer of a cup of canteen tea, they ground to a halt again beside a vaguely classical edifice in a quiet side street not far from the Bayswater Road, where Mackintosh repeated his double-yellow-line-and-police-business routine before leaving the car.

'This is Westminster,' he said heavily. 'Here they tow you away before you can get the kids out of the back seat.'

'It is a bit more hairy than when I worked here,' Mower said. 'I'm glad I came down on the train.'

'Believe it, mate,' Mackintosh said. 'Now then, this is the

place I thought must be our boy's salvation – or not, as it's turned out. The Congregation of the Blessed. Pastor: the Rev Stephen Pemberton Wright. And it looks as if the place is open even if it is a Wednesday morning so we're in luck.'

The two officers went up the steps and tried the handle of the heavy wooden doors between columns and pediment and found they obligingly swung open. Inside, a lofty white space was filled with rows of chairs facing a solid wooden pulpit, and a wooden dais and benches which looked as though they were designed for a choir, while the walls were covered with framed biblical scenes in garish colours. At the other end was what looked like a large tiled communal bath, with wooden steps leading up to its rim and down into the slightly murky-looking water. The place was warm and clean and well decorated; unusually so, Mower thought, for the base of a sect which he guessed had no truck with more established churches. As far as the two officers could see, the place was empty, but as they walked towards the pulpit, their footfalls echoing on the tiled floor, a door at the side opened and a heavy, middle-aged man, with a shock of untidy grey hair, came in. He did not seem especially surprised or pleased to see them and made his way slowly between the rows of chairs until they met in the central aisle, where he placed himself squarely in front of them.

'You look like policemen,' he said. 'Am I right?' Mower and Mackintosh showed him their warrant cards and he waved them into seats before turning a chair to face them, placing himself heavily in it as though movement was painful. His fleshy, grey face seemed to pale slightly with the effort but the eyes, bright blue above heavy violet bags, were sharp and alert.

'And you are, sir?' Doug Mackintosh asked. Their host was not in clerical dress but wore a comfortable, worn-looking pair of old-fashioned grey flannel slacks and a slightly threadbare woollen sweater of muddy brown with a polo neck.

'Stephen Wright,' he said. 'This is my church. How can I help you, gentlemen?'

'Have you been here long, Mr Wright?' Mower returned question for question.

'About twenty years, since the church opened. This used to be a non-conformist chapel, Unitarian, I believe, but it fell into disuse. It was in serious disrepair, sadly, but in spite of property prices round here, we were able to renovate it, with the help of some generous friends.'

'Are you part of a wider group? I can't say I've ever heard of the Congregation of the Blessed,' Mower ventured.

'We began years ago meeting in private houses for prayer and Bible work, but felt that we needed our own large meeting place eventually... But can I ask what brings you here? I'm sure it's not a casual visit, gentlemen, and I have other matters which need my attention.'

'Of course, sir, I was just interested...' Mower left the statement hanging, as if he might have ambitions to become one of this unprepossessing pastor's congregation.

'We're interested in someone who we think came here about eight or ten years ago, sir,' Mackintosh broke in. 'We thought at least you might remember him and possibly know where we can find him now.'

'One of my congregation?' Wright asked.

'We think so. A black lad, about twenty at the time, name of Leroy Jason Green. Ring any bells, sir?'

Wright glanced down at his hands, which were joined

almost as if in prayer, and did not answer immediately.

'May I ask why you want to trace him?' he asked, and when the two policemen gazed at him stolidly without response, he shook his head. 'No, I suppose not,' Wright said sadly.

'You knew him?' Mower snapped, his approach much less friendly now.

'I did,' Wright said. 'He came here regularly for a while and I believed at the time that he was one of our successes. He had been in trouble with the police in the past, been in prison, I believe, but once he found Jesus I thought he had turned a corner in his life. I had high hopes. He was an intelligent young man. I prayed...' He gazed almost pleadingly at Mower and then Mackintosh, but when he met no response his gaze turned sadly to his hands again.

'D'you know where he went when he left London?' Mower asked.

'I don't, I'm afraid. One Sunday he was here and the next he had gone. I never saw him again.'

'Is there anything else you can recall which might help us to trace him?' Mower persisted. 'It's very important we talk to him as soon as we can. We've spoken to his family but they have no idea where he is.'

Wright raised his eyes to the ceiling this time as if in search of divine guidance.

'It's just possible, I suppose...' He hesitated. 'He struck up a friendship with one of our benefactors. A successful man who contributed most of the cost of renovating this place. He came occasionally to services here and seemed to take an interest in Leroy. I know he was associated with various projects for young people in trouble. It's just possible that he took Leroy onto one of those schemes, gave him a start in

terms of employment or training, something of that sort. He
might have had contact with him after we did.'

'And this benefactor is...?' Mower snapped.

'A man called David Murgatroyd, a devout Christian. I
believe he's gone on to greater things these days. You should
be able to trace him. He did very well in the city, I believe, and
has become quite a philanthropist.'

'Bingo,' Mower exulted under his breath without letting his
expression alter by even a fraction of an inch.

'Anyone else you can think of?' he asked, but Wright shook
his head.

'It's only a possibility,' he said sorrowfully. 'I don't feel I
have been of great help to you, or to Leroy. I will pray for the
young man and hope that the trouble he seems to have fallen
into is not too great.'

'Was that a result?' Doug Mackintosh asked as he and
Mower went back to the Met officer's car which was being
hovered over by a slightly uncertain traffic warden.

'Police,' Mackintosh snapped and the woman backed off
with an attempt at a smile.

'Oh yes, that was a result,' Mower said. 'A very useful lead
indeed. Can you do me a real favour and drop me off at King's
Cross? I need to get back sharpish.' As Mackintosh set off
again with a slightly grudging shrug, Mower pulled out his
mobile and thumbed in DCI Thackeray's number, with a
satisfied grin.

Laura Ackroyd hung up her office phone with a hand that was
shaking uncontrollably and glanced around at her colleagues.
But no one seemed to have picked up the shrill voice that had
just assailed her for five minutes with a stream of invective

which made her shudder. Even worse was the feeling that the woman at the other end of the phone had some justification for her fury in view of the appalling news that she had rung to pass on to the *Gazette,* at the same time as cursing reporters and all their works.

Laura got to her feet unsteadily and on the way to Ted Grant's office touched the crime reporter, Bob Baker, on the shoulder.

'You'd better hear this,' she said, her mouth dry, and motioned him towards Grant's glass enclosure, where the editor could be seen flicking through the latest efforts of his staff with a typically dissatisfied expression on his face. He glanced up when the two reporters tapped on the half-open door and edged into his cluttered sanctum.

'You look as though you've lost a fiver and found a brass farthing,' he said to Laura, who knew that her face must reflect her distress.

'I've just had Debbie Stapleton's partner on the phone,' she said, her voice strained as she fought back tears. 'Debbie's taken an overdose and been rushed to the infirmary. Her partner's blaming us, Bob in particular but me too, apparently, and she's not going to do it quietly. She says she's already done an interview for local TV tonight. I'd say she's going to kick up as much of a stink as she possibly can. The *Gazette's* not going to come out of it very well.'

'Nor are Peter Maxwell and his academy friends,' Bob Baker put in defensively. 'They're the ones who decided to persecute the woman. It's no good trying to shoot the bloody messenger.'

'There are messengers and messengers, Bob, and you're not one I'd like delivering to me,' Laura said, throwing caution to the winds. Bob opened his mouth to retort angrily but Ted Grant broke in.

'Enough already,' he said. 'Let's not waste time blaming each other. Laura, did this so-called partner – does she have a name by the way? – did she mention Maxwell or Murgatroyd? Has she got them in her sights as well?'

'Her name's Maggie Benwell, and she's going to spread the blame as widely as she can, that was very clear. She's blaming us for outing Debbie on the front page, and the school and the council for suspending her and putting an end to her career. She's virtually accusing us all of hounding Debbie to death. She's got everyone in her sights – the *Gazette*, the council, Murgatroyd, the lot. The only thing she didn't mention was that she apparently took off herself and left Debbie on her own to face the crisis. I didn't reckon that was very supportive behaviour either.'

'How to you know that?' Grant asked sharply.

'I spoke to Debbie earlier today to warn her that the national press might be landing on her doorstep any minute, in particular Vince Newsom, who we all know is not the most gentle of ministers to the walking wounded. She was there all on her own and sounded bloody terrified.'

'Right, where is this Benwell woman, at the moment?'

'She didn't say, but I expect she's at the hospital,' Laura said.

'So get down there, try to make contact and persuade her that we don't make the news, we just report it. Bob, you get up to their cottage and see what you can winkle out up there. There's bound to be a copper or two you can chat up. And the neighbours. See who did turn up from London. I'm sure we can give this a bit of a spin in the direction of ruthless paparazzi from the nationals if we try hard enough.'

'And what about Maxwell and Murgatroyd?' Laura asked. 'They've got some hard questions to answer, haven't they? Maggie Benwell's right about that, at least. They've behaved disgracefully.'

'I'll talk to them myself,' Grant said cautiously. 'It's not that unusual, you know, for head teachers to get booted out if they've been running a crap school. Ms Stapleton can't have been too surprised at that possibility.'

Laura stared at her boss open-mouthed.

'You're going to let them off the hook,' she said, her stomach tightening. 'All that stuff – crazy God-botherers, bullying, sex discrimination, homophobia – that I've been researching, and now a woman driven to suicide, and you'll let it ride?'

'I'll talk to them,' Grant snapped. 'As I hear it, this may be the least of Peter Maxwell's troubles, so leave it to me, will you?'

Laura felt the colour drain out of her face as a wave of nausea overtook her. She spun on her heel without another word and made it to the cloakroom just in time. As she splashed cold water on her face and gazed at herself in the mirror, hardly recognising her own reflection, she knew that she had to make some more hard decisions quickly. Her whole life, she thought, and that of her baby, were in limbo, and she could no longer carry on like this. She pulled her mobile out of her bag and thumbed in Michael Thackeray's number.

'I must talk to you,' she said softly when he responded. 'Please, please come home tonight.'

For a moment she thought her plea was going to be

rebuffed, but then the familiar voice came back, filling her with euphoria for a second.

'About eight,' Thackeray said. 'I'll see you then.'

Half an hour later she left the *Gazette* building, unsure whether she ever wanted to cross its threshold again.

CHAPTER SIXTEEN

Laura woke up alone in bed the next morning, puzzled for a moment at the sounds of movement in the living room next door. Then the events of the previous afternoon and evening came flooding back and she groaned faintly. Everything, both professional and personal, seemed to be falling apart, and as the first wave of nausea, which was becoming a regular morning occurrence, hit her, she buried her head under the bedclothes and closed her eyes.

Within minutes she felt a hand on her shoulder and peered out of her cocoon to find Michael Thackeray, already fully dressed, standing by the bed holding a cup of tea in his hand.

'I brought you this,' he said awkwardly. 'When Aileen was pregnant she found it helped.'

Thackeray had stayed the night after an evening of inconclusive wrangling over the future, but had chosen to sleep on the sofa, and she had not objected. They both knew that if they found themselves in bed together the sexual chemistry that there had always been between them would prove irresistible, and that would not solve their problems.

Thackeray sat on the edge of the bed as Laura sipped her tea disconsolately.

'I have to go to work now,' he said. 'This murder case I'm working on looks as if it may blow up into something much bigger than we anticipated. There may have been other similar killings elsewhere.'

'A serial killer?' she asked, but her heart was not really in the question. There was too much else on her mind.

'Possibly,' Thackeray said. 'You've had contact with this man David Murgatroyd, haven't you? What's he like?'

Laura looked at him in astonishment for a moment.

'Surely you're not looking at him for your murder, are you? He's some sort of born-again puritan. I can't see him going dogging in the woods.'

'No,' Thackeray said, smiling faintly. 'But he does seem to have had some contact years ago with someone we're interested in. I want to see whether he knows where he is.'

'Well, he doesn't like answering questions, that's for sure,' Laura said. 'I wish you luck. The man's a bastard, if you want my opinion. It was his religious bullying put Debbie Stapleton in hospital.'

'You take these things too hard, Laura,' Thackeray said. 'Do you want me to come back tonight?'

'If you want to,' Laura mumbled.

'I do want to. I hate to see you like this, you know that.'

'You know what to do about it,' Laura said bitterly.

'Yes,' Thackeray said, but would not meet her eyes. 'Are you going to work today?'

'No,' Laura said flatly. 'I'll call in sick. I want to go to the hospital again to see Debbie Stapleton. And I want some time to think.'

Thackeray sighed and ran his hand gently over her face and hair, spread in a red cloud over the pillow, before kissing her on the cheek.

'I won't get much time to think today,' he said. 'But I will see you later. I love you, Laura, you know that. Take care.'

Laura lay back on the pillows with her eyes closed long after she heard the front door of the flat close. For all Thackeray's solicitude, and she never doubted for a moment that it was genuine, she knew that he was still deeply ambivalent about committing himself to another child. And she could see no way of shifting him. To all intents and purposes she was on her own in this.

Eventually she crawled out of bed, called the office to tell them she was not coming in until later, showered and dressed and contemplated going down to the infirmary to see how Debbie Stapleton had fared overnight. She had made the same journey the previous afternoon, at Ted Grant's insistence, though with absolutely no confidence that she would discover anything of use to the *Gazette*. In that expectation, at least, she had been proved right, but after she had failed to extract any information at all from the press-relations manager she had found herself back in reception where a woman she vaguely recognised was sitting alone in a chair against the wall, red-eyed and twisting a handkerchief in her hand. Their eyes met, and the woman suddenly leapt to her feet as if she had been stung.

'You're that woman from the *Gazette*,' she had said vehemently. 'Debbie said you had red hair. What the hell are you doing skulking around here like a ghoul? Haven't you and your friends done enough damage?'

'You must be Maggie,' Laura had come back quietly,

realising this would be a difficult situation to defuse. At least Maggie had not returned to the ranting attack she had launched on the telephone. 'I'm sorry about all this, but you must realise that Debbie invited me to school to tell me what was going on there. I really don't think I can be accused of harassing her. How is she, by the way? Is she going to be OK?'

'It's taken me hours to find out,' Maggie Benwell had said, her face contorted with bitterness. 'Apparently they only issue bulletins to 'family' – and I'm not 'family', am I? I had to go to the hospital management to convince them that I'm effectively her next of kin before they'd tell me she was recovering. But she's taken bloody paracetamol and that can have long-term effects. She's not out of danger yet. But I don't want you printing that in your bloody newspaper. Let us have some privacy, for God's sake.'

'I don't think this story is going to stay out of the *Gazette* whatever I do,' Laura said. 'She has a lot of campaigners like Steve O'Mara on her side, all of them out to stop David Murgatroyd, and they'll make capital out of what's happened, I should think. She's in the middle of a very public battle, I'm afraid, Maggie, and that's going to be even more true now.'

Maggie Benwell had turned away and sat down again, dabbing her eyes and then twisting her handkerchief in her hand.

'I wanted us to go for a civil ceremony, then I'd have some rights. I should be up there in the ward with her instead of down here like a bloody pariah.'

'Is she in intensive care?' Laura had asked.

'Yes, and they're strict about visitors up there. Relatives only.'

'I'm sorry,' Laura had said, turning away, feeling defeated, leaving Maggie to her sad vigil alone.

This morning, feeling drained and still nauseous herself, she had driven down into the town centre and made her way to the infirmary, hoping against hope that Debbie's condition had improved overnight. And when she inquired at reception she was relieved to hear that the head teacher had been moved to one of the main wards and could have visitors. She took the lift to the third floor and ventured cautiously onto the ward and immediately saw Maggie Benwell at Debbie Stapleton's bedside at the end of the ward. The two women spotted her almost immediately and exchanged a few words and Laura was not surprised to see little warmth in either of their eyes as she approached.

'I'm not on duty today,' she said cautiously, wanting to avoid another tirade from Maggie. 'I was in town and wondered how you were...?' Debbie Stapleton was leaning back against her pillows, ashen-faced and with dark circles beneath her eyes, one hand clutching her partner's.

'You warned me what would happen,' she said so quietly that Laura had to strain to catch her words. 'Thanks for that, at least.'

'I shouldn't have gone off like that,' Maggie said. 'I should have realised...'

Debbie squeezed her hand hard.

'You're here now,' she said.

'What are you going to do about the council and these academy people?' Maggie asked, clearly still in no mood to let anyone off the hook. 'Is the *Gazette* going to expose how they've been behaving?'

Laura sighed.

'I don't know,' she said honestly. 'I hope so, but I wouldn't bank on it.' She thought of Ted Grant's cosy relationship with many of Bradfield's movers and shakers, who seemed only too ready to take David Murgatroyd's plans to their hearts, and guessed that his victims stood little chance of a fair hearing. She could just imagine the whispered conversations about hysterical women and emotional reactions even without any of the covert homophobia which would no doubt also rise to the surface like scum on a stagnant pond, and she shrugged.

'I'll see what I can do,' she said, as she got up to go, content that Debbie was back in the safe hands of her lover. And if I get nowhere with that, she thought, I may well call it a day myself.

Sir David Murgatroyd arrived at Bradfield's central police station with his solicitor in a top-of-the-range BMW precisely five minutes before the hour of his appointment with Superintendent Jack Longley and DCI Michael Thackeray. He glanced at his watch as he got out of the car.

'Half an hour, Dixon,' he said to the driver. 'I should think that would be more than adequate, don't you?' He glanced quizzically at his lawyer who scurried round the back of the car to fall into step beside him.

'More than enough, I should think, Sir David.'

They were shown quickly from reception to Longley's office and offered chairs across from Longley's desk, arranging impeccably tailored suits to their satisfaction as Thackeray took the report Sergeant Mower had prepared on his trip to London to a seat at the table underneath the window overlooking the town hall square below.

'It's good of you to come in, Sir David,' Longley said with

what Thackeray felt was a touch too much deference in his voice. 'But my officers feel that you might be able to help us in a matter of identification.'

Murgatroyd raised an eyebrow at that but his solicitor filled the slight pause.

'My client is very happy to help in any way he can, if it is within his power,' he said.

'DCI Thackeray is the senior investigating officer in this case, so I'll leave him to pursue this with you.'

'Thank you,' Thackeray said, flicking through his file although he knew exactly what it said since he had picked it up from his desk as soon as he got into the office. Mower had been hovering by the door, with excited eyes, and had followed him into his office.

'I think we may have a lead to this bastard,' he had said. 'At least a link with Bradfield, even though our man seems to be a Londoner born and bred.' Thackeray had read his report carefully and then nodded.

'We need to talk to this man, Murgatroyd,' he said. 'I'll see the super as soon as he's in and tell him what we've got. It may be that Murgatroyd's not even in Bradfield. He seems to have interests all over the country, but we'll get hold of him somewhere. Hopefully he'll remember our Leroy, may even know where he is now.' But it had turned out that Murgatroyd had been at home at Sibden House, had agreed readily enough to an interview and had arrived at the station with his solicitor precisely at the time agreed.

'If I may inquire exactly what case we are talking about here?' his solicitor now addressed himself to Thackeray. 'Your officer was not very explicit on the phone, apparently.' The two men waited for Thackeray's answer with expressions of mild curiosity on their faces.

'As you may know, we are investigating the particularly brutal murder of a young woman whose partially buried body was found two days ago on a lonely stretch of moorland between Bradfield and Manchester.' An expression of surprise flickered across the solicitor's face and he glanced at his client, who remained completely impassive.

'You mentioned a question of identification...?' the lawyer asked, more tentative now as he took on board information that had obviously been a shock to him.

'Yes, we have forensic evidence that leads us to wish to question a man called Leroy Jason Green who was living, some nine or ten years ago, in West London,' Thackeray said, watching Murgatroyd closely. 'Did you ever meet Leroy Green, Mr Murgatroyd?'

Murgatroyd met Thackeray's gaze directly for the first time and he shrugged slightly.

'Not that I can recall,' he said. 'Is there any particular reason why you think I might have done?'

'You both had some connection with a church in Bayswater, I understand,' Thackeray said. 'Do you remember that?'

Murgatroyd continued to stare at Thackeray blankly for a moment and then slowly nodded.

'You must mean Stephen Wright's worthy effort? What did he call it – the Congregation of the Blessed? Something like that? I do remember Stephen. A good man, if somewhat disorganised. But a bit out of his depth, I always thought, with some of the young people he recruited from Notting Hill and Paddington. Is this young man Leroy one of his lost sheep? It is possible I met him without taking his name on board. I take it he's West Indian?'

Thackeray nodded.

'By descent,' Thackeray said. 'Mr Wright seemed to think that he might have joined one of the training schemes you were involved in yourself at that time. Do you remember him in that context?'

'Not individually, no,' Murgatroyd said with what sounded like genuine regret. 'There were a lot of young black men on those schemes. Some went on to make a success of their lives, others didn't. Presumably if Leroy Green is now a murder suspect, he was one of the ones we failed with. I have always thought, looking back, that I was too preoccupied with my business interests at that time to give the charitable activities I was involved in as much attention as they deserved. But then, if I hadn't done that, I certainly wouldn't have been able to become involved in education as heavily as I am today.'

He offered a self-deprecating smile and glanced at his solicitor.

'I do have a photograph that might jog your memory,' Thackeray said. 'Green has a criminal record.' He took the police snapshot of a sulky-looking prisoner from his file and handed it to Murgatroyd, who did little more than glance at it before handing it back.

'I'm sorry, but no,' Murgatroyd said. 'This is all a very long time ago, Mr Thackeray, and I really don't think you can expect me to remember every youngster who went to Stephen Wright's church, much less the even greater number who Mr Wright tried to help in other ways. My input was largely financial not personal. I did my best to help, but was not really actively involved.'

'This is what our computer people think he might look like after ten years or so,' Thackeray persisted, handing

Murgatroyd another picture which Murgatroyd studied briefly again.

'Have you met that man, or anyone who looks like him, more recently, in Bradfield perhaps?' Thackeray pressed him. But Murgatroyd shook his head again.

'Sorry,' he said.

'You're sure?'

'Absolutely.'

'Is there anything else my client can help you with, Superintendent?' the solicitor said, closing his own file with a snap of finality. Longley glanced at Thackeray who shook his head slightly.

'Thank you for coming in, Sir David,' Longley said and watched as Thackeray opened the door for them and summoned a passing constable to escort them out of the building.

'Not much joy there, then,' Longley said. Thackeray shrugged.

'I'm not sure I believed him,' he said. 'But we'll have to take his word for it for the moment.'

'Keep me up to speed, Michael,' Longley said. 'I'm already getting hints from the top that there are complaints coming in from some of the men you brought in yesterday for further questioning. Not that I want that to stand in the way of your investigation in any way, but tread carefully with these people. They can't all be guilty and some of them can make our life uncomfortable in one way or another.'

Thackeray looked at his boss for a moment without speaking.

'I'll take that in the spirit in which I'm sure it's meant,' he said, and walked out, closing the door very firmly behind him.

Sergeant Kevin Mower waylaid him on the way downstairs to his own office.

'Has Murgatroyd gone, guv?' he asked. He was clutching a sheaf of papers in his hand and looked as excited as his perpetually cool exterior ever allowed.

'He says he doesn't recall Green in any shape or form,' Thackeray said.

'Well, that could be bullshit,' Mower said. 'Take a look at this and see what you think.'

Thackeray waved Mower into his own office where the sergeant spread a photocopied sheet of newsprint onto the DCI's desk, together with the artist's impression of what Leroy Green might look like ten years after his police mugshot had been taken. The page, which had been taken, Thackeray noticed, from a copy of the *Bradfield Gazette* of a week previously, included a photograph of a group of people outside Sutton Park School, above a brief item on the academy plans over Laura Ackroyd's byline.

'So?' he said, reading the caption underneath the photograph. This identified the head teacher, Debbie Stapleton, Sir David Murgatroyd and Councillor Peter Maxwell, all of whom he recognised. It had been taken as Murgatroyd arrived to make his first visit to the school after the local council gave provisional approval to the academy proposal, and there were half a dozen people clustered behind the main party, none of whom looked familiar to Thackeray.

'Look here,' Mower said, pointing to a blurred image at the very back of the group. 'How like our computer impression is that?' he asked.

Thackeray pulled the computer image from his own file and laid it close to the newspaper photograph where a solitary dark face was half obscured by a figure in front of him. He glanced at Mower doubtfully.

'There's a resemblance, I suppose,' he said cautiously. 'Find out who he is. Don't be fooled by the colour of his skin. It could be anyone, a teacher or a governor at the school, perhaps. There's not necessarily any connection with our inquiry. But it's certainly worth a couple of phone calls, one to Laura, if you must.'

'I'll get a digital image of the picture from the *Gazette* if I can and see if we can enhance it,' Mower said. 'The other thing you need to know is that we've got an interesting result from forensics. It's very tentative as yet, but they think they've found DNA on the body itself that is not the same as the traces they've got from the fingerprints. In other words, they think at least two people have been in contact with the body. It'll take a while to confirm – the traces from the fingerprints are minute, you know how it goes. But they thought we would want to bear it in mind.'

'Good, we'll bear it in mind,' Thackeray said. 'Then we can do some elimination. We've got too many people under suspicion at the moment. If we can persuade some of them to give us a sample voluntarily so they can rule themselves out, everyone will be a whole lot happier, including the super.'

'Getting a bit close to the golf club, is it, guv?' Mower asked with a grin. 'Or his cronies in the Clarendon bar?'

'That thought's unworthy of you, Kevin,' Thackeray said, with a wry smile. 'But I think it's safe to say that if we offer some of our doggers a way of eliminating themselves from a murder inquiry, they'll jump at it.'

'I'm sure you're right, guv,' Mower said.

Back in the murder incident room, he did a quick check on

how far detectives had progressed with their various tasks. Ten minutes later DCI Thackeray came down to the incident room himself to conduct the day's review of the progress in the case and to discover that a few more new elements had been thrown into the mix.

'We may have got something significant from our trawl through misper records,' Mower said. 'We asked other forces if they had any missing women who had been involved in swingers or dogging groups and we've had a few possibles. Obviously it's hit-and-miss. Not every investigating officer would have asked questions like that of grieving husbands or boyfriends. But there are half a dozen where questions were asked and which seem to bear some similarities to Karen Bastable's disappearance. None of them has ever been seen or heard from again, and in a couple the male partner was suspected of unlawful killing for a time, but there were never any charges. We've asked all the areas involved to send us full details.'

'So you think there's possibly a serial killer out there who's generally made a better job of hiding the bodies?' Thackeray asked.

'It looks like a possibility,' Mower said. 'But as to who it is, the only identification we have is still the fingerprint evidence from the plastic wrapping Karen was found in.'

'Right,' Thackeray agreed. 'So our top priority has to be tracking down Leroy Green. Any progress there?'

'Again, we've circulated other forces, and looked at all the databases, but without any positive response so far. There's no record that he's dead, but no other record of him, either, for the last nine years that we can trace. No driving licence or vehicle registrations, his NI number hasn't been used, he's not come to police attention in any way, he hasn't joined any of the services. He's either gone abroad or very successfully gone underground.'

'With a new identity, perhaps?' Thackeray said.

'That's not easy for a lad of nineteen, twenty to organise,' Mower objected.

'Did he have a passport?'

'Yes, issued when he was sixteen for a school trip. But it's long expired and hasn't been renewed,' Mower said. 'He could have gone abroad for a while, but he would need a passport to get back into the country, and we know he was here in Yorkshire just days ago. That wasn't a blurred or partial print they found, it was a good clear image. There's no doubt he was there when Karen's body was parcelled up like that. He's an accessory if not a killer.'

'Anything else?' Thackeray glanced around his assembled detectives who appeared to be in sombre mood.

'I was looking at the Internet,' Mohammed Sharif said. 'There are sites run by various groups with unusual sexual preferences.' The Asian DC's deadpan delivery gave nothing away to indicate his personal views of such activities, but none of his colleagues had any doubt that he had found this particular inquiry profoundly troubling.

'That includes doggers?' Thackeray asked.

'Yes, it does, though there's nothing specific to this area, sir. But it might be somewhere someone who wanted to set up a group would start. I reckon the next step is to make contact with some of these other people – see if anyone knows anything.'

'Absolutely right,' Thackeray said. 'If there are networks, our man may well be exploiting them to find new victims, using the groups to make contact with women for his own purposes. Make that a priority, Omar.'

Sharif nodded.

'And his purposes might be...' Sharif hesitated. 'He likes perverted sex, or he hates it?'

'You never know with these psychos,' Mower said. 'What's going on in their heads is a mystery and no psychologist I've ever come across has ever explained it adequately. Fortunately in this case we've got some good, strong forensic leads, so we don't need to go delving into perverse motivation just yet. Just follow your Internet links, Omar, and see where they take you. OK, guv?'

Mower glanced at Thackeray for approval and received a brief nod. The sergeant knew that the DCI would not hesitate to call in a forensic psychologist if he thought it was necessary but, with only one body and strong leads to follow, that point had not yet come. Old-fashioned detective work looked as though it might yet get a result and, as the briefing ground to its inconclusive end, Kevin Mower and the rest of the team were clearly keen to get on with it.

CHAPTER SEVENTEEN

'His name's Winston Sanderson, and he's David Murgatroyd's gofer, right-hand man, gatekeeper, whatever,' Laura Ackroyd said, glancing again at the photograph she had printed off the *Gazette*'s database for Kevin Mower, who was sitting across a table in the Lamb that lunchtime. 'From my point of view, the man's a complete menace. He guards Murgatroyd like a well-trained Rottweiler. You'd think bloody Sir David was some sort of premier-league footballer, he's that well protected.'

'Perhaps he's had some bad experiences with the tabloids. Not everyone is keen on this business of selling off state schools to dubious millionaires, after all, especially not the religious ones,' Mower said, sipping his pint reflectively. He had been shocked, when Laura joined him, to see how pale and unwell she looked but he did not quite know how to broach the subject too directly.

'Maybe,' Laura said dubiously. 'It looks as if tabloid culture's claimed another victim in Debbie Stapleton. Did you hear about that?' Mower nodded.

'She's going to be all right, isn't she?'

'I think so,' Laura said. 'She's out of intensive care, though there's various nasty little pieces appeared in the London papers which won't make her feel any better when she reads them. I'm not sure I'll ever forgive Bob Baker for starting this all off.'

'The man's only fit for a tabloid himself. I don't know why the *Gazette* puts up with him.'

'Ted Grant not only puts up with him but encourages him, because at heart Ted's a tabloid vulture himself,' Laura said. 'He's never got over some brief stint he did on the *Globe*. Everything up here on a local rag is just a pale shadow of what he'd really like to get up to. But I can't see him ever leaving. No one else would have him now. So we're in for years of him getting more bitter and frustrated.'

'I'm sure you're right,' Mower said. 'So Sanderson is Murgatroyd's minder, protecting him from the likes of Bob Baker? Is that right?'

'Seems to be. Though Sir David seems to be a little more open to my approaches. I have met him, with Sanderson's reluctant approval.'

'No doubt the result of your undoubted charms,' Mower said. 'But why do I get the impression that this man Murgatroyd is not bringing much except trouble to Bradfield?'

'My feeling entirely, though I can't take sides so openly in reporting it. But it's difficult to see how the protesters are going to get their case over to the powers that be with the remotest chance of success, let alone win the battle. The council stands to gain too much from this academy scheme: a brand new school to replace a crumbling ruin and, if he keeps his promises, a whole lot of troublesome kids taken off their hands. Councillor Peter Maxwell thinks it's Christmas with bells on.'

Mower laughed and then thought better of it, burying his face in his glass again. Laura was doing no more than sip at her vodka and tonic, he noticed.

'What?' she said, quick to pick up on his hesitation.

'Let's just say that Councillor Maxwell has got a few other things on his mind just now that I couldn't possibly tell a reporter about,' he said. Laura gave him a sharp look.

'And what, exactly, am I supposed to make of that?' she asked.

'Anyway, tell me what you know about this man Sanderson? Is he local?' Mower knew he had gone too far, and shifted the subject sharply.

'No, I don't think so. He sounds like a Londoner. Though I can't say he's ever got very personal. He seems to think the sun shines out of David Murgatroyd, though. Gods' gift, in Sanderson's view.'

'Can I show you something, strictly off the record?' Mower asked carefully.

'I suppose so, if it'll help,' Laura said.

Mower pulled the police mugshot of Leroy Green from his inside pocket and spread it out on the table.

'D'you think that could have been Sanderson nine or ten years ago, when he was about nineteen, twenty?'

Laura studied the photograph carefully for a moment and then shook her head.

'It could be, I suppose,' she said. 'But I couldn't be sure.' She smiled faintly. 'And I do know enough black people not to think they all look alike,' she said. 'But this is just a boy. Sanderson's a grown man. There's a slight resemblance, perhaps, but I couldn't identify him from this.'

'OK,' Mower said, hiding his disappointment. 'It was just a hunch.'

'I didn't think Michael allowed hunches,' Laura said quietly. 'Especially if they could be jumping to racist conclusions.'

'The odd one gets through,' Mower said.

'Is this part of your murder investigation?'

'Off the record, yes,' Mower said. 'But the whole thing looks as if it might blow up into a national investigation. It looks as if there are some other cases with similarities to Karen Bastable's death. One in Peterborough, another in Swindon, one in Preston and a few other places.'

'You mean a serial killer?'

'Well, it's only a possibility at the moment,' Mower said. 'It needs a lot more work on it yet. A well-travelled serial killer, if that's what we decide is really going on, and that's unusual. So don't get too excited. It's another hunch at the moment, if it's anything. But don't worry, the *Gazette* will be the first to know if we get anything definite.'

'If you're right, and Sanderson is your suspect, that list of yours sounds very like the list of places where Murgatroyd has set up his academies. That would put Sanderson in the right place, possibly even at the right time. I've no idea how long he's been working for David Murgatroyd.'

'That's a long shot, but worth checking out,' Mower said. 'Enough to let us talk to him, anyway.'

'Glad to have helped,' Laura said. She finished her drink. 'I'd better get back to work. I've a lot on.' She hesitated for a moment.

'Well, thanks for that,' Mower said. 'Don't tell the boss that

I was being indiscreet, will you?' Mower drained his glass and was astonished when Laura glanced away, her eyes full of tears.

'Chance would be a fine thing,' she said.

'What is it, Laura?' Mower said, putting a tentative hand over hers on the table. 'You don't look your usual blooming self. Have you split up or something?'

'Not quite,' Laura said. 'At least I don't think so. But it's a close-run thing.'

'Oh, shit,' Mower said. 'But I'm glad you told me. I might have put my foot right in it... If it's any comfort, I don't think the boss is a happy bunny, either. In fact, now I come to think of it, he's seemed seriously distracted the last few days.'

'So he bloody should be,' Laura said, jumping to her feet, her face suddenly flaming. 'I'm sorry I wasn't much help with your pictures, Kevin. It's good to see you.' And she swept out of the pub, copper hair flying, drawing admiring glances as she went.

DCI Michael Thackeray was sitting at his desk, apparently staring into space, when DS Kevin Mower reported back.

'I had a chat with Laura,' he said tentatively. 'She says the black guy in the *Gazette*'s picture is Murgatroyd's PA, name of Winston Sanderson. And she doesn't reckon he looks much like our mugshot from ten years back, I'm afraid, though he could have been in some of the places where there've been similar disappearances. I'll check out his background, just in case. And bring him in for a chat, if I can find him. We really need to eliminate a few people from this inquiry. Not all the doggers can have had contact with Karen, but some of them must have done. We need to know who.'

'Have you started asking them for voluntary DNA samples?' Thackeray asked.

'In hand, guv,' Mower said. 'Laura did say that she thought Sanderson was a Londoner, incidentally. That may mean something or nothing. And there's an overlap between where Sanderson has been involved in setting up these new schools and our similar cases.'

'Check it all out,' Thackeray said irritably. 'At this rate we'll be getting another force coming in to review our progress and as far as I can see we're getting nowhere.'

'Guv,' Mower said and turned to go back to the incident room and then half turned. 'I thought Laura was looking very pale,' he said. 'Is she not well?'

The sudden anger on Thackeray's face took Mower by surprise. He knew he'd crossed a line that had been unspoken between them for years, but had hoped it would be taken for no more than friendly concern. But his boss did not erupt in the way Mower expected, though he looked for a second or two as if he might. Instead he ran his hand through his hair and shrugged with a weariness that made Mower think he should be inquiring about his health as well as Laura's.

'She'll be OK,' he said. 'It's just a winter bug. Nothing to worry about.'

'Right,' Mower said and turned away again to hide the disbelief in his eyes. He had seen Laura and the DCI at odds before, but this time, he thought as he left the office, it looked terminal.

When the sergeant had gone, Thackeray resumed his agonised reverie. He must, he thought, have something constructive to say to Laura this evening when he kept his promise to go back to the flat. But when he faced himself squarely in his mind's eye, he had to confess that he was no nearer to deciding what he wanted to do than he had been on the day she had told him that she was expecting a baby. The thought of another child filled him with joy, but the thought of making himself vulnerable to the loss of another child filled him with an even more overwhelming panic. He could still see no way of reconciling the two.

Laura drove out of Bradfield feeling a slight sense of exhilaration. The call from Sir David Murgatroyd had come out of the blue.

'I promised to invite you up to Sibden,' he said. 'I have a window this afternoon if you'd like to come. Tea and cakes, I suppose, would be appropriate, d'you think? I think my housekeeper could manage that. A small indulgence in recompense for being so elusive earlier on?'

'But Winston Sanderson said...' She did not hesitate to express her surprise at this unexpected turn of events. And after her chat with Sergeant Mower, she did not think she wanted to meet Sanderson face-to-face again so soon, although she had mentally discounted what seemed like far-fetched police suspicions of Murgatroyd's PA. To her mind, it could be a case of someone in CID seizing on any available black face, however blurred, that might fit the charge sheet. If she had been on normal speaking terms with Michael Thackeray, she thought, she might have remonstrated with him, but what drove her now was to prise out of Murgatroyd some sort of normal reaction to Debbie Stapleton's suicide attempt. If the man was human at all, he must be blaming himself to some extent for that, although she had serious doubts about whether she could persuade him to admit it.

'Winston? Oh, you don't need to worry about Winston.' Murgatroyd laughed. 'He's overprotective on occasion, as you know. Anyway, he's away at the moment. He has to be in London for me today. Nanny need never know.'

Laura had glanced at her watch.

'Yes, that's fine then,' she said. 'I could be with you in about half an hour? Is that OK?' She grabbed her coat and her tape recorder, glanced towards Ted Grant's office but could see that he was head-to-head with the marketing manager so thought better of interrupting him in what was obviously aggressive mid-flow, and left the office to drive the ten miles up the Maze valley to Murgatroyd's home.

The gates swung open smoothly, as did the front door when she rang the bell, and she found herself face-to-face again with David Murgatroyd in what was obviously his country gentleman mode, khaki drill trousers and a checked shirt, open at the neck, and a chunky, light blue sweater. He seemed much more relaxed than when they had last met in Sheffield and Laura guessed that might be because he felt less threatened on home turf. It might just be possible, she thought, to get him to open up about his own traumatic childhood here.

'Come in, Laura. It's good to see you again,' he said, waving her through into the spacious sitting room where Winston Sanderson had taken her the last time she had come to Sibden House. 'I'll get us some tea in a minute. I'll have to do it myself, I'm afraid. I'd quite forgotten my housekeeper was taking the afternoon off to go to a funeral. But I'm sure I can cope.'

'I'm sure you can,' Laura said. 'This place must take a lot of staff to run.'

'Especially the garden,' Murgatroyd said. 'Are you interested in gardens? The rain seems to have stopped so we could take a turn around later. But first let me make tea and we can continue where we left off in Sheffield. I felt a little – what should I say – dissatisfied with our discussion there.'

'You gave me enough to complete my feature,' Laura said. 'Although I could still add a paragraph or two if you feel that there's anything we haven't dealt with. It's not going in the paper until the beginning of next week. After all, the situation has changed now.'

'In what way?' Murgatroyd asked, his tone hardening slightly and the smile no longer quite reaching to his eyes.

'You must have heard what happened to Debbie Stapleton,' Laura said, seeing no reason to pull her punches with this man. 'She's still seriously ill in hospital. Surely you must feel some responsibility for that.'

Murgatroyd was silent for a moment.

'I would have thought you and your colleagues were much more to blame for her situation,' he said. 'It was the *Gazette* which put her personal life all over the front page.'

'You were about to take away the job she loved,' Laura objected. 'It was that which caused the crisis in her life, I think.'

'She was at liberty to apply for the new headship,' Murgatroyd said, angry rather than defensive at Laura's assault. 'In fact, she did apply.'

'But you didn't shortlist her, presumably because of her sexuality. You wouldn't have appointed a lesbian, would you, even without all this publicity? That wasn't ever on.'

Murgatroyd spread out his hands in surrender.

'You're right, of course. I wouldn't have appointed her. You know the Christian position on homosexuality. She could never have run one of my academies.'

'Not all Christians take that view,' Laura objected.

'The Bible is quite clear on the matter,' Murgatroyd said, flatly. He gazed at Laura for a moment until she began to feel slightly uncomfortable, and then he relaxed again and smiled.

'Let's not get into an argument,' he said. 'I invited you up to show you the house and garden, not to argue about my local problems. I thought we'd finished with all that. I'll make some tea and then show you round. Is that all right?'

Laura shrugged resignedly. She was obviously not going to get anything more useful for her feature article so she might as well let this man with his abhorrent views give her his tour so that she could decently make her escape.

'Fine,' she said. 'Let's have tea.' She glanced at her watch. 'I don't have a lot of time.'

Murgatroyd got up and made his way to the door.

'Did you inherit that red hair from your mother?' he asked unexpectedly. Laura half turned in her chair, slightly thrown by this suddenly personal turn in the conversation. But she half smiled.

'From my grandmother,' she said. 'It skipped a generation.'

'Yes, it does that sometimes,' Murgatroyd said, as he left the room, closing the door behind him. While he was away Laura got up and walked around the spacious sitting room, glancing at the bookcases, filled with leather-bound classics which did not look as if they had ever been opened, and studying the paintings – originals in oils which seemed slightly old-fashioned even to her untutored eye – almost as if the room had been designed to order quite recently to a template established in the 1950s rather than later. None of the furniture looked antique or even as if it had been handed down from parents to son. It was newish but Maples, not Habitat, good quality but traditional, as if the owner's taste had been set in stone a generation or more before his time.

Murgatroyd came back quite quickly, carrying a tray with a pot of tea and a plate of buttered scones.

'Mrs Bateman left everything ready for us,' he said. 'She is, as they say, a treasure. Will you pour?' Laura did as she was asked and sipped her tea thoughtfully. Murgatroyd had also fallen silent, although Laura was uncomfortably aware that those unusual blue and gold eyes were watching her with an intensity that she suddenly decided she did not like.

'Did you refurbish the house completely when you came back to it?' she asked, to break the spell.

'Completely,' he said. 'I wanted a clean sheet.'

'It must have held a lot of unpleasant memories for you after what happened to your mother,' Laura ventured. Murgatroyd did not answer immediately. His face seemed to close down and age before her eyes, before he shook himself slightly and gave an impatient grunt almost of exasperation.

'You don't understand,' Murgatroyd said. 'It was what happened to my baby sister that was important. She didn't inherit my mother's red hair either. It was what happened to her that I couldn't forgive, what I've never forgiven.' He stared intently into his teacup while Laura finished hers.

'Shall we have our walk round the garden now?' Murgatroyd asked, and somewhat brusquely handed Laura her jacket, which she had taken off and laid beside her on her chair. She put it on, deciding suddenly that she would go straight back to her car when she had taken a token walk round the grounds. For some reason she felt her confidence in the situation beginning to drain away. Murgatroyd suddenly seemed an oppressive presence and she wondered if he had sent the housekeeper away deliberately. For all his fervent claims to moral superiority, she decided she no longer trusted him.

She followed his lead to the back of the house where he unlocked a door into a conservatory.

'My mother had this built,' he said. 'One of the few good things she did in her life.' The room had been closed up and was hot and stuffy, green blinds on the windows half down giving a dim, underwater light. Laura felt a slight wave of nausea, mixed with relief that feeling unwell might give her the excuse she needed to get away.

'I was there, you know,' Murgatroyd said over his shoulder and he moved between the potted plants towards the garden doors.

'I'm sorry?'

Murgatroyd stopped and turned back towards her.

'I said I was there with my mother and sister when she walked into the lake. She left me in the car, but when I saw what was happening, I ran after them. I tried to get the baby off her. But she fell out of my mother's arms and I couldn't find her. I tried and tried but the water was too deep and too dark. I lost hold of her. They said later that she'd been tangled up in weeds below the surface.'

'That must have been terrible for you,' Laura said, fighting off a growing desire to throw up. 'And your mother drowned too?'

'She went in deeper and deeper. I swam out to her. I was a good swimmer even then. I made sure she drowned. It was what she wanted. And what she deserved. A life for a life, though I don't think I thought quite like that then. I was only a child myself. But I knew with a passion that if Jennifer was dead I wanted my mother dead, too.'

Laura gazed at Murgatroyd, her vision swimming, wondering if she was really hearing this man confess to matricide.

'I'm sorry,' she said, her voice sounding faraway. 'I don't feel very well.'

'Sit down for a moment,' Murgatroyd said, pulling up a wicker chair into which Laura sank gratefully.

'It's nothing,' she said. 'It's just that I'm pregnant. I'll be all right in a minute.' But as she gazed up at Murgatroyd's piercing eyes, she knew that she wouldn't. He stroked her hair tentatively as her eyes closed and darkness engulfed her.

'Such beautiful hair,' he whispered. 'Such beautiful auburn hair.'

CHAPTER EIGHTEEN

Michael Thackeray was surprised to see no lights on in Laura's flat when he pulled up outside at seven that evening. He had expected her to be at home waiting for him. He glanced at his mobile phone, but there were no messages, so he thumbed in Laura's number, only to find that she did not answer her phone, which was unusual. Ted Grant expected his reporters to be on call 24/7, all part of his fantasy existence as a high-octane editor, and Thackeray experienced a twinge of anxiety as he listened to the voice message on Laura's phone again, just to make sure.

He let himself into the flat and it was obvious from the dirty breakfast dishes still stacked in the sink that Laura had not been home since she had left for work. Perhaps she was driving, he thought, and would be back any minute. He took off his coat, switched on the TV news, and tried to put the problems between the two of them out of his mind until she came home. But the screen took up only half of his mind, and as the minutes ticked by he became more and more concerned.

Eventually he pulled out his phone again, and after failing

to reach Laura, put a call through to the Mendelsons. Vicky picked up, sounding harassed, and he could hear a child crying in the background. Naomi Laura, he thought, close to panic, the sound threatening to pull him apart. He took a deep breath.

'It's Michael,' he said quietly. 'Sorry to bother you, but do you know where Laura is? Is she with you?'

'I've no idea,' Vicky said, and hesitated, as if wanting to say more, but reluctant to commit herself. 'Hasn't she got her phone on?'

'Of course not, or I wouldn't be asking,' Thackeray snapped.

'I'm sorry,' Vicky said, her voice faint and the sobbing child suddenly much closer to the receiver. 'Sorry, David's not home and Naomi's not well. She's got a bad cold.'

'Has she told you how she's feeling?' Thackeray asked, desperate now.

'About the baby, you mean? Yes, we've spoken about it.' Vicky's voice was becoming more chilly. 'I thought you'd be delighted about that, both of you, I mean. But apparently not. I can't understand that, Michael, to be honest.'

'Has she told you what she's going to do about it?'

'A termination, you mean?' Vicky asked sharply. 'I don't think she wants that.'

'I just thought...she's not come home...'

'You thought she might be in hospital? Without telling you?' Vicky sounded incredulous.

'I just don't know what to think. She said she'd be here, at the flat, tonight, so we could talk...'

'I'm sorry, Michael,' Vicky said. 'I really am. But I don't know where she is, or what she's planning to do. I haven't seen her for a couple of days, and this is something you have to sort out between you. You know what I think. But I'm sure she wouldn't have arranged anything drastic without a word.'

'No, I'm sure she wouldn't,' Thackeray said, trying to sound confident and failing miserably. 'I'm sorry to bother you. I hope Naomi's better soon.' And he cut the connection abruptly. He did not have Joyce Ackroyd's number in his phone so he looked it up in the phone book, not remembering until he had listened to the number ringing unanswered for several minutes that Laura's grandmother was away on a visit to Laura's parents in Portugal.

'Damnation,' he said, as he cut the connection again. He flung himself back onto the sofa and considered his options. He could call Ted Grant to ask whether Laura had been sent unexpectedly on some assignment. Mobile phone signals could be intermittent in the hills of Yorkshire and that might explain why she had failed to reach him to tell him she would be late. But to do that meant exposing himself and Laura to the no doubt intrusive inquiries of her boss. Or he could pull rank and ask his own colleagues to try to trace her which, as she was only a couple of hours late, would expose him to some derision down at the station and longer-term gossip about his private life. Or he could just wait. He glanced at his watch with a sigh. It was ten past eight. He went into the kitchen and made himself a sandwich and a cup of coffee, but he found it almost impossible to eat. He switched the TV on again and flicked from channel to channel in a vain attempt to find something that would occupy his mind but there was nothing there that remotely overcame his growing conviction that he had forced Laura into doing something desperate. He glanced towards the cupboard where Laura kept her drinks, but he knew that if he set hands on her vodka he would empty the bottle and compound every problem that was already tormenting him. But as he gritted his teeth for a long wait, his mobile rang and he grabbed it with shaking hands, only to find that it was not Laura, but Sergeant Kevin Mower, at the other end. He could hardly bring himself to respond coherently, but what Mower was saying eventually got through to him, if dimly.

'We picked up Sanderson heading down the M1, guv,' Mower said. 'Suitcases packed in the back of the car. He says he wants to make a statement. I thought you might like to come in.'

'Give me fifteen minutes,' Thackeray said, his mind jerking into full consciousness, in spite of himself, as if it had been whipped back to life. 'I'll be there.'

Winston Sanderson was sitting in an interview room with a uniformed constable in attendance when Thackeray and Mower came in. He glanced up at them with a half smile which looked almost rueful.

'You took your time,' he said. 'I thought you were keen to get this case sorted.'

'Has he been cautioned?' Thackeray asked Mower, who nodded.

'Says he doesn't want a solicitor,' Mower said.

'Are you quite sure about that?' Thackeray asked Sanderson.

'Quite sure,' Sanderson said, looking almost at ease in his bleak surroundings.

'And you've volunteered to make a statement about the death of Karen Bastable?'

'That's right.'

Thackeray settled himself into one of the chairs opposite Sanderson and watched him closely while Mower switched on the tape recorder, slotted two tapes into it, and recorded the identities of those present.

'Let's get this quite clear,' Thackeray said, when the sergeant had finished the preliminaries. 'Do you confirm that, although you are known as Winston Sanderson, your real name is Leroy Jason Green, formerly of the Notting Hill area of London.'

'That's right,' Sanderson said, again with a slight smile. 'Seems I couldn't get away from him after all.'

'So what exactly do you want to tell us, Mr Green?' Thackeray asked. 'Take your time. And think carefully about what you are saying.'

'My boss let on that you were looking for me. You even asked him if he knew Leroy. He had no idea, of course. He never made the connection when I turned up on one of his training schemes with a different name.' He laughed this time, as if he had pulled off some particularly piquant practical joke. 'But I remembered him from seeing him once or twice with the old Rev Steve at that church I went to for a while. I couldn't believe it when he offered me a job. Anyway, I guessed I must have made some sort of mistake when he said you were looking for Leroy Green and somehow you'd linked Karen with some long-ago bad boy and his criminal record. Couldn't believe it. I thought I'd been so careful. But there you go.'

Sanderson's attitude set Thackeray's teeth on edge when he remembered the mutilated body he had last seen on Amos Atherton's table, tortured and mutilated into little more than a slab of raw meat. How could this well-dressed, self-assured young man, with his easy charm, have turned into the sort of monster who was capable of that level of depravity? Thackeray had never quite believed in the possibility of a real-life Jekyll and Hyde but it seemed as if he might just possibly be facing exactly that.

'You don't deny that you concealed Karen Bastable's body on Staveley Moor?' Thackeray asked.

Sanderson shrugged, his face more serious now.

'You obviously know I did, though I don't know how you know. What was it? A fingerprint? I wore gloves but I think I took them off for a moment when I got some dirt in my eye. It was wild up there. Stupid mistake.'

'So tell us everything that happened the night Karen disappeared,' Thackeray said.

Sanderson leant back in his chair and closed his eyes for a moment, as if rerunning a mental film of the events of that night.

'I was driving up near the forest,' he said. 'I'd been over to Lancashire for the boss, to Preston—'

'Preston?' Mower broke in, recalling the painfully collated list of missing women who just might be this man's other victims. 'Why Preston?'

'We have a new academy there,' Sanderson said, with no sign that he regarded the place as of any particular significance. 'Anyway, I decided to take the country route back, over the moors. When I started coming down it was dark but not very late and I noticed these cars going into the trees, one, two, three, after each other. I was curious, wasn't I? I wondered where they were going. So I followed them. They parked up in a circle in a clearing, and I stopped just a little way back to watch, just to see what they were doing. They ended up with quite a few cars there, in a big circle, and people got out, and then it got quite exciting.'

'You mean sexually exciting?' Thackeray asked.

Sanderson nodded with a little giggle.

'You have to admit a no-holds-barred orgy's a bit of a turn-on. I'm not quite such a saint as my boss.'

'So you joined in?' Thackeray's distaste was written all over his face and Mower could see the tension in his jaw and the clenched fists, which he had carefully hidden under the table.

'Nah,' Sanderson scoffed. 'Not then. Later. Most of the guys made off pretty sharpish, but the girls stayed behind for a gossip. Like they do. Comparing notes, little slags. Karen was the last to leave. I stopped her before she got into her car and persuaded her to come with me for a bit more fun and games. She didn't object. Quite liked the idea, I think. It's not just a myth, you know.'

'What isn't?' Thackeray asked sharply.

'That some white women fancy black men,' Sanderson said, almost as if talking to a five-year-old.

'So, you picked her up. Where did you take her?' Mower pressed.

'I couldn't really tell you,' Sanderson said. 'Just further back up onto the moors where I could park the car out of sight. I told her I was taking her to my place but that would never do. The boss wouldn't put up with women visiting, would he? Not at his precious Sibden House. That place is sacred, a sort of mausoleum to his dead sister. Anyway we found somewhere quiet. But then she got a bit stroppy. Didn't like some of the games I wanted to play. So I tied her up. And after that it's all a bit of a blur. I came round lying beside her in the heather, or what was left of her. So then I did go back to Sibden and got hold of some stuff to wrap the body in. Bin bags and that. I reckoned I needed to dump her much further away. I was just too close to home.'

'You took her with you in the car to Sibden House?' Thackeray snapped, but Sanderson shook his head.

'Not likely,' he said. 'Not in the state she was in. I went back for her, wrapped her up, snug as a bug, and then drove as far as I could in the opposite direction to bury her. I was mortified when she turned up so quickly. I thought it would be months, years maybe, before she was found up there. Like those kids on Saddleworth Moor. I suppose the papers will call me another Ian Brady, but I'm obviously not as good at hiding bodies as he was.'

'This is not a bloody beauty contest,' Mower said suddenly, surprising himself with his fury and banging his hand on the table between them until it shook in spite of its legs being bolted to the floor. 'You sick bastard.'

Sanderson shook slightly, though whether in amusement or fear it was difficult to tell. Thackeray put a restraining hand on Mower's arm and waited until he had calmed down slightly.

'And the weapons you used? You had those with you?' Thackeray asked, his own voice like ice.

'Old habits die hard. I had a knife.' Sanderson shrugged. 'I told you. I can't remember the details. I must have lost it completely at some point.'

'Can you recall why you cut off her hair?' Thackeray asked.

Sanderson looked at him blankly for a moment and then laughed.

'I really don't like red hair,' he said. 'I'd have taken the bottle-blond one for preference, but she went off in a car with her friend, didn't she? Safety in numbers, they must have thought, I suppose. Dead right, as it turned out.'

'And what did you do with Karen's hair? It wasn't with her body. Where did you hide it?'

'It's somewhere up on that blasted heath,' he said. 'Blown to the four winds I expect. What does it matter?'

'Oh, it matters,' Thackeray said. 'We'll take a break there, Mr Sanderson, as there are some other matters we want to talk to you about. Perhaps you can tell us where your car is. We'll want that for forensic examination.'

Sanderson told them where to find his parked car, and they left him, subsiding now in his seat, swaying slightly with his eyes shut, apparently oblivious to the uniformed constable who came back into the interview room to watch over him.

'What do you make of that guy, guv?' Mower said. 'Apart from the fact that he's seriously stoned, I mean. All that giggling. The custody sergeant who booked him in should have spotted that.'

'You think so?' Thackeray asked sharply. 'You should have mentioned it sooner. If he's under the influence of drugs the whole interview's worthless as it stands.'

'I reckon the whole interview's worthless anyway,' Mower said. 'He's told us nothing about Bently Forest that he couldn't have picked up from the press. And he conveniently can't remember where or how he killed her. It's cobblers, isn't it, guv?'

'But his fingerprint was on the plastic bag,' Thackeray said. 'We have that. So we have him. He's involved.'

He suddenly spun on his heel and went back to the interview room where the PC looked up in surprise when the door opened again so soon.

'I'll resume our interview in the morning, Mr Sanderson,' he said. 'In the meantime, we can offer you a meal and a night in a cell until we're ready for you again. See to it, Constable, will you, please?'

Blackness, nothing but blackness. Laura drifted back to consciousness, aware first of all that she could not see and, gradually, that neither could she move. She blinked a couple of times, to make sure that her eyes were actually open, but it did nothing to reveal anything but utter darkness. Only gradually, as she flexed her arms and legs, did she realise that she was tied down in some way to a flat surface, arms to her sides, ankles fastened together. She felt a tide of panic beginning to engulf her and she moaned slightly, but as she heard her own gasping breath she realised that at least she had not been gagged. But that fact, when she'd caught her breath, offered no comfort at all. If she had been left here to scream for help, all that implied was that no one could possibly hear her.

The silence was as profound as the darkness. Try as she might, she could hear absolutely nothing at all. There was no movement of air, although she gradually became aware of a sweet, slightly metallic smell which seemed familiar although she could not place it. As silent and dark as the grave, she thought, and another wave of panic swept over her, making her gasp and her heart thump uncontrollably, when she considered the possibility that she was actually in a coffin. But even though she could not reach out to feel the edges of her prison, she did not think she was anywhere as enclosed as that. The sense of suffocation which swept over her, she thought, was more in her own head than in any real inability to breathe, and gradually she made herself take small, regular breaths again and she felt a chill as the sweat which had soaked her began to dry.

There was a sense of space, she told herself firmly, even without the evidence of her eyes to back it up, and wherever she was was cool but not bitterly cold. As far as she could tell she was still wearing the coat she had put on to go out into Murgatroyd's garden and she was not physically uncomfortable, just immobile, and she knew that there must be a malign purpose behind that. She was being kept here for something, and when she allowed the thought of Karen Bastable's fate to intrude, she moaned again.

She licked her lips and realised she was very thirsty. Whatever Murgatroyd had used to knock her out had left her mouth dry and furry. She wondered how long it took to die of thirst, and she wondered how long she had been here, immobile and unconscious – hours, days? She did not think it could be long as, apart from her dry throat, she was not particularly hungry or even uncomfortable. But at the back of her mind she knew that there was something she should remember and it remained tantalisingly just out of reach in the fog of her brain. She flexed her muscles again against whatever was tying her down, but there was no give anywhere, and even if she managed to wriggle a limb free, she did not know what she would do next. In the complete darkness, even trying to step off whatever she was fastened to would require a leap of faith she did not think she could summon up.

Michael must be looking for her by now, she thought. He would be at the flat, as arranged, wondering where she was. And then the crucial fact that she had not been able to recall filtered slowly back into her conscious mind. She had not told anyone where she was going, had she? She was bitterly sure she had not. Ted Grant had been busy and she had left the office without a word to anyone else. She groaned again. Michael might be looking for her but he had absolutely no idea where she had gone, and nor did anyone else. Murgatroyd had all the time in the world, she thought, to do whatever he wanted to do, and she had very little doubt what he intended.

She had no idea how long she lay there trying not to let her imagination run riot amongst the horrors she might be facing, or their inevitable conclusion, but despair was never far away, and when she finally heard a sudden sharp noise, she shrank into the hard surface beneath her, as if she could minimise herself in the teeth of whatever was to come. She recognised the click of a key in a lock, and a dim light as a door close to her head opened, and then she was dazzled by a much stronger light as a switch was pressed.

'You're awake. That's good.' She recognised David Murgatroyd's voice although she had screwed her eyes shut against the glare and it was a minute before she could see him standing close to her at the side of what seemed to be a high bed. He said nothing, watching her with no obvious expression in his gold-flecked eyes. Then she realised that he was holding a knife in one hand and with a sick certainty she realised that the smell that had tantalised her with its familiarity was the meaty smell of a butcher's shop.

'Why are you doing this?' she whispered, her eyes fixed on the shining blade of the heavy kitchen knife. 'What have I ever done to you?' She glanced around what turned out to be a small windowless room, which she guessed was a cellar.

Against a wall was a table with an array of tools and knives on it, and above a carefully arranged display of photographs which looked like blown-up family snapshots, some in black and white and some in colour. All of them featured a tall, beautiful young woman, with flaming red hair, sometimes with a small boy, sometimes with the boy and a young baby, and suddenly she understood where Murgatroyd's claim that he had killed his mother had led him.

Murgatroyd seemed to spot the comprehension in her eyes.

'She was a whore,' he said flatly.

'And Karen?'

'Another whore. They all were, all those women.'

'But I'm not,' she said. 'I'm not one of those women. I'm not a whore.'

'I don't believe you,' Murgatroyd countered and Laura swallowed hard, trying to control her trembling limbs as she realised that she was to become just one more in what must be a grisly sequence of killings. He turned away, selected a large pair of scissors from the table behind him and grabbed hold of her hair.

'No,' she said faintly, but he was not to be deterred as he pulled her copper curls in hanks away from her head and began to hack them off. And this, Laura thought with certainty, catching the manic look in his eyes, would just be one of the preliminaries. When he had finished, he gathered up the bundle of hair carefully and put it in a box under the table which seemed to be already full of a red-gold cloud.

'But I'm not a whore,' she said, with as much firmness as she could muster. 'Whatever your mother did, or the rest of them, that's not me. I am loved and wanted, and so is my baby. Are you going to kill us both just because of a casual resemblance? Is that what God wants? Another innocent death like your sister's? That can't be right.'

Murgatroyd looked at her, his expression inscrutable, and then opened the scissors and held the sharp blades against her throat as she flinched and turned her head away so as not to let him see the fear in her eyes or the tears that slipped down her cheeks.

'It's a strange God who murders unborn babies,' she whispered as she felt one of the blades slice into her neck.

And suddenly, as suddenly as he had appeared, he was gone, and she was in darkness again as the door closed behind him. She took a deep breath, sure that he soon would be back, and aware of a trickle of blood beginning to soak into her shirt collar. She might have shaken his resolve for a moment, she thought, but he would not dare let her live now that she could identify him. His only realistic choice was to continue what he had begun.

CHAPTER NINETEEN

Michael Thackeray had hardly slept, and felt the gritty-eyed and fuzzy-brained results when he went back to police HQ the next morning. He had waited until after midnight for Laura, trying her phone at intervals and finally calling anyone he could think of who might know where she was, spreading anxiety he did not want to spread and to absolutely no avail. No one, friend or colleague, knew where she was heading after she left the *Gazette*'s offices the previous afternoon. Finally, exhausted, he had flung himself onto the bed fully clothed and slept fitfully until the first streaks of dawn woke him through the curtains Laura had carefully chosen for their bedroom. His first thought was Laura, but she still wasn't answering her phone. He got up, swallowed a scalding black coffee and set off for work before seven.

To his surprise, he found Sergeant Kevin Mower already in the CID office, hunched in front of his computer screen.

'I've firmed up these other disappearances,' Mower said, over his shoulder. 'Dates, places, circumstances and, as far as possible, sexual history. There are six that happened close to

Murgatroyd's academies, all around the time that Sanderson would have had reason to be in the area concerned. All the places seem to have had some dogging activities going on at around the same time. There's more than enough here to start questioning him about exactly when he was where. Then, I reckon we need to start looking at his computer. He had a laptop with him. If he accessed dogging sites, or even set them up himself, it'll all be in there on the hard disk. As we said early on, it's a brilliant way for a predator to pick up women in a totally anonymous environment where no one will want to come forward as a witness.'

Mower swung round towards the DCI and tried not to look as horrified as he felt when he took in his dishevelled, unshaven appearance.

'Are you all right, guv?' he asked. 'You look as if you had a rough night.'

Thackeray's first instinct was to rebuff this incursion into his private life but he was suddenly overwhelmed with immense weariness and knew he had to tell someone what was going on in his life or he would go mad.

'Laura's disappeared,' he said. 'I've hardly slept. I need to file a missing person report.'

'Jesus,' Mower said. 'When did this happen?'

He listened without comment as Thackeray spelt out what had happened the previous day.

'I thought she looked very stressed when I saw her the other day,' was his only comment when the DCI had finished.

'My fault,' Thackeray said. 'If she's gone off somewhere voluntarily, it's all my bloody fault, as usual. She's pregnant. And I was giving her a hard time about it.'

'And if she hasn't gone voluntarily?' Mower said sharply,

an appalling thought striking him. 'Look at this, guv.' He turned back to the computer and brought up a page of photographs of six women.

'They all have red hair,' he said quietly. 'If that bastard Sanderson's a serial killer, he picks out women with red hair. Maybe he had more reason than we imagined to be haring down the M1 with all his luggage in the boot of his car yesterday.'

Thackeray sat down at the desk next to Mower's and buried his face in his hands. Mower glanced around the CID room, to make sure that they were still alone.

'Let's take this a step at a time, guv,' he said. 'Take your coat off and tidy up a bit and then go down to uniform and report her missing. There's no reason to think she hasn't just taken some time off to sort her head out.'

'With her phone off?' Thackeray asked, desperately trying to find a glimmer of hope somewhere.

'Maybe she doesn't want to talk to you just now.'

Thackeray nodded gloomily, accepting the justice of that.

'While you sort all that out, I'll get Sanderson back up to an interview room and we can press him really hard this morning on all this other stuff. And ask him about Laura, just in case he's broken the pattern. Which I don't honestly think is very likely, guv. You know what these bastards are like. If they go out looking for tarts, amateur or professional, that's generally what they find. And if that's what's happened to this lot, I can't see that Laura could be at risk. Why should she be?'

'You know she's had some contact with Sanderson. She's been chasing an interview with his boss for a week. She knows the bastard.'

'Sure, we'll push him then, won't we? We've got enough

already to charge him with something on the basis of the fingerprint alone. We can afford to press him now on the rest. And ask him about Laura as well.'

Thackeray sighed heavily and ran a hand across his greying hair. Mower, he thought, had taken control and he half resented, half felt grateful for that.

'I'll see you downstairs in ten,' he said.

Sanderson turned out to be much more subdued after his night in the cells. His face was drawn and there were dark circles under his eyes. Thackeray guessed that he had had as little sleep as he had had himself, and if he had been high on drugs the day before he certainly was not high now. But when they asked him again whether or not he wanted a solicitor he shook his head.

'Let's get on with it,' he said dully. 'I've told you what you wanted to know about Karen. You've got your confession. Why don't you just charge me, for God's sake? Let's get it over with.'

'Oh, I think we've only just begun, Mr Sanderson,' Mower said, after acknowledging a nod from Thackeray. He put a bulging file of computer printouts on the desk in front of him. 'Let's start with Linda O'Hear, twenty-six years old, missing from her home in Peterborough since she vanished five years ago. Do you remember her?'

Sanderson stared at the two detectives with a blank expression.

'I've never heard of her,' he said. 'I don't know what you're talking about.'

'How long have you worked with David Murgatroyd on his schools programme?' Thackeray asked.

Sanderson shrugged.

'Eight, nine years,' he said. 'He advertised the job just as I finished on his training scheme. I knew his name, of course, though I'd never met him again, after the church, that is, and thought it would be a laugh to work for him. I think he fancied a black PA. Reckoned it did something for his street cred. Not that he ever guessed how much street cred I actually had back in Notting Hill. It was only later that I got my head round the sort of man he really was. How much good he was doing, you know? And making no fuss about it. All that. I never planned to stay with him so long. It just happened. I was hooked. He became my religion.'

'So you stayed, and if we asked you if you've ever been to Peterborough, or Swindon, or Leeds, or Derby or Oldham, you'd agree you had.' Mower consulted his file ostentatiously.

'I suppose,' Sanderson said. 'I generally go where the boss goes. What's that got to do with Karen Bastable?'

'So if we ask your boss where you were on which dates over the last few years, there'll be a record somewhere?'

'Yes, yes, you can ask him, but he's away at the moment. He's abroad.'

'And we already know you're familiar with Preston. You said you'd been there the day Karen disappeared,' Mower pressed on.

'Yeah, yeah, so what?' Sanderson asked, looking genuinely bemused. Could he be that good an actor, Thackeray wondered?

'So tell us all about the red-headed women you picked up at sex parties in those places, Leroy,' Mower snapped. 'Just like the party you claim you stumbled on accidentally in Bently Forest.'

'What?' Sanderson said, looking amazed now. 'What the hell are you talking about?'

'There's always a pattern to serial killings,' Thackeray said. 'It's a great pity it sometimes takes a long time to emerge. But in this case, we've got there in the end. You've told us about Karen and how you picked her up at the dogging meeting. You've told us you cut her hair off because you hated redheads. So now tell us about the six other women who disappeared in similar circumstances, every one of them a redhead, every one of them a dogger. Linda O'Hear, Kelly Smith, Jan Wooldridge…do I need to go on?'

'I've never heard of any of them,' Sanderson said. 'I don't know what you're on about.'

'We've started looking at your computer, Leroy,' Mower said. 'If you found those doggers' parties online we'll find a record of it, believe me. You've coughed to Karen's killing. What's the point of not telling us about the rest? You're going down for life anyway. You must know that.'

'What is this? What are you doing, trying to set me up, trying to clear your books or something? I don't know anything about any women in these other places. I don't know what happened with Karen. Somehow I lost it. I was out of control. I can't even remember exactly, I told you that. But it was a one-off, believe me.'

'Were you stoned, like you were last night?' Mower pressed.

'No, no, I don't remember.' Sanderson buried his face in his hands. 'I don't know,' he said. 'It's all a blur.'

'And now we have another redhead missing,' Mower said. 'Another young woman you've met. Where is Laura Ackroyd, Leroy? What have you done with her?'

'The reporter woman who's been pestering the boss? She's missing?' Suddenly Sanderson's demeanour changed, he looked suddenly sick and grey and began to tremble. To Mower's alarm, Thackeray jumped to his feet and went around the table to take hold of Sanderson by the scruff of the neck, pulling his head back until their eyes were only inches apart.

'Where is Laura, you bastard?' he hissed. 'Tell me what you've done with her.'

'Nothing, nothing at all,' Sanderson whispered, hardly able to speak as his collar cut into his windpipe. 'I don't believe this. It can't be right.'

'Steady, guv,' Mower said. Thackeray released his grip but still stood over the prisoner, waiting for an answer. There were tears in Sanderson's eyes now.

'Tell us,' Mower snapped. 'Tell us everything.'

Sanderson slumped forward across the table and nodded but took a few seconds to find his voice again and when he spoke it was in a whisper.

'I thought it was a one-off,' he said.

'Louder, for the tape,' Thackeray snapped.

'I thought it was a one-off,' Sanderson said, slightly louder. 'I found him with Karen…'

'Who? Who did you find?' Thackeray broke in again.

'The boss, my boss. I got back and found him in the grounds at Sibden, at the side of the garage. She was dead and he was in a dreadful state, covered in blood, incoherent, kept rambling on that she was a whore and God hated whores… I got him indoors and put him under the shower and then into bed. Then I burnt his clothes and then got rid of the body, exactly as I told you. Wrapped it up and took it up onto the moors and buried it.'

'You made yourself an accessory to a brutal murder, just

like that?' Thackeray's expression was incredulous.

'It didn't seem like that at the time. It seemed like a nightmare that wasn't connected to real life. He never mentioned it again. It was as if it had never happened. Maybe he couldn't remember. But I thought I could watch him, make sure it never happened again. I thought it was an isolated thing, a sudden madness. But then, when you started looking for me it looked as if it was coming too close to home, and I reckoned I could vanish if I got back to London. I'd done it once, I could do it again. And you'd go on looking for someone who didn't exist. You'd assume I'd killed her and keep on looking for me, not bother with anyone else.'

'You reckoned without motorway cameras,' Mower snapped. 'You were doing ninety-five.'

'Yeah, yeah. Stupid mistake,' Sanderson said. 'So when they stopped me, I had a choice, didn't I? Grass him up or let you go on thinking I did it. You had the fingerprint, after all. I did bury the body. And I wanted him to go on doing what he was doing, not killing, of course, not that, but he does so much good stuff. I wanted him to go on doing that. He's a good man. It was a no-brainer, really.'

'You decided to take the blame?' Mower asked. 'You'd do a life sentence for this bastard?'

'You don't understand,' Sanderson said, with total accuracy as far as the two detectives were concerned. 'You don't know him. You don't know how he changes people's lives. And I didn't know there were others,' Sanderson whispered. 'I truly didn't know that.'

'You said Murgatroyd's away,' Thackeray said. 'Is that true? Could Laura have gone up to Sibden to see him?'

'I've tried and tried to keep them apart. I knew he was

fascinated by redheads, but I never knew why.'

'Is he away?' Thackeray snapped.

'No, he's not away. He was at Sibden all day yesterday. He might have arranged to see her after I left, I suppose. I didn't tell him I was taking off and not intending to come back. He doesn't usually do that, make his own appointments, I mean, but he might have as it was her.' He shrugged helplessly, his eyes full of horror as if he had only just begun to appreciate the depth of the pit he had fallen into. 'Dear God,' he said. 'I hope he didn't. He's not safe, is he? He's never going to be safe again.'

'Come on,' Thackeray said explosively to Mower. 'Get this bastard back to the cells. We'll find her, even if I have to take his house apart brick by bloody brick.'

The police arrived at Sibden House mob-handed: a transit van full of uniformed officers, two carloads of detectives. There was no response when they tried the keypad on the electronic gates and Thackeray waved to a burly constable with a ram to force the lock before they roared up the drive and decanted twenty officers onto the gravel drive in front of the portico. There was no sign of life anywhere along the sunlit sandstone facade and again no response to the bell or a repeated hammering on the solid wooden double doors, and again Thackeray authorised a forced entry. Leaving half a dozen men to search the grounds, the rest made their way into the echoing entrance hall, where Mower dispatched half of them to search the upstairs floors and the rest to explore downstairs. There was not a sound to be heard before heavy boots began to tramp around the premises, and no shout that might indicate that anyone might have found anything of interest to the police.

'It's odd the alarm isn't on,' Mower said, glancing up at the flickering sensor in a corner of the hallway where they stood waiting for developments.

'Maybe someone left in a hurry,' Thackeray said. He resumed his nervous pacing up and down the tiled floor. 'I can't believe she would have come up here without telling anyone,' he muttered, pulling out his mobile and thumbing in Laura's number again. Somewhere not far away a telephone rang, and Thackeray glanced at Mower in wild surmise.

'Find it,' he snapped.

Mower opened the door into an extensive sitting room where the sound of the call instantly became louder, although when they glanced around they could see no sign of a phone. Eventually Mower walked across the room to a sofa and pulled a mobile out from underneath the brocade pelmet where it had been lying completely concealed. He handed it to Thackeray, his mouth dry.

'It's hers,' Thackeray said, his voice cracking. 'Look, so many missed calls, all mine. So where the hell is she?'

They went back into the hall and Thackeray strode out onto the steps at the front of the house, desperately scanning the rolling park and gardens for signs of anything to indicate that Laura might have been there, but within minutes a uniformed officer came running round the side of the house.

'What sort of car did Miss Ackroyd drive, guv?' he asked.

'A black Golf,' Thackeray snapped.

'There's one of those in the garage at the back. And we've found a locked door which looks as if it leads down into some sort of cellar or store. We thought you'd like to see before we smash the door down.'

Thackeray and Mower raced down the steps and around the side of the house where they found the officer in charge of the ram and another couple standing outside an unobtrusive door close to the garages.

'OK,' Thackeray said, his heart thumping as the door splintered and gave way.

'Let me, guv,' Mower said, pushing his way in front of his boss and going through the doorway first. But inside there seemed to be only a cluttered storeroom, and it was not until they began to search more closely they found that the junk half hid another locked door, where the ram-wielding officer performed his function yet again. Beyond were stone stairs leading down into pitch darkness. Thackeray himself found a light switch and they made their way down the stairs in single file into another room, empty apart from a tall shape in one corner which swung gently in the draught from the door. Taking a sharp breath, Mower crossed the room and took the weight as one of the uniformed officers tried to unhook a rope from a hook in the ceiling. When he succeeded, Mower carefully lowered the body of a man to the floor and turned it over onto its back.

'Murgatroyd?' he asked Thackeray.

'I've never met him, but I guess so,' Thackeray said, his mouth dry. 'I've seen photographs.'

'He's been here some time,' Mower said. 'We don't need to be heroic and try to drag him back to life. No chance.'

'So where's Laura?' Thackeray said so quietly that Mower could barely hear him. Mower glanced around.

'There's another door,' he said. 'This is like one of those puzzles, boxes within boxes.' He tried the next door and it swung open easily revealing an even smaller space with little more than a bed and a table, where another immobile body lay. Thackeray pushed past the sergeant with a strangled cry as the light went on revealing Laura strapped to the bed, face ashen, eyes closed, with a dark pool of blood at her neck, dripping steadily onto the floor.

'She's alive, guv,' Mower said, feeling for a pulse. 'Just.' He turned to the officers crowding in behind them.

'Get a fucking ambulance!' he yelled. 'Quickly.'

Michael Thackeray sat beside Laura's bed watching the steady drip making its way down the long plastic tube and into her hand, as he had for hours, long after the doctors had finished the blood transfusions which they hoped would save her. Prayers from long ago came unbidden into his head as he watched her immobile body under the hospital sheet, at first barely breathing. With memory beyond control, he recalled sitting by his mother's bed as she slipped into final unconsciousness, leaving him bereft and his father embittered, after watching the slow ravages of MS take her, inch by inch, away from them. If that happened again, to another woman he loved, he could not bear to even contemplate the consequences for his own life.

Laura had not opened her eyes since they had found her in Murgatroyd's cellar, although the doctors had been encouraging after they had treated her. The slash to her neck had nicked an artery, but she had been found in time, they said, the transfusions would do their work. And her breathing, he noticed at last, had perceptibly become more regular, until he had begun to tell himself that she was now sleeping more or less normally. She was still a deathly white, and he could barely bear to look at the dressing beneath her ear or at her head, where her hair had been hacked away. The nurses had gently wiped away the smears of blood and brushed what was left over her bare scalp, but he felt the loss of her cloud of copper curls as much, if not more, than he knew she would when she saw herself again in a mirror.

He felt rather than heard someone behind him, and turned round to find an anxious-looking Kevin Mower hovering by the door to the private room they had given Laura.

'How is she, guv?' the sergeant asked quietly.

'As well as can be expected,' Thackeray said. 'You know they never commit themselves.'

'I came to give you a quick update...'

Thackeray got to his feet wearily and followed Mower out into the corridor.

'There was another room beyond where we found Laura,' Mower said. 'Empty, but with a very patchy concrete floor. I've got them started on breaking up the floor and they've already found one body, not far down. It's pretty obvious there'll be more. Six, at a guess. It looks as if he took them back to Sibden, killed them in the room where we found Laura, and then buried them in the one beyond that. He could have gone on indefinitely, I guess, if he hadn't attacked Karen Bastable before he got her indoors.'

'Any theories about why he might have done that? What does that bastard Sanderson say now?'

'Still says Murgatroyd was incoherent beside the body when he found him, but thinks he said something about her struggling free and he had to use the knife to stop her getting away. Presumably, once he'd started on her, he couldn't stop, he was out of control, and killed her where she lay, instead of taking her indoors. If he hadn't done that, we'd never have got near him. He could have carried on indefinitely.'

'You've charged Sanderson?'

'Oh, yes, guv. He'll go away for a very long time.'

'He was nearly as warped as Murgatroyd himself,' Thackeray said. 'How could you cover up a crime like that and actually feel good about it?'

'All part of God's higher purpose, according to his latest statement,' Mower said. 'Some God.'

Thackeray glanced back into Laura's room, and Mower put a hand on his arm.

'Get back to Laura, guv,' he said. 'Everything's under control back at base. I'll keep you posted.'

'Thanks, Kevin,' Thackeray said. And to his joy, when he turned to take up his watch beside Laura's bed, he found her green eyes were open and she was watching his approach with every appearance of relief.

'How are you feeling?' he asked.

She shook her head slightly.

'Tired,' she said faintly. 'Have I been asleep for long? I'm very tired.'

'Quite long, yes,' Thackeray said, his mouth dry. 'But you're all right now. You're going to be all right.' Laura nodded, and winced as she tried to move her neck.

'And the baby?' she whispered. 'Is the baby all right?'

Thackeray nodded wordlessly.

'They say the baby's all right,' he said. He took her hand, unable to speak, and she seemed happy to lie for a while with her eyes half shut.

'Have you caught him?' she whispered at last, almost as if she had been reviewing what had happened, and Thackeray wondered how much she actually remembered. He did not want to push her back into the horror. There would be plenty of time for that later, much later, he thought.

'We've got him,' Thackeray said. 'He won't ever hurt anyone again.'

'And Debbie? Is she all right? He did a vicious job on her as well, you know.'

'She's recovering,' Thackeray said. He took her hand.

'And with you? What made him stop short?' he asked. 'Have you any idea?'

'It was the baby. He couldn't kill the baby at the end,' she said simply. 'I reminded him of his mother, and the baby must have reminded him of his sister.'

'Is that what he told you?' Thackeray asked, astonished into asking one more question.

'I told him,' Laura said, with a crooked attempt at a smile. 'I told him he couldn't murder us both. That wouldn't be right.'

'That was very clever psychology,' Thackeray said, kissing her hand. 'The baby saved your life. You have no idea how good that makes me feel.'

'Really?' Laura whispered.

'Really,' he said. 'For all three of us.'